Always Be Mine

Barb Evans

Published by Barb Evans. PO Box 3030 YARRUNGA VIC 3677

barbevans.author@gmail.com

Printed and bound by IngramSpark. Australia: Ingram Content Group AU Pty Ltd, Melbourne, Victoria. US: Lightning Source LLC, La Vergne, Tennessee / Allentown, Pennsylvania / Jackson, Tennessee, United States. UK: Lightning Source UK Ltd, Milton Keynes, United Kingdom. Europe: Lightning Source UK Ltd, with facilities in Germany, France, and Spain.

The authorized representative in the European Economic Area is Lightning Source France, 1 Av. Johannes Gutenberg, 78310 Maurepas, France. compliance@lightningsource.fr

Cover Art by Keri Arthur using Shutterstock images and Barb Evans' photos.

Internal Art by Keri Arthur using Shutterstock images.

Ebook ISBN: 978-1-7645839-1-6

Print (paperback) ISBN: 978-1-7645839-2-3

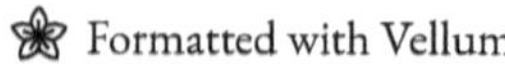

This book is dedicated to my wonderful partner, Bob, for his patience, love, and support.

I couldn't have done this without you.

Acknowledgements

A book doesn't make it to the outside world without the involvement of a number of people.

My unending gratitude to Keri Arthur. This book would never have seen the light of day if not for her encouragement, guidance, friendship, and her invaluable advice to 'finish the damned book'.

I also want to thank Debbie Phillips of DP Plus for making my words shine.

Part One

One

APRIL 2008 - KATHERINE

Katherine held her father's hand, determined not to cry. His death was close, and their time together precious. There would be plenty of time for tears. Later.

"Promise me, Katherine." His feeble grip tightened, and he struggled to prop himself up on one elbow, a sharp intake of breath hissing through gritted teeth. Lines of pain deepened around his mouth and eyes. "Don't listen to your mother. She never understood. Never approved. Promise me you'll pursue your dream. You're thirty-three and have talked about it for years now. This is your chance to make it happen. I know you can do it." His voice, while quiet and edged with pain, held an urgent quality that commanded attention. And compliance.

Katherine's throat burned, giving a strangled, tormented croak to her voice. "I promise, Dad." She swiped at the tears sliding down her cheeks and wiped her hand on her jeans. *Hold it together, Katherine.*

Her father settled back in his bed with a groan and nodded. "That's good." A faint smile formed on his face, and he closed his eyes.

Katherine squeezed his hand gently and looked down at their hands. Hers, still youthful and smooth, his thin and bony, his almost translucent skin marked with age spots. His eyes were now dull and yellowed, his once clear voice now faint and breathy. He looked so frail, so old. He was only sixty-eight, but cancer had ravaged his body, making him look twenty years older.

She caught sight of their reflections in the darkened window. How different they now were. Once her father's hair had been dark and curly like her own, but as he'd aged, his hair had grayed and then thinned from the rounds of chemotherapy he'd endured.

His eyes opened again, and he smiled and winked at her. For a moment, the years fell away, and instead of the tired, gray-haired man in blue-striped pajamas, he was again the father who picked her up and carried her on his shoulders when she was a little girl. The father who laughed with her, encouraged her, and taught her. The father who comforted her when she was sad. Her rock. Her idol. She smiled back at him and leaned over, kissing him softly on his cheek.

"I love you, Dad." The dam holding back her tears was close to breaking, so she swallowed hard and sat back in her chair, again just holding his hand.

His eyes fluttered closed again, and his labored breathing evened to a more regular rhythm. For now, he slept, something he would do more and more of as he inched inexorably closer to death. Two days ago, monitors filled the room with their incessant beeping and whirring, but since there was nothing more the team of doctors could do, her father asked for the machines to be removed so that he could spend his final days in peace. So now his room was quiet. Deathly quiet.

Katherine picked up a notepad from the side table and scribbled a quick note below the logo for the Royal Cornwall Hospital, Truro.

Dad,

I mean it.

I promise.

All my love, always,

Katherine.

Each time she left his bedside, she feared it would be the last time she saw her father alive. *Please no, don't let it be. I couldn't bear it.* Tears trickled down her cheeks as she kissed her father's forehead and placed the note beneath his hand where he would find it when he woke.

If he woke.

Two

THREE WEEKS LATER

Katherine placed a yellow rose on her father's grave, its brightness a sharp contrast to the red-brown earth that marked his final resting place.

The funeral for Norman Walters, two days before, had seen the small church packed with mourners, and she'd been unable to say her own private farewell, having been whisked away by her mother almost as soon as the graveside service was over.

Now, alone at her father's grave, her sorrow overwhelmed her; her heart ached as though shattered into a thousand shards, each one relentlessly stabbing inside her chest. Her throat burned, every breath like acid. How would she get through this? The man who loved her, supported, encouraged her, was gone. How would she face life without him? The single yellow rose blossomed into a bouquet through the kaleidoscope of her tears.

"I miss you so much, Dad."

Katherine crouched and placed her fingertips on the grave as if touching her father's forehead. She bowed her head, letting her tears fall, the strains of "How Great Thou Art" drifting from somewhere else in the cemetery. As the hymn finished, Katherine sighed, stood, and wiped her eyes.

"I love you, Dad."

She trudged along the path to the cemetery gate. Around her, new life burst forth; trees budding with new leaves, daffodils blooming, birds beginning their mating rituals. Yet, for Katherine, the season held no joy or fascination this year. How could she rejoice in the new spring when her father was no longer with her? As she closed the gate behind her, she glanced at her watch. She'd arranged to meet her mother to choose a headstone, and she mustn't be late. Once that was done, she would head back to her tiny flat in Tavistock and try to rebuild her life.

And, of course, keep the promise made to her father.

Three

SEPTEMBER, 2008

Katherine took a sip of her take-out coffee and studied the listings in the realtor's window, hoping to see something new. Something that hadn't reached the internet real estate sites yet. She longed to move out of her cramped, rented flat to her own place, but she'd seen nothing she liked, or more to the point, that she could afford. Her father had left her enough money to buy a small cottage and support herself for a year or two to pursue her dream of being an author, and she'd made him a promise. But as yet, she hadn't found the right place at the right price. She didn't want or need a big, modern house in the suburbs. Something small and quiet in the country would suit her just fine.

"Excuse me."

The voice startled Katherine, and she jumped. "I'm sorry, I was just wool-gathering." She moved aside from where she'd been blocking the door.

The man laughed. "So I see." He pushed the door open, triggering a tinkling bell. "Are you looking for something in particular?"

"I, um...," she stammered, appraising him. Probably mid-thirties, immaculately dressed in a dark-blue suit, knife-edge creases in his trousers, highly polished black shoes, crisp white shirt; perfectly groomed light-brown hair, and ice-blue eyes.

"I've seen you a few times looking in the window." He thrust out his hand. "Jonathan Irving, at your service. And you are?"

She glanced down at the proffered hand and tentatively shook it. "Katherine Walters."

"It's a pleasure to meet you, Katherine. Now, why don't you come in and tell me what you're looking for?" He cupped her elbow and guided her through the door and to a large wooden desk bearing an oversize, ornately carved nameplate bearing the name 'Jonathan Christian Irving'. The keys he tossed onto the desk were on a keyring that bore the three-pointed star of Mercedes-Benz.

He pulled out a chair, and Katherine sat perched nervously on the edge of the seat. The telephone on the desk rang, and Jonathan raised his voice. "Mark, can you get that, please?"

Katherine turned to look. On the other side of the office, a slightly overweight, balding, middle-aged man picked up a phone, and the strident ringing stopped.

"Sorry about that," Jonathan said."Now. Can I offer you a coffee?"

Katherine held up the coffee cup she still carried.

Jonathan tittered like a schoolgirl. "Of course." He loosened his red-spotted tie and sat at the other side of the desk in a chair notably larger, higher, and grander than the visitors' chairs.

Everything about this man pointed to his belief in his superiority. The Mercedes, the larger than average desk, the over-the-top nameplate, and the throne-like chair. His entire demeanor exuded privilege.

He leaned toward Katherine. "So tell me, what kind of property are you looking for?"

Katherine took a deep breath. "Well, I'm wanting a cottage in a quiet area." She looked down at her hands. "Somewhere I can write without being disturbed."

Jonathan gave her a beaming smile and clapped his hands together. "A writer. How marvelous! So, do you have a specific location in mind where you want to live? For instance, does it need to be within walking distance of shops and the like?"

"Goodness, no." Katherine laughed. "I have an old Land Rover, so it can be off the beaten track as long as it's quiet and has phone reception, electricity and running water."

"I see." Jonathan screwed his face up into a frown of concentration, leaned back, and steepled his hands. "Hmmm, well, I can't think of anything suitable that we have on our books at the moment, but I will keep you in mind if something comes up."

"Thank you; that would be wonderful." Katherine rose.

"Wait, don't go yet," Jonathan said. "Tell me more about what you would like, and I'll make some notes." He opened a drawer, rummaged for a few seconds, and pulled out a notebook, which he pushed across the desk to Katherine. "Better start with your phone number so I can contact you." He held out a pen.

Katherine sat again and took the pen, noting that even something as mundane as a ballpoint pen could exude luxury. At least it did when it bore the little white star emblem on the top of a Montblanc pen. Not for Jonathan the cheap pens from the local newsagent or, as in her case, charity pens she'd bought to support the Red Cross or British Heart Foundation. She printed her name and phone number at the top of the page, then returned the notebook and pen to Jonathan.

"So, tell me about your ideal home. Such as how many bedrooms, modern or something older, etc."

"I haven't really got a shopping list of needs and wants, other than what I'd already told you. Quiet, phone reception, electricity."

Jonathan scribbled notes, all the while smiling and nodding.

"But I need it to have two bedrooms; one for my mother," Katherine said.

Jonathan's smile vanished, and his shoulders drooped. "I see. You live with your mother." His tone changed from warm and welcoming to cold and dismissive.

"Good heavens, no." Katherine shook her head. "I couldn't live with my mother; it's just that she may stay a night or two from time to time."

Suddenly Jonathan's warmth was back, along with his nodding. "Okay, I understand. A 'guest room', as it were."

They chatted a while longer before Katherine checked her watch. "Gosh, I must get back to work. Thank you for your time."

Jonathan hurried around the desk to Katherine as she rose. "It was my absolute pleasure, Katherine." He put a hand on the small of her back, so close beside her, she caught a whiff of his aftershave. Fresh citrus, an almost soapy scent with a hint of spice. "I do hope I can help you find your dream home soon."

Once on the street, Katherine walked back to her office. Jonathan seemed very nice, charming even, except for that one odd moment when she mentioned her mother. And he was a bit too free with his hands, first touching her arm, then the small of her back. Still, if he found her dream home, she'd forgive him.

Four

JONATHAN

Jonathan watched Katherine as she walked away down the street, her hips swaying beneath her tailored black skirt, her long black curls bouncing around her shoulders in contrast to her pale blue shirt. She reminded him so much of... but no, he wouldn't think of *her* anymore. Couldn't allow himself to think of *her*.

This was the one. She had to be. He'd waited so long. Katherine was younger, of course, but that didn't matter. What mattered was the way she looked. Much more like *her* than even the last one. Perhaps this one wouldn't betray him.

He whispered her name, "Katherine". Even her name was perfect. It sounded so... so... right, somehow. He closed his eyes, imagining entwining his fingers in those dark curls, pulling her head back, his mouth on hers. "Katherine," he whispered again. When he opened his eyes, she'd disappeared from view. He sighed wistfully and returned to the office. Mark sat, feet up on the desk, engrossed in a telephone conversation, his back to Jonathan.

Safe.

Jonathan slid open his bottom drawer and took out a photograph. He held it below his desk, where only he could see it. The woman in the photo stood beneath an arch of roses, the scarlet blooms framing her body in sharp contrast to her dark, flouncy curls. Her black lace bra not quite able to contain her full breasts, the tiny matching pants only just covering her pubic hair. One hand reached as if to pluck a rose, the other by her side. Her scarlet lips pursed in a kiss. A kiss meant for him.

His pulse beat faster as he traced the outline of her body with his finger. His eyes drifted closed, and he stroked the erection that threatened to burst his zipper as he remembered. Her nipples stiffening as he sucked and nibbled them. Her moans of desire as she pushed his head down. Down over the soft skin of her belly and further, the scent of her strong...

The bell jingled.

"Shit." His erection withered as reality snapped back. He shoved the photo back in the drawer and slammed it closed. He glanced down and made a quick adjustment. Satisfied that all was as it should be, he stood, plastered a smile on his face, and walked toward the prospective customer.

"Hello, I'm Jonathan Irving. May I be of assistance?"

Five

KATHERINE

A week later, Katherine's phone rang while she was in the middle of proofreading the editorial for the *Tavistock Tribune*. Absently, she reached over and declined the call, only for it to ring again almost instantly. Again, she rejected the call. When it rang a third time, she switched off her phone.

Twenty minutes later, her proofreading finished, she switched her phone back on. Eight missed calls, all from the same number. *Someone's eager to get hold of me.* She checked her voicemail. "Katherine, it's Jonathan Irving. I have to talk to you urgently. I'll keep trying, but please call me back as soon as you get this." Before she'd even had a chance to call back, her phone rang again. She answered.

"Katherine. Finally. It's Jonathan. You didn't answer or call me." He sounded breathless.

"I'm at work and was in the middle of something. But I'm free now. What can I do for you?"

"It's what I can do for you. I think I've found your house, but we must act quickly. Can you come to my office?"

She glanced at her watch. Four o'clock. There was nothing urgent left she needed to work on today, and she could come in early tomorrow, so it wouldn't hurt to leave now. "Yes, I can be there in five minutes."

"Great, I'll meet you out the front."

Jonathan was indeed waiting for her, nervously bobbing from one foot to the other. He looked up and waved as she approached. She stopped a couple of feet away from him, but he closed the distance between them in a single stride and clasped her forearm. "Katherine, how wonderful to see you."

Katherine moved back, dislodging Jonathan's hand from her arm. "You said you've found a house for me."

"Yes, yes. I think it's perfect and I can't wait to show it to you."

"Tell me about it."

"It's got two bedrooms and a separate studio, which I think would be perfect for your writing. The kitchen and bathroom have been recently renovated, so you've got modern amenities in a beautiful old stone cottage, and it's in a very peaceful setting. You must come and see it." Jonathan's words tumbled out of his mouth in an excited babble.

"What, now?"

"Why not?"

"Well, for one thing, I don't have my car. I walked to work."

"That doesn't matter; we'll take mine. I'm so excited about this, and I'm sure you'll love it too."

"Why the hurry?"

"It hasn't hit the open market yet, and the owner's asking price is very reasonable indeed, but I fear once it reaches the market, there will be several interested parties, and it may end up going to auction, and the price will rise beyond your budget. But if we act now, and lock in a contract, you'll get a bargain."

"Well, what are we waiting for? Let's go."

Jonathan again put his hand at the small of her back and guided her to a very classic Mercedes-Benz convertible, its deep burgundy red exterior gleaming in the sunshine, its roof down, exposing the luxurious pale cream leather interior. It probably cost more than Katherine would earn in ten years. Again, another show of his belief in his superiority. Jonathan opened the passenger door. Once Katherine was seated, he handed her the tongue of the seatbelt and waited until she fastened it before closing her door. He trotted around and got in behind the wheel.

"Lovely car," Katherine said.

"Yes, it's a classic. They don't make them like this anymore. Solid steel, not plastic like so many modern cars. Sure, it doesn't have all the bells and whistles of modern cars, but I love it. It's a pleasure to drive." He started the motor and pulled away from the curb.

Katherine leaned back, enjoying the warmth of the sun, but as the car picked up speed, her long black curls whipped her face, and she fought to control them. Jonathan brought the car to a stop and took a baseball cap from the glove compartment. "We've got about half an hour's drive. You might want to tuck your hair up, unless you want me to put the top up."

"I'll tuck it up." Katherine took the cap, which bore the slogan 'Irving and Wallace—the REAL Estate People' on the peak, twirled her hair into a knot, and managed to contain most of it beneath the cap. "So, where are we going?"

"The cottage is on the edge of Dartmoor, one of the few freeholds within the national park."

Katherine's eyes widened. "Really?"

Jonathan glanced across at her and grinned. "Well, you wanted seclusion."

The convertible hugged the road through twists and turns while Katherine discreetly studied the man beside her. His clean-shaven face bore the ruggedness of someone who spent a lot of time outdoors. His short, light-brown hair was much more suitable for driving a convertible than her own long, curly locks. He smiled often, showing white, even teeth between lips that her mother would have said were made-for-kissing. Today, he wore no jacket, and his rolled-up shirt-sleeves exposed strong, tanned forearms and well-manicured hands. He held the steering wheel in his right hand while his left rested on the gear stick. No wedding ring and no telltale mark where one may have recently been. A bracelet of plaited leather encircled his left wrist, above which he wore a tattoo: several stars arranged in a cross.

"It's the Southern Cross," Jonathan said.

Heat crept up from the base of Katherine's neck, and she darted a glance at him. His eyes twinkled, his mouth set in a smug, self-satisfied grin. Not unlike one particular Cheshire Cat.

"Like on the Australian flag," Jonathan said. "My best mate was

Australian, and we went surfing Down Under when we left university. He was killed. I got this done as a memorial to him."

"I'm so sorry."

"Don't be. I don't mind talking about it now, but it cut me up badly when it happened and for a good while after."

"What happened?"

"Shark. We were at Bells Beach. I caught a wave and rode it all the way in, and when I turned around, Dave was gone." Jonathan's voice became a distant monotone. "I scanned the surf and saw his board in the water. A huge part of his board was missing, and I knew. The coast guard searched, but they never found him."

"How heartbreaking. It must have been horrible."

"Yes. Yes, it was." He lapsed into silence.

They'd left the town behind and were now surrounded by fields of sheep and cattle grazing on the lush grass. The car juddered over a cattle grate, and the wildness of the moors stretched endlessly before them. Ahead, The Coachman's Rest stood beside the road; its whitewashed walls complemented by hanging baskets of purple and yellow flowers.

"That's so pretty." Katherine swiveled in her seat to look again as they passed, her skirt riding up above her knees as she did.

"Perhaps we could try it out for lunch on Sunday," Jonathan said.

Katherine took a quick glance at him, trying to determine his intent. His gaze appeared focused on her legs, so she hitched her skirt down and left his comment dangling, unanswered. He couldn't be asking her out, could he? Hopefully, it was just part of his sales agent pitch.

Six

Beyond Merrivale, the road climbed, and near the top of the rise, Jonathan turned right over a narrow stone bridge. The road meandered past a farm and a disused quarry. Jonathan pointed to a road on their left. "That leads to Princetown. It's probably the closest town to the cottage."

As they rounded a bend, Jonathan pulled to the side of the road and pointed. "That's it."

A low stone wall surrounded a two-story gray stone cottage, dwarfed by the majestic tor standing sentinel over the surrounding moor. Behind the cottage stood a grove of trees—which Jonathan informed her was the orchard—and further on, a path led over a small stone bridge and continued across the moor. To the left of the bridge, a small stream tumbled over a low waterfall, sparkling in the sunshine. How wonderful it would be to sit beside it with her laptop, listening to the gentle babbling of the water as she wrote. She hadn't even seen the house yet, and already it felt like home.

Katherine gasped. "It's absolutely lovely."

"You can't see the studio from here. It's just beyond the bridge, but hidden by the trees," Jonathan said. "It's what made me think this would be perfect for you." He put the car in gear and pulled back onto the road. Only a short distance further, he turned through a gap in the stone wall into a gravel courtyard and stopped.

"We're here." Jonathan leaped out of the car and rushed around to open her door. Katherine got out, her eyes never leaving the cottage. It called to her, and she knew in her heart it would soon be hers.

The exterior of the house looked in good order. No slates missing from the roof as far as she could tell. The chimney pots were intact and even straight. The windows were quite small, which was disappointing but expected, given the age of the cottage. But no way would her budget stretch to major renovation work. Jonathan opened a big, heavy oak door that creaked on its hinges. Katherine stepped over the threshold. A sudden chill swept from her ankles to the top of her head, tightening her scalp before shivering back down her body.

"It always feels cold when you walk into an empty house," Jonathan said. "Come on, I'll give you the tour."

He launched into sales agent mode, turning to face her, his back to the stairs. "This leads to the living area." He flung his right arm out in a grand gesture, like a game show host displaying the prizes on offer. "While this is the kitchen." His left arm repeated the gesture so that for a moment he stood with both arms outstretched like a priest bestowing blessings, before dropping his arms back to his sides. "The staircase leads to a small landing, off which are the two bedrooms and the bathroom. Let's start with the kitchen, shall we?" He gestured toward his left and stood back for Katherine to precede him.

Katherine gazed around the surprisingly modern kitchen with its wall oven and dishwasher, its white-flecked stone countertop, white backsplash tiles, and white cabinetry. "It all looks so new."

Jonathan nodded. "It is. This and the bathroom are fairly recent renovations." He opened a door almost hidden in the wall and stood back. "This leads to the cellar. There's no electricity on at the moment, and it's pretty dark down there."

A gust of damp, musty air rushed up at Katherine, and she peered into the gloom. "It's a bit creepy." She pushed the door closed.

"Right, let's see the rest." Jonathan led her back to the hallway and up the stairs. "This would probably be a guest bedroom." He opened a door. "Not much of a view from here."

The room was pleasant, though, with its view over the front courtyard and countryside, and it would be big enough for when her mother visited. Carpeted, which was certainly a bonus.

"Here's the bathroom." Jonathan opened another door.

Katherine glanced around the room. A good-sized bath and separate shower. Her mother would approve. She always hated the shower-over-the-bath idea, particularly after she once slipped in the bath, caught her toe on the faucet, and broke both the tap and her toe. The fact that Katherine's father fell about laughing at the time didn't help, of course.

"And this is your bedroom." Jonathan's voice came from further along the landing, where he held open the remaining door.

She walked into the room and stopped, staring at the jaw-dropping vista before her. She clasped her hands together in front of her chest. "How magnificent!"

Enormous windows afforded the most stunning view of the moors. Sunlight filled the room with its cheerful warmth. Beyond the orchard, and a roof that must be the studio, the vastness of the moor stretched endlessly away into the distance to the left, while to the right, the tor dominated the landscape, its crags and clefts shadowy and mysterious even in the bright sunlight. She opened a window and leaned out. "It's amazing! I love it." She turned back to Jonathan, tears of happiness misting her eyes. "I want it. It's perfect."

"You haven't even seen the living room or the studio yet." Jonathan laughed.

"Well, lead on!" This was everything she'd dreamed of and more. She had to have it.

The living room boasted an enormous fireplace big enough to roast a whole pig.

"Katherine?" Jonathan said, putting his hand on her shoulder.

She shook her head and moved away. "Sorry, sometimes my imagination runs away with me. I'm prone to daydreams."

"So I see. Shall we continue our tour?"

Seven

French doors led to a sunny conservatory and from there to a paved patio, also bathed in sunshine.

Katherine clapped her hands. "This is absolutely wonderful. Show me the studio."

As if her exuberance was infectious, Jonathan threw open the doors with a flourish and led her across the patio to an archway covered in climbing roses, the blossoms faded now, only a hint of deep red left this late in the year, but in full bloom, they'd be stunning. Beneath the arch stood the orchard gate.

As they walked through, Katherine noted apple, pear, plum, and even a quince tree, all laden with fruit. Perhaps she could supplement her as-yet non-existent writer's income by selling preserves. At the bridge, Katherine looked over into the crystal-clear water, again dreaming of sitting beside the stream with her trusty laptop.

"Here we are, the studio," Jonathan called to her, and she hurried to catch up. He opened the top half of a stable door, then reached inside and unbolted the bottom.

Even the buildup of grime on the large window couldn't diminish the fabulous view of the tor, the moor, the ponies and sheep scattered like confetti amid the heather.

A sturdy wooden table and chair stood in the middle of the studio, both covered with a thick layer of dust. She ran a finger through the dust and absently wiped it on her gray skirt. How many people before her had sat at this table? And for what purpose? This is where she would write her novel. Here or beside the stream. It was perfect.

She gripped Jonathan's arm. "I mean it, Jonathan. I want it. When can I move in?"

Jonathan laughed and slipped an arm around Katherine's shoulders. "Well, we'd better head back and sort out the paperwork."

On the way back to Jonathan's office, Katherine chatted excitedly about her new home, where each piece of furniture would go, and the extras she'd have to purchase. An hour later, she'd signed the contracts, and the cottage was almost hers. She would organize the deposit as soon as her bank opened in the morning.

"So, settlement would normally be twenty-eight days from now, but would you like me to see if you can move in sooner?"

"Would you? That would be wonderful."

"I'll telephone the owner and see if I can persuade him. I've got your number here, and I'll call you as soon as I've spoken with him."

"I'll need to engage a solicitor too, I guess."

"No need to do that. I can organize all the conveyancing for you, save you all that unnecessary expense. Get things done a lot faster, too."

"Hmm, I don't know. Can you? Are you sure? That would make things easier, but I don't know..."

Jonathan reached across and patted her hand. "You leave everything to me. We're not your normal realtor. We pride ourselves on handling every part of the purchase process. It's all part of the service."

The bell jingled as Katherine left the office. She walked a few steps down the street and stood a moment, looking skyward.

"I'm doing it, Dad. I'm keeping my promise."

That evening, she couldn't sit still; even two-thirds of a bottle of wine didn't quell her exuberance or her anxiety while she waited to hear from Jonathan. While she would love to move in straight away, realistically, there were things she needed to do. Like resign from her job for one thing. The cottage had cell phone reception, so that would at least keep her in contact with the outside world until she worked out what she needed and got organized. She'd spotted a landline phone, but that would probably need to be reconnected.

A little after nine, her phone rang, and she almost fell off the sofa, dropping the phone on the floor as she scrabbled to answer it with a very breathless, "Hello."

"Katherine, it's Jonathan. Good news. I've spoken with the owner, and he's quite amenable to you moving in as soon as you like. I asked how much rent he wanted per week until settlement, but he brushed it off. 'I'll be glad to get rid of it, ' were his words."

"Gosh, that's wonderful news. I'll get the deposit organized as soon as the bank opens tomorrow and give notice to vacate here, and I'd better start packing."

"I can help you pack."

Katherine cringed a little. How did she answer that?

Jonathan chuckled. "Only kidding, of course. But please call me if there's anything else I can do for you."

"Thank you, I will."

Katherine hung up the phone, leaped to her feet, and danced around her living room, whooping with joy.

Eight

Once Katherine had visited her bank and organized the deposit, she made her way back to work. It was time to hand in her notice. While she was eager to start her new life, a certain amount of trepidation had her stomach in knots. This was a big step. No, not a big step, a monstrous leap into the unknown. What if it all went wrong? What if the burning flame inside her to write fizzled out before she'd finished her novel? What if her writing was simply no good?

Her father's voice rose in her mind. *You can do it. You need to believe in yourself and give yourself a chance*

She swallowed down the lump of sorrow that rose in her throat every time she thought of her father. There was no one she could talk things over with, nobody to reassure her. Certainly not her mother, and Katherine was never one for making close friends. Not the confide-in types, anyway. But a promise was a promise, and there was no way she'd let her father down. So she steeled herself and knocked on her boss's open door.

"Got a minute?" she asked as he glanced up from his desk.

Half an hour later, it was done, and Katherine locked herself in the ladies' room and cried. Not with tears of sadness, but with the relief of getting this far. "No going back now, Dad," she murmured. "I hope you're right."

Of course, I'm right, Katherine. You know the old saying, 'father knows best.'

She giggled nervously. Did others do this? Carry on conversations with their dead relatives?

She emerged from the bathroom and made her way back to her desk, trying to concentrate on the piece she was supposed to be editing, her mind wandering to all the things she needed to do before she left work for the last time. She'd given two weeks' notice, but it would fly by.

Later that afternoon, her boss called an impromptu staff meeting where he announced Katherine's decision to leave, which, of course, led to the inevitable question. What was she going to do?

Katherine took a deep breath and, with every ounce of courage and bravado she could muster, said, "Well, I'm going to write a novel."

For a few seconds, nobody spoke, and Katherine cringed, wishing she could take back her words. What were they thinking? Was this the dumbest idea ever? Did they wonder if she'd gone mad?

But then Rebecca cheered, and Maddy joined in. Katherine relaxed. Her colleagues surrounded her, patting her on the back, wishing her well, encouraging her, and she knew she *had* made the right decision. She told them about the cottage she'd put a deposit on and about Jonathan.

"He's gorgeous, isn't he?" Rebecca said, with a faraway look in her eye. "When Craig and I sold our flat, Jonathan handled the sale. He did everything. Mum and Dad bought their house through him, too. Same thing, he took care of every little detail. He's very professional."

Rebecca's glowing praise of Jonathan quelled any misgivings Katherine had of letting him handle the legal side of her purchase.

Nine

Her last day at work seemed to be an endless round of people dropping by her desk to say goodbye, with promises made to keep in touch. But eventually, it was time for her to leave. She slung her bag over her shoulder, picked up the bouquet of soft pink dahlias and white nerines from her boss, a box containing several notebooks and pens she'd received as farewell gifts from Rebecca and Maddy, and left the office. As soon as parking restrictions had ended, she'd nipped home to change into jeans and a T-shirt and to fetch her car, snagging a parking spot only a short walk away from her office. She stepped out onto the street to find Jonathan waiting outside.

"I thought you might need a hand," he said, taking the box from her.

"Thank you. That's very thoughtful of you, but I'm parked right there." She pointed to a slightly worse-for-wear green Land Rover. Katherine dug her keys out of her bag and unlocked the passenger door, then placed the flowers on the seat.

"Are you having a farewell dinner or drinks somewhere nice?" Jonathan asked.

"No. My boss wanted to organize something, but it's not my scene. Besides, I have to go home and pack."

"But you can't let your last day of work go without some sort of celebration. At least let me take you for a drink. Come on. You'll still have plenty of time to pack, and I can help."

Katherine made an involuntary exasperated 'tut' sound, which resulted in Jonathan's jaw clenching, his eyes glaring. Dammit, she'd hurt his feelings, and he was only being kind. Quickly, she said, "I really have to start packing, but I guess one drink won't hurt."

The corners of Jonathan's mouth twitched in a cocky smile. "That's my girl," he said, placing Katherine's box of gifts on the floor of the Land Rover. "Where shall we go?"

Katherine glanced up the street. "How about The Cornish Arms? It's the closest." She'd have a quick drink with Jonathan, then grab some fish and chips from Mickey's across the road, and head home.

The bar was already buzzing with patrons as was usual for a Friday night, most standing around in groups, drinks in hand. Katherine spied a small table in a corner and made a beeline for it while Jonathan went to get drinks. She opted for cider, afraid that if she asked for wine, Jonathan would bring a bottle and then she would be obliged to stay longer.

Jonathan returned with not only drinks but a couple of menus tucked under his arm. "Thought we could make a night of it; have dinner." He put the drinks down and slid a menu in front of Katherine. "The special today is lamb korma with rice and poppadoms."

Katherine shook her head. "I don't have time for dinner, only a drink. I want to get home."

Again, Jonathan's mouth set in a firm line. He snatched the menu from in front of Katherine and slapped it face down with a bang. An awkward silence fell between them. *This man is not used to people saying no to him.* Katherine took a sip of her cider. "Mmm, that's nice. Thank you," she said, hoping to soothe his bruised ego.

"Glad you approve," he said, with a smile so forced it looked more like a grimace.

Katherine hated conflict, always had, and there were many times she'd backed down to keep the peace, and this was another of those times. "I'm really sorry I can't stay for dinner. I've got so many things to do, and my mind is a whirl. Perhaps some other time."

Jonathan's face softened a touch. "Yes, another time."

Katherine chided herself for giving in, yet again. She must learn to stand up for herself.

They chatted amiably. About the real estate market, Katherine's new home, and good places to eat, and after they finished their drinks, Katherine pushed back her chair. "I must get on," she said, getting to her feet. "Thanks for the drink and the chat. It's been fun. I've got the removal truck booked for Tuesday, so I guess I'll see you then to pick up the keys."

She wanted to grab a fish supper, but Jonathan insisted on walking back to her Land Rover. So, she made a show of fumbling in her bag for her phone and waited until Jonathan was out of sight before ducking into the chippy. Back at her flat, she poured a glass of wine and sat on the sofa to eat her dinner.

One thing she definitely needed to do was to call her mother. She'd been putting it off, knowing full well her mother would give her a lecture on the futility of it all, how irresponsible she was being, how she should be forging a proper career, not faffing about writing a novel. Et cetera, ad nauseam. And her mother would no doubt slip in a few remarks about how Katherine should also focus on finding herself a husband.

Her fish and chips finished, she poured herself another glass of wine and called her mother.

The conversation went much as Katherine had expected.

Ten

Katherine spent the next few days sorting out and packing up her flat. Even though it was tiny, it was amazing the amount of stuff she'd accumulated. Admittedly, she still had things she'd brought with her when she moved back from Manchester, which she had never unpacked. Should she be ruthless and toss out stuff now, or take it all with her and sort it out when she unpacked in her new home? She decided on the latter.

By Monday evening, everything was ready to be moved, with only a few things left to finish on Tuesday morning before the removal van arrived.

Katherine left the removal men, Roy and Doug, loading furniture and boxes into their van, and went to pick up the keys to her new home.

Jonathan looked up and smiled as she entered the office. He got up and came to greet her.

"Katherine! Lovely to see you."

Katherine extended her hand, expecting Jonathan to shake it, but Jonathan caught her by the shoulders and kissed her cheek instead. She backed away awkwardly, heat creeping into her cheeks. "Hello, Jonathan."

"I'll bet you're excited. Moving in today."

"Yes, I am, rather. I came to get the keys while the removal men finish loading my stuff."

"Right. Well, I'd better get them." He strode back to his desk and returned a few moments later. "By the way, the phone should work now; I got it reconnected for you. I've put a tag on the keyring with your new number, and I've labeled each of the keys for you." A large, glittery initial 'K' dangled from his finger, along with several keys.

Katherine took the keys, clasping them in her hand. Her stomach fluttered. She hadn't been this excited since her first date. "Thanks, Jonathan, for everything. You've done so much for me. I'm indebted to you."

He walked with her to the door, again his hand pressing into the small of her back. "It's a pleasure, my dear Katherine. All part of the service. I was about to step out and get a coffee. Will you join me?"

"No, I can't, sorry. I've got to dash. I told the men I would only be ten minutes."

Jonathan's smile disappeared, and his voice turned cold. "Perhaps another time."

"Yes, another time," Katherine said and hurried away, leaving Jonathan standing in the open doorway.

Eleven

The rush of cold air hit Katherine again as she opened the front door to her cottage. She couldn't wait to build a fire and dispel the chill. She brought in the box of essentials she'd carried with her. Cleaning cloths, polish, matches, fire-starters, and a bag of logs and kindling from the hardware store in Tavistock. Once the fire was burning well, Katherine went into the kitchen. The cellar door stood open, and she closed it. She set to work wiping out the cupboard shelves and bench tops so that she could unpack straight away.

A rumble from outside announced the arrival of the removal van, and she hurried outside to greet the men. Over the next hour, she directed the placement of pieces of furniture, the hanging of pictures, and the stowing of boxes.

"I'd keep this door closed if I were you, Miss. There's a definite chill," Roy said, pushing the cellar door closed.

Finally, everything had been unloaded, and Katherine watched the removal van lumber its way down the road. The van disappeared around a bend, and she was alone. Completely alone. For the first time in her life, there was nobody around her. What if she were in trouble? Who would she turn to if she needed help? Where would she go? Where was her closest neighbor?

Back inside, with the door closed, she stood a moment. Had she done the right thing? She closed her eyes, and her father's face smiled at her. That encouraging, you-can-do-it kind of smile. The tension drained from her. Yes, she could do this. She opened her eyes and clapped her hands excitedly. "Yes, Dad, I've started my new life. No excuses now. Time to work on that novel."

But first, she needed to unpack. The kitchen seemed like a good place to begin; at least she could then make a cup of tea.

Katherine stepped into the kitchen and stopped, her exuberance draining away as the chill from the open cellar door curled around her ankles. *Hmph. I'm sure I closed it properly last time*. She jiggled the latch. It seemed in order, but she closed the door with an extra hard slam. *There. Definitely closed this time.*

She set to work, singing softly to herself as she unpacked. When the final kitchen box was empty, she stretched and looked around her. Crockery and glassware in the dresser, earthenware pot beside the stove, full of the utensils she used when cooking. Pots and pans stowed, groceries in the cupboard, perishables in the fridge. Finished. At last.

"Right, time for that cup of tea." She boiled the kettle and made her usual lemongrass-and-ginger tea and sat at the table.

Creeeaaak! The noise behind her brought Katherine to her feet in an instant, her chair falling to the floor as she stood and spun around in one motion. The cellar door swung open, the darkness beyond it seeming to move toward her. Frightened now, Katherine backed away from the yawning darkness, her hip bumping the corner of the table. She cursed in pain and stumbled, tearing her eyes away from the cellar door as she did. The spell broken, she scolded herself for being so silly. It was merely a door with a wonky latch that wouldn't stay closed, and it had moved to the top of her fix-it list.

She walked to the door, swung it shut, and wedged a kitchen chair under the door handle. "There, now let's see you get THAT open!" She sat again and sipped her tea, but this time she sat facing the cellar door, which stayed mercifully shut.

Her tea finished, she put the cup into the dishwasher and headed upstairs to make up the bed and unpack her clothes. A stack of boxes greeted her, and she groaned. Did she really have all this stuff?

Singing softly, she opened the box marked 'bed linen' and made up the bed. Would it seem strange sleeping here tonight?

Gravel crunched outside, and Katherine bounded down the stairs and opened the front door. Jonathan waved as he got out of his car and picked up a bunch of flowers from the back seat and presented them to her.

"To welcome you to your new home," he said.

She took the bouquet from him; pink carnations surrounded by a haze of baby's breath. "They're lovely. Thank you, Jonathan. That's so kind. Would you like to come in? Perhaps a cup of tea?"

"Yes, please!"

Katherine emptied her earthenware pot of its kitchen utensils and filled it with water. It would have to do until she found a vase. She placed the flowers on the table and made fresh tea, English breakfast this time.

Jonathan looked around the kitchen. "Wow, this looks great. Really warm and homely. I love that dresser. Is it an antique?"

"I think so. It belonged to my grandmother, but I don't think it was new when she got it. I don't know too much about it, I'm afraid." Katherine handed Jonathan a cup of tea and apologized that she didn't have a biscuit or some cake to accompany it.

"That's okay, I'm sweet enough." He laughed nervously and looked away and then back at Katherine, a puzzled, inquiring look on his face. "What's with the chair?"

"I kept finding the door open, probably got a wonky latch or something, so until I fix it, the chair will suffice."

"I see. Have you been down in the cellar yet?"

"No, not yet. There's no light; it probably needs a new bulb. I figure it can wait until I sort the rest of the house out. I'll head to town in a day or two for supplies, and I'll grab a couple of light bulbs."

Jonathan's eyes sparkled with eagerness, and he seemed about to speak, so she quickly added, "I need to check out Princetown anyway.

Get myself a post office box, organize to have my mail re-directed, and the like."

Jonathan's face fell into a forlorn expression, his shoulders sagging along with it. "I hoped... but you're right, Princetown's closer, I guess."

Guilt pinged Katherine's conscience despite her not wanting to encourage Jonathan's attention. She still wasn't sure if his motives were purely professional courtesy or if he was hoping for something more. Behind his charming demeanor, she sensed he was rather spoiled and selfish. Time to change the subject. "Any idea of the history of the area?" she asked.

"Hmm, not very much," Jonathan said. "The tor behind the cottage was once a quarry. You can still see remnants of the crane mounts. You need to watch your step if you wander around there. One particular place is a very sheer face, and if you fell..., well... promise me you'll be careful." Jonathan looked directly at Katherine. "I'd hate to lose you."

Katherine averted her gaze and tried to sound casual as she laughed. "Believe me, I'll be careful, I'd hate to lose me, too!" *Is he really flirting with me?*

Twelve

JONATHAN

Jonathan's knowledge of the cottage was actually far greater than he'd told Katherine. He'd owned the house for years. Under an alias, of course. A name he'd often used in the past when wanting to hide his true identity. Many times over the years, he'd walked the length of the tunnel from the old railway halt to the cellar when the others were tenants.

He'd made mistakes with each of them, allowed them too much freedom, too much independence, instead of controlling them. He looked down at the tattoo on his arm and sneered. Just as well it wasn't Chloe's name instead of the Southern Cross. After all he'd done for her, she'd scurried back to Australia without even saying goodbye.

Then came Sarah, who didn't resemble *her* as much as Chloe had, her hair being shorter, but she'd been more submissive. That was until... well, at least she didn't leave him. Not really. He hadn't allowed her to leave, but the end result was the same.

He'd been on the phone when he'd first seen the woman he now knew as Katherine looking in the window at the advertised properties, and knew instantly she was perfect. It was like fate was hollering through a megaphone that this was the one who would finally replace *her*. He'd rushed to end his call, but by the time he'd hung up and dashed to the door, there was no sign of her. When he re-entered the office, Mark told him the woman had dropped in the previous week while Jonathan was out of the office. She was looking for a quiet cottage in the country, but she didn't leave her name or number.

So he waited, constantly watching for her. He mustn't let this one escape his net. He'd made the mistake of renting the cottage to the others, but realized now that if he could persuade this one to buy his cottage, well, that would keep her well within his grasp and make it much harder for her to up and leave.

Then he'd seen her looking in the window again, and she was simply perfect. Chloe and Sarah were mere imitations, but Katherine could have been *her* twin. When *she* had been younger, of course. But he must be careful; he must ensnare Katherine completely before springing his trap. Then at last, he could forget *her*.

Thirteen

KATHERINE

Katherine stretched and glanced at the bedside clock; it was almost 9 a.m. She'd slept late, but why was it so dark? Disoriented, she got out of bed and walked over to the window. Dark clouds hung menacingly low, obscuring the tor. While yesterday the scene was bright and sunny and filled her heart with delight, today that same view seemed brooding, gloomy, and melancholy. *There goes that walk on the moor.*

Once showered and dressed, she headed downstairs. The fire still smoldered, so she stoked it, put more wood on, and soon had it blazing again. She stood for several minutes, warming herself in front of the flames. If she needed a fire now, when it was late summer, what was it going to be like in winter? Perhaps she'd better look into getting central heating installed.

Her stomach rumbled. Katherine made a pot of tea, two slices of toast smothered in marmalade, and took her breakfast into the conservatory. She powered up her laptop and connected to her email provider.

Two new emails awaited her. First, a note from her mother, welcoming her to her new home and hoping to visit before too long. 'I'll just give you time to get sorted first, dear.'

Katherine groaned; she loved her mother dearly, but she was hard work sometimes. Firing off a quick reply, she promised that her mother was welcome to visit when Katherine had settled in, but it might take a few weeks. She had a lot to organize.

The other email was from Jonathan. Again, welcoming her and trusting that she'd be happy in the cottage. He closed by saying that he would love to take her to The Coachman's Rest for dinner one evening soon. It seemed more and more that Jonathan was interested in her, but she wasn't interested in him, not romantically. He was nice enough, but somewhat bland. Not her type at all; not that she'd figured out what her type was, but Jonathan certainly wasn't it. Perhaps she wouldn't reply to his email for a day or two.

Rain pelted the glass roof of the conservatory, and Katherine looked away from her screen. It was so gloomy outside it seemed like night had fallen. Through the heavy rain and the darkness, she could only just make out the gate that led through the orchard. Suddenly, a flash of lightning lit up the room, followed a split second later by a loud thunder crash. She uttered a small scream, jumped, and plopped back into the chair, then relaxed and giggled nervously. It was only a thunderstorm.

May as well finish unpacking and get the place into some semblance of order. She turned off her laptop, reached for her cup, but another bolt of lightning froze her to the spot. Her eyes widened in shock and disbelief. The brightness of the flash etched a picture into her mind like a monochrome photograph.

And that photograph was very, very wrong.

Fourteen

On the path, right by her orchard gate, a sinister figure stood watching her. She gasped; a sharp intake of breath, her hand covering her mouth, stifling the scream rising in her throat, her heart clamoring a zillion beats a minute. She hurried to the door and checked it was securely locked, then stood and watched.

Watched and waited. Her unblinking stare riveted to the spot where she'd seen the mysterious stranger, waiting for the next bolt of lightning. When it came, her eyes widened, taking in every detail. The figure was gone; the path deserted. She waited once more. When lightning again rent the sky, the path was still empty.

Did she imagine it? Was it a trick of the light, or had someone actually been there? The silhouette burned into her mind had certainly looked like a man. An ominous figure in a wide-brimmed hat and wearing a long, flowing coat, just as she imagined The Man In Black from Stephen King's *Dark Tower* series would look, and very reminiscent of the garb worn in those old black-and-white horror movies she'd devoured during her teenage years, *Jamaica Inn*, and *The Hound of the Baskervilles*. She shuddered. Wasn't that hell-hound supposed to haunt Dartmoor at night? She and her high-school friends, Charlotte and Amy, used to scare themselves silly with stories of witchcraft, vampires, devil worship, and human sacrifice. Many of them told by candlelight during storms such as the one going on around her right now. One night, during an intense storm, they had been playing with a Ouija board, convinced they'd raised the spirit of Black Sam Duggan, a notorious pirate, betrayed by his crew, and thrown alive into a quicksand bog where he'd sunk without a trace, his spirit now said to roam the county seeking revenge. As thunder raged and the wind howled, the candles had blown out, plunging the room into darkness. Then, when a bolt of lightning illuminated the landscape, Katherine had seen a figure outside dressed in a long coat and a wide-brimmed hat. She'd screamed and raced from the room, upending the Ouija board and sending the planchette flying across the room. That vision had haunted her nightmares for many years, and now he was back.

But where was Katherine's stranger now? Was he even real, or was he a ghost? Maybe the ghost of Black Sam Duggan still searching for his treacherous crew. Had she imagined the figure? She had no answers, only doubts. She checked every door and window, ensuring each was locked or securely shut. If there was someone out there... she closed the curtains on each window. At least the figure would not be able to see her. The conservatory did not have curtains, so she retreated to the living room, bolting the door between it and the conservatory.

Katherine sat and waited for the storm to pass. Eventually, the thunder diminished to a deep rumble from far off. Opening the curtains, she looked out. Lightning still flashed in the distance, but no longer threatening. The rain had eased, the sky beginning to lighten. She relaxed a little; no menacing figure anywhere to be seen. Maybe it had simply been her imagination. But she'd realized how completely alone she was, and incredibly vulnerable.

Fifteen

That night, in her dream, she'd tried to run from the sinister figure as he chased her, but even though she ran as fast as she could, her legs pumping, a stitch forming in her side, panting for breath, she made no progress. It was as if everything was happening in slow motion. She looked behind her, and there he was, clad in his long coat, his wide-brimmed hat, his eyes blazing like laser beams in the dim light. He laughed as he chased her. A laugh of pure evil. Katherine ran on. When she looked behind her again, he was right behind her, his hand stretching toward her, his impossibly long arm seeming to extend further and further until he grabbed her hair, spun her around, and pulled her towards him. His arms enveloped her, his face dipping toward her, his lips drawn back to reveal his pointed teeth. Teeth that dripped blood. He laughed again, his foetid breath hot on her face. Breath that smelled of the grave.

Katherine screamed and struggled and woke, the bedclothes tangled around her. She heaved a sigh of relief that it had only been a dream. A dream that had seemed so real, as nightmares often do. The same nightmare she'd had all those years ago after the Ouija board incident.

She lay a while in the warm comfort of her bed, letting her breathing and heartbeat return to normal. Even though it was still early, she knew she'd get no more sleep that night, so she might as well make a start to the day.

Later, with her unpacking finished, Katherine surveyed her new home with a sense of satisfaction and pride. Everything was in place. Well, everything except the bundle of empty boxes and the kitchen chair still wedged under the cellar door.

With a sense of trepidation, Katherine removed the chair and opened the cellar door. Again, the cold rush of air made her shiver. She flicked the light switch, but nothing happened; not that she expected it to. It didn't work yesterday, so it would have been a miracle if it worked today. Still...

She went in search of her torch. She must remember to get a supply of spare batteries as well as bulbs.

The torchlight did little to penetrate the darkness, its beam illuminating only a few steps down. Treading carefully, she made her way, wishing she'd worn a jacket; the air seemed to get cooler as she went down. At the bottom of the steps, she shone the torch around the small cellar. As she moved closer to the far wall, she found another set of steps leading off to the left. She directed her torch beam downward. She couldn't see the bottom, but while the steps from the kitchen to this point were concrete, this next flight was stone. And judging by the indentation in the middle of each step, well worn. How many feet had trodden these steps? And why?

Well, she'd come this far, may as well go on. She started down, taking slow, careful steps, shivering again; definitely a lot colder down here.

Finally, she reached the bottom of the steps and took a deep breath, forcing her shoulders to relax.

The sub-cellar appeared larger than the one above, and certainly chillier. Cobbled stones lined the floor, and shelves ran down each side of the room. On one shelf, several stone flagons stood amid a thick layer of dust. Were they old cider flagons? Perhaps there was still cider in them. She tapped the side of one with the butt of the torch. The hollow thunk told her it was empty. Same with the next one. The third lay on its side, its cork on the floor beneath.

She retrieved her bundle of boxes and stacked them on a shelf, coughing at the cloud of dust that puffed up around her.

A cold draft swirled around her legs, and she shivered violently. As quickly as it came, it was gone. She shone her torch around one last time and headed back upstairs. She must remember to keep a jacket by the door, it's so cold.

~

Katherine set off along the path to the studio. If she was serious about writing, she needed to make a start, and what better place for a writing retreat than the studio? With no phone or internet, and free from distractions, there was only her, her laptop, and her imagination. The prospect thrilled her, but first the studio needed a good clean.

Yesterday's storm had blown away, leaving the countryside sparkling in the morning sunshine. Katherine breathed in deeply, delighting in the fresh scents of rain and heather. A few white puffy clouds dotted an otherwise perfectly blue sky. A perfect fall day. She couldn't remember being this happy and excited. In the orchard, she plucked an apple from a tree and bit into it, her mind drifting back to when she was a little girl, sitting quietly in a corner of the kitchen, munching on an apple from a huge pile, while her mother and grandmother made jams and jellies. During apple season, they made some kind of apple dessert almost every day. Her grandmother made baked apples filled with dried fruit, cinnamon, and nutmeg. As for Katherine's mother, she made the best apple pie in the world. Beautiful, buttery pastry with a fluffy apple filling. Katherine's stomach growled, and she giggled. *Must stop thinking about food.*

She came to the small bridge and stopped halfway across. Upstream, the water cascaded over rocks to a pool beneath, and from there, it flowed steadily on. Where did it end up? Did it join the Walkham River and on to the Tavy, or did it join the Meavy and eventually the Plym? Either way, it was odd to think that the water flowing beneath her bridge would end up out to sea at Plymouth. What was that game she'd played with her father? Poohsticks. That was it. They would each throw a stick into the water on one side of the bridge and rush over to the other side. The first stick to come out from under the bridge was the winner.

"I miss you, Dad," she whispered, her eyes filling with tears, her joyous mood replaced by a great heart-wrenching sadness.

She brushed away her tears and gazed at the water below, catching sight of a large fish, sort of greenish-brown with dark spots. Perhaps this was a trout? She knew very little about fish. Her one and only fishing trip with her father had cured her of the idea of catching her own dinner. She'd been happy enough when a fish took her bait and she carefully reeled it in. But her happiness soon turned to horror when her father told her she must kill it.

That's all part of the deal, Katherine, he'd told her. *You catch it, you kill it.*

Looking down at the poor, helpless creature, its mouth opening and closing as it gasped, had made Katherine sick to her stomach. Having to stun it and bleed it. It was too horrible to think about. She forced her mind away from the scene unfolding in her memory and made her way to the studio.

As she put her bucket of cleaning tools on the ground and opened the top half of the stable door, the hair on the back of her neck prickled. Was she being watched? Heart racing, remembering the man from the storm, she spun around, her eyes darting from right to left.

Nobody.

Stop being so jumpy.

Beyond the studio, the path meandered toward the tor, and Katherine ventured on; her promise to get started on creating her writing retreat forgotten in her desire to explore. After living in a tiny flat with no garden, save for a couple of sad-looking plants on her window ledge, the whole of Dartmoor surrounded her cottage for her to enjoy.

A sheepdog bounded toward her, its shiny coat rippling as it ran. Would it attack? How would she defend herself? Fortunately, the animal stopped a little way from her and sat, its tongue lolling out of its mouth as it panted. It looked happy.

"Hello, boy. What a good dog you are," Katherine said, trying for the friendly approach, hoping she wasn't misreading the dog's demeanor.

The dog's tail wagged and thumped the ground.

"FELAN!!" a voice thundered. "HERE!" A loud whistle cut through the air, and the dog scampered off toward the tor. Katherine smiled, watching the animal as it ran, envying its speed and grace.

Her smile disappeared in a gulp of horror when the dog approached the tor, for standing near the peak was the figure from the storm. The same long, flowing coat. The same wide-brimmed hat.

Sixteen

Panicked, Katherine sprinted down the path to the studio and looked back when she reached her door. The stranger still watched her. The day had lost its warmth, and she shivered as the chill of fear crept over her.

Who was he? Why was he watching her?

Her cleaning could wait. She ran back to her cottage and powered up her laptop. Sitting in the conservatory, she trawled the internet for any history of the area. She read about the quarry that once existed nearby; the one Jonathan had mentioned, and about a railway that used to run between Yelverton and Princetown some years ago. There had been a stop—or halt, as it was known—right here at Ingra Tor. In fact, the road that led to her house was sited beside what was once the railway track.

Who built her cottage, and why? Was it the owner of the quarry? The railways? Perhaps the library in Princetown held some answers.

~

Katherine returned to the studio the following day, determined to go ahead with her cleaning. She scanned her surroundings as she walked, looking for any sign of The Stranger, although what she would do if she encountered him, she hadn't a clue. Was she brave enough to confront him? Demand to know why he was watching her? Probably not. She was a coward at heart and avoided unpleasantness wherever she could. Better to avoid him altogether, if possible.

A half smile turned up the corners of her mouth. Her subconscious capitalized how she thought of him—The Stranger—the words in her mind written in a deep, arterial blood red, pulsating, and dripping. Obviously harking back to Charlotte, Amy and the Ouija board, not to mention one too many horror movies.

A little way along the path provided a good view of not only the tor, but the surrounding moors as well. She looked around, watching for any movement. Not a soul in sight. She was completely alone. Thank goodness.

Back at her studio, she picked up the bucket she'd left the day before and opened the door. Not only was the layer of dust even thicker than that on the shelf in the cellar, but the window was also filthy, both inside and out. This was going to be a bigger job than she'd expected. When was the studio last used, and for what purpose? Was the previous owner an artist of some kind? Perhaps a writer like herself. A vision rose in her mind of an old man dressed in a velvet coat, a ruffled collar, quill in hand, seated at this very table, scrawling sonnets on sheets of parchment. *Stop daydreaming, Katherine, or you'll never get the studio clean.*

She emptied her bucket of its furniture polish, window cleaner, scrubbing brush, and an assortment of rags, then took the bucket to the stream for water. As she approached, she saw a large fish, perhaps the same one as yesterday. It darted away from her. "Don't worry, little fishy," she told it, "I won't hurt you."

Back at the studio, she dumped a good measure of window cleaner in her bucket and started with the window. She scrubbed, she rinsed, she polished almost every surface, making numerous trips to the stream for fresh water. By the time she finished, the window sparkled, the table and chair gleamed, but her jeans and shirt were filthy. Over the years, smoke from the fireplace had discolored the stone mantel, and no amount of scrubbing was going to get that clean. Besides, it added a certain amount of character to the room. She must remember to bring a barrow-load of firewood next time. It would be lovely to sit here and write with the crackle of a fire, particularly when the cooler days of winter arrived, although she'd need a light of some description. She should look at getting power connected. Ha, maybe she'd better get her book written and published before she started spending that kind of money.

She packed up her cleaning bits and bobs and set off toward the cottage. Again, she stopped at the bridge and looked into the water. The fish was in his usual spot. On an impulse, she called out to it.

"Hi, Norman; it's me, Katherine." But Norman was not much of a conversationalist, choosing instead to flick his tail and hide behind a rock. She'd been thinking of her father the first time she saw her fishy friend, and it seemed right, somehow, to name it after him.

Her father had always encouraged her to write, even as a little girl. Back then, she'd written stories about fairies and ballerinas, ponies and puppies. But now, in her thirties, she wrote about women with courage, who faced their struggles and came through. Sometimes along the way, they fell in love, but mostly, like her, they didn't.

It's not that Katherine wasn't interested in the opposite sex. She liked men, had had her fair share of dates, even a surprise proposal of marriage on a second date, but she hadn't found that special someone with whom she wanted to share her life.

She'd always read her work aloud as part of her editing process, and up until recently, it was her father to whom she'd read, but now Norman the fish would be her sounding board. If people thought her crazy, reading to a fish, so be it.

Katherine's mother never understood her desire to write, nor her father's encouragement of it. Her mantra had been, "Stop filling the child's head with silly nonsense, Norman." To which her father would reply, "Fiddlesticks, Jacqui. Katherine has a talent for writing, and you know it." At which point her mother would usually 'harrumph' and flounce out of the room.

Her mother always appeared jealous of the close relationship

Katherine shared with her father. In fact, all the arguments between her parents usually found Katherine planted squarely in the middle; her father taking Katherine's side against her mother. When Katherine announced to her parents that she was to study creative writing at the University of East Anglia, her father hugged her and congratulated her, but her mother's reaction was quite different.

"How utterly ridiculous," her mother said, directing her tirade at her husband. "This is all your fault, Norman. You and your silly bloody stories, always encouraging the girl. I warned you, didn't I? She should be thinking of a proper career, not swanning off to learn creative writing." As usual, she stomped out of the room and up the stairs.

When Katherine finished her degree and landed a job as an editorial assistant with a publishing company, her mother reluctantly conceded that perhaps her study had been worthwhile.

For Katherine, however, it was all very well editing other people's articles and copy, but what really set her heart on fire was writing her own stories. So, she wrote under a pseudonym and was lucky enough to have had several short stories published in magazines. She was prudent enough not to mention this to her mother, of course, but her father was still her sounding board, so she read every new story to him before releasing it to the outside world.

Her parents were living in Tavistock when her father became ill, and Katherine moved from Manchester to be near him. She'd rented a small flat in town and taken a job as a proofreader at the *Tavistock Tribune*. When his illness progressed to the point where he needed twenty-four-hour care, her father was transferred to the Royal Cornwall Hospital in Truro. Her mother moved to Truro to be closer to him, and when he ultimately passed away, she stayed on. She'd grown up and gone to school in Truro and still maintained a good network of friends in the area. Katherine stayed on in Tavistock.

She shook herself back to the present. *Gosh, I've got to stop this or I'll never get my novel even started, let alone finished. Better get my skates on!*

Back at the cottage, she changed into clean clothes and dumped the dirty ones in the washing machine, then gathered the things needed to make a start on her novel. Laptop, of course, a spare battery, as there was no electricity in the studio, and no phone. That would keep her focused. No wasting time on social media. She packed a box with other things she would need. Notepads, pens, pencils, and her most cherished book: *On Writing* by Stephen King, her favorite author. She especially treasured it, as it was the last birthday present her father gave her. He'd written on the fly-leaf: *Believe in yourself. You can do it.* She loved his quiet encouragement and his solid belief in her.

She made a thermos flask of lemongrass-and-ginger tea, found a packet of chocolate digestive biscuits, grabbed a jumper in case it got cold, and set off for the studio.

As she crossed the little bridge over the stream, she called out, "Hi Norman, it's me, Katherine." Norman didn't return the greeting. "Bit quiet today, Norman?" she called and giggled. People will definitely think I've lost my marbles. But people talk to their pets all the time, so why shouldn't she talk to a fish?

Before she entered the studio, she scanned the surroundings for any sight of The Stranger, relieved there was no sign of him. She settled herself at her table, switched on her laptop, poured herself a cup of tea, and opened the packet of biscuits. She took two and scrunched the packet closed. A sip of tea, a crunch into her biscuit, and her laptop was ready. She opened a new project file, sat a moment gathering her thoughts, and then set to work, her fingers flying over the keys as the story unfolded in her mind.

The afternoon wore on. Every once in a while, Katherine stopped writing, got up and stretched, only vaguely aware of the shadow of the tor creeping closer as the sun sank lower in the sky.

Hours later, her laptop beeped and a 'low battery' warning popped up. Katherine saved her work, stretched, and looked up. She froze, mouth open, eyes wide, heart pounding in her chest. The Stranger stood on top of the tor, motionless, watching.

Seventeen

What should she do? There was nowhere to hide, no one to call for help.

As if realizing she had seen him, The Stranger strode down off the tor and out of sight. Now, Katherine didn't know where he was, and somehow, that was worse than knowing he was watching her. Where was he? She moved to the window, pressing her forehead against the glass, but still no sign of her tormentor.

Footsteps crunched on the gravel path outside, and Katherine spun around, frantically looking for something, anything, to use as a weapon. She grabbed her laptop and held it above her head.

"Katherine? Anybody home? " A cheery voice called from outside.

Jonathan! Thank God. She put the laptop back on the table and opened the door.

"My God, Katherine, are you okay? You look like you've seen a ghost." Lines of worry etched Jonathan's face.

"He... he... on the tor," Katherine stammered, her heart thumping her chest so hard she struggled to breathe.

Jonathan grasped her shoulders. "Who? What's wrong?"

Katherine leaned against Jonathan, and he folded his arms around her, stroking her hair.

"It's okay, you're safe," he murmured. "Who frightened you? Can you tell me?"

His voice was soft, reassuring, albeit a little patronizing. Katherine's heart slowed, and she relaxed a little, comforted by Jonathan's embrace.

"The Stranger. On the tor, he just stood there, staring at me, then he disappeared. I heard footsteps. I thought it was him."

Jonathan hugged her tightly before releasing her. "Stay here." He strode outside, but returned a minute later, shaking his head. "There's no one there. Are you sure you didn't imagine it?"

Katherine gaped at Jonathan. Didn't he believe her? "Of course I'm sure. I've seen him before. When I first moved in, the day of that big storm. He was standing by the orchard gate, watching."

"What makes you think it's the same man?"

"I recognized his hat and coat. It's one of those long, oilskin-looking things, and his hat is sort of like a cowboy hat, but the brim is wider. He looked like something out of an old horror movie." No way was she going to tell Jonathan about the night of the Ouija board and her resultant nightmares.

Jonathan shrugged. "Well, there's nobody there now, anyway."

Katherine gathered her things together. She'd done enough writing for the day; it was time to go back. "So what brings you all this way, Jonathan?"

Jonathan's cheeks flushed, but he still managed to look smug. "Um, well, I was simply wondering how you were getting on... after that storm..."

"I'm fine, Jonathan. You really didn't have to come over; you could have just telephoned. Although I'm glad you came."

Jonathan turned away, looking out of the window. He was silent for a moment, then took a deep breath. "Would you have dinner with me tonight?"

Eighteen

Oh no. She didn't want to encourage Jonathan, but she also didn't want to hurt his feelings. He'd been so kind to her; she shouldn't be heartless. Perhaps once would be alright.

He turned to face her, his brow lifted in a question, and Katherine looked away.

"That would be nice," she murmured.

"What about The Coachman's Rest? In Merrivale."

"Yes, alright. I can meet you there, about seven?" She looked up at Jonathan, whose face now wore an expression reminiscent of cats and cream. *Lord, what have I done?*

"I could drive you..."

Katherine cut him off. "No, that's silly. You'd have to drive me all the way back here again. Much more logical for me to take my car. Save you all that driving."

"I don't mind. Really."

"That's okay, Jonathan. Thank you for the offer, but I'll drive." She spoke firmly, hoping that would be the end of the matter. The last thing she wanted was an awkward farewell on her doorstep late at night. Or worse, Jonathan insisting on a nightcap.

"Well, okay if you must." Jonathan's shoulders slumped, and his face traded its smugness for a crestfallen expression.

"I'm done here. Shall we go back to the cottage?" Katherine edged toward the door.

"Can I help carry anything?"

"No, that's fine, thanks."

Jonathan closed the stable door, and they walked along the path together. Crossing the bridge, she called, "Hi, Norman; it's me, Katherine, and my friend, Jonathan."

Jonathan looked at her, his forehead wrinkled, brows knitted together. "Huh? Who's Norman?"

"Norman is a fish. He lives by the bridge."

"You've called a fish Norman?" Jonathan's tone mocked her.

"And what's wrong with Norman? I named him after my father." Katherine spoke sharply, defensive of her fishy companion and her father.

Jonathan held his hands up in surrender. "Nothing, nothing. I'm just not used to people naming fish. What does your father think of you calling a fish after him?"

Katherine hung her head. "My father's dead," she whispered, her voice breaking into a sob.

Jonathan put his arm around her. "I'm so sorry, I didn't know."

She leaned against him a moment, glad of his comforting arm, before she walked on.

The two remained silent for a while, but as they passed through the orchard, Jonathan stopped, admiring an apple tree laden with red-and-orange-blushed apples.

"That's a Cox's Orange Pippin," Katherine said. "Said to be the finest of the dessert apples. Have one if you like."

Jonathan plucked one off the tree and bit into it, juice running down his chin, which he swiped away with his free hand as Katherine laughed. "Delicious, but I mustn't spoil my appetite for dinner." He threw the rest of the apple away and looked around. "Good lot of fruit on the trees. What will you do with it all?"

"Lots of things. Apple crumble, jams, jelly, pies. Might even try my hand at cider if I've enough apples. Then, of course, there's all the plums."

Jonathan looked directly at Katherine, his eagerness crystal clear. "I simply adore apple crumble. It's my favorite pudding of all time."

Katherine squirmed under his gaze, knowing where this would lead if she didn't head him off. Her emotions were mixed. She liked Jonathan, had gladly taken comfort when he offered it, but she didn't want a relationship with anyone at the moment. "You're more than welcome to take as many apples as you want, then you can make apple crumble as often as you like."

Jonathan seemed to deflate, his eager manner gone in a flash. "Thank you," he said in a voice that held very little enthusiasm.

Katherine walked into the living room and put her laptop on the coffee table. Jonathan plopped himself, uninvited, on the sofa, his arms spread out along the backrest. Was he angling to stay while she got ready? That wasn't happening. She wanted a shower and to wash her hair, and she wasn't about to do that with him still in the house.

She left the living room and walked toward the front door. "I'll see you about seven," she called back over her shoulder.

Jonathan emerged from the living room, looking at Katherine with his sad puppy eyes.

"Look, Jonathan. I want to have a shower. I can't go out for dinner looking like this." She indicated her messed-up hair, her dirty jeans, and shirt.

"You look beautiful."

"No, I don't, so stop trying to be nice. Go! I won't be long."

Jonathan trudged toward his car, and she closed the front door behind him and leaned against it. Why, oh why, did she agree to this? She locked the door and dashed up the stairs to the bathroom, turning the shower on to warm up while she stripped off her clothes. Stepping under the water, she let it run down over her face and sighed. *Mmm, that's good.* She shampooed her hair, applied conditioner, and combed it through, carefully removing a couple of stubborn knots.

A final rinse, and she turned off the shower. She dried herself, squeezing the water from her hair, wrapped a towel around her body, and made her way to her bedroom. Through the window, the late afternoon sun shrouded the moor with shadows. She turned on the light and sat at her dressing table to dry her hair, then applied a little make-up and a dab of perfume.

She chose clothes and laid them out on the bed. Underwear, jeans, a linen shirt. The setting sun hovered a sliver above the horizon, bathing her room in its golden glow. She moved to the window to watch it set, letting the towel fall to the floor as she dressed, watching the sun sink lower. When the last tiny sliver disappeared, and she could no longer see outside, just her own reflection in the window, she pulled on a pair of boots and surveyed herself in the mirror. Yes, she'd achieved the look she wanted. Smart and casual, not dressy. This outfit shouldn't give Jonathan any encouragement.

Nineteen

JONATHAN

Jonathan drove away from Katherine's cottage, frustrated that she'd insisted on driving herself to Merrivale. He'd planned to get her a little tipsy, get her guard down, and take her home, where he could seduce her, make love to her, and claim her as his own. But she'd decided on being Miss Independent. So he'd have to bide his time for a little while longer.

He stopped out of sight of the cottage, took a pair of binoculars from the glove compartment, and got out of the car. The late afternoon sun behind the tor threw long shadows, and he kept to these as he crept closer to the object of his desire. Once in sight of the cottage, he knelt beside a gorse bush and adjusted the focus of his binoculars in order to see Katherine's bedroom window clearly. Her light was on, but he couldn't see her.

Dammit.

He waited.

After several minutes, with still no sign of her, he lowered the binoculars, but at the last second, his peripheral vision detected movement, and he again trained the binoculars on her window. There she was, a towel wrapped around her body, her hair falling in curls around her shoulders. My God, she was beautiful, even with her back to him.

A stirring in his groin gave rise to an erection that grew harder as he watched. Katherine now stood at the window. Perhaps she was looking for him, thinking about him, and their date tonight. His breathing quickened, his erection straining to be free of its confines. God, he wanted her.

Katherine dropped the towel, and his eyes widened, his mouth agape as he cried out with shocked pleasure at her naked body. His erection throbbed at this vision of loveliness, then bucked and spilled.

"Oh, shit." He dropped the binoculars, undid his trousers, and yanked them down before his fluids soaked through them. His underwear was already sodden. He kicked off his shoes, pulled off his trousers and laid them on the heather, then removed his underwear, and used them to dry himself as best he could. No way could he wear them again, and there wasn't time to go all the way back home and change before meeting Katherine. Her image floated into his mind again, arousing him, and he wrapped his hand around his already stiffening penis, stroking up and down with slow, but firm movements. Was his beloved still naked? Light continued to spill from her bedroom window. Maybe he'd be in luck. Still stroking his now fully erect penis, he picked up the binoculars with his other hand and focused them on Katherine's window. Damn. She was almost fully dressed. Nowhere near as exciting. He dropped the binoculars and closed his eyes, summoning back the image of her nakedness, imagining himself touching her—his stroking grew faster—tasting her—faster still—her mouth on him. Then to take her, claim her, plant his seed inside her. With a guttural grunt, he climaxed, his semen spilling onto the heather.

He relaxed for a few minutes, cleaned himself up, and pulled his trousers back on. Would Katherine notice his lack of underwear? He'd never gone 'commando' before; it was quite liberating. Perhaps he'd do it more often.

Katherine's window was dark. If she left immediately, she might see his car on the roadside. He'd have to hurry. He pulled his shoes on and ran back to his car, panting, a stitch in his side, but no time to rest. If he was to remain unseen, he needed to leave now. He sped away, his powerful Mercedes eating up the road ahead while he kept one eye on the rearview mirror, looking for her lights.

At the car park of The Coachman's Rest, he brought the car to an abrupt halt. Made it. Exhausted from running and the adrenaline rush from his breakneck driving, he lay his head on the steering wheel. He allowed himself a few minutes to recover before getting out and leaning against his car, legs crossed at the ankles, trying for a casual, carefree pose.

It wasn't long before lights approached from the direction of the moor. When they turned into the car park, he did a mental check of himself. Yes, he was ready. Tonight, he would begin his seduction.

Twenty

KATHERINE

Katherine pulled her Land Rover in beside Jonathan's Mercedes. He'd been casually leaning against his car, but now he rushed toward her. No doubt intending to open her door for her. She hastily got out herself, thwarting his gallantry.

"Hello again," she said.

Jonathan gave a nervous laugh. "Hi."

"Have you been running? You seem flustered." In fact, he looked rather rumpled, not a bit like the immaculately dressed young man she'd come to know. What had he been up to?

He looked away. "No, no. Of course not. I'm just really glad to see you." He brushed the knees of his dark gray trousers. "Goodness, look at the state of me. You'll think I'm a vagabond."

"Well, I did wonder..."

His head snapped up, and he glared at her. Then his face softened, and he smiled. "You're teasing me, aren't you?"

"Of course I am."

"I didn't have time to go home and change. Mark needed some files and couldn't find them. I've been down on my knees in the store room searching for them. I'm really sorry."

Something in his tone, his hurried speech, and the way he avoided her eyes as he spoke struck her. *He's hiding something.*

The Coachman's Rest looked different at night. A golden glow spilled through the windows, and old-fashioned carriage lamps illuminated the car park. Tiny fairy lights twinkled around the stone porch, giving it a magical appearance. This would look fantastic blanketed in snow. If the food was good, perhaps she'd bring her mother here for Christmas lunch.

Jonathan opened the door and held it for Katherine to enter. The rustic interior boasted a stone fireplace in which a roaring fire blazed, its warmth being enjoyed by a black-and-white cat snoozing on the hearth. Easy chairs upholstered in rich red velvet stood on either side of the fire, inviting you to sit a spell. All it needed to complete the picture was a Christmas stocking hanging from the mantel.

The inn was a picture-postcard Devon pub with its oak beams and real beer taps. Bottles of various colors and sizes lined the back wall, while above the bar itself, glasses of various shapes and sizes glittered in the light. The bartender put down the glass he had been polishing and smiled. "Hello and welcome. What can I get you?"

Jonathan put his foot on the brass rail running along the length of the bar and smiled at Katherine. "Now, what would you like to drink? Perhaps a cider?"

"Yes, a cider would be good."

"I'll get these; you choose a table." Jonathan addressed the barman. "I'll have a pint of Jail Ale, please, and my girl would like a cider."

Katherine bristled and gritted her teeth. How dare he refer to her as 'his girl' indeed? But rather than make a scene in front of the barman, she walked away and surveyed the tables. A cozy booth in the corner looked inviting, but it would be too easy for Jonathan to sit close to her, so she opted for a table with chairs opposite each other. Much safer.

Jonathan arrived with the drinks and placed them on the table. He sat, picked up his beer. "Cheers."

Katherine reached for her glass, turning it around and around in the pool of condensation forming at its base. "Look, Jonathan, there's something I need to get clear right from the start. I am not *your girl*. Understand?"

Jonathan laughed and waved a hand dismissively. "Oh, that. I didn't mean it that way. It came out wrong. What I meant to say was 'my friend'. I'm sorry."

Katherine nodded, unconvinced. "Okay, as long as we're clear." She picked up her cider and took a drink. Fresh, crisp, not too dry. "Mmmm, that's nice."

"I'm glad you like it. It's Devon Red. The barman recommended it."

"He chose well." Katherine took another sip.

"Thought about what you'd like to eat yet?" Jonathan asked.

"No, not really. Any thoughts yourself?" She looked at the blackboard menu above the fireplace.

"Well, I'm told they make fabulous pies, so I might try the steak and kidney."

Katherine scanned the menu. "Yum, they've got trout. One of my favorites. I'll have that."

"I like a girl who can make a quick decision." Jonathan looked lovingly at her.

Katherine squirmed under the intensity of his gaze and took another sip of her cider. Agreeing to come out with Jonathan was a bad move. He'd taken it as her being interested in him. She didn't believe for a moment his excuse for referring to her as 'his girl'. How could she extricate herself without hurting his feelings?

The awkward moment was averted by a waiter arriving to take their order. Jonathan ordered for both of them. The waiter scribbled on her little notepad, smiled at Katherine, and left.

"So, tell me about yourself." Jonathan sat back, crossing one leg over the other.

"Not a lot to tell. I'm a writer, but you already know that."

"What do you write?"

Katherine looked down at her hands as she toyed with her glass. "Well, my last job was mostly proofreading, but I've written a few short stories, and I've just started my novel. Today, as a matter of fact."

"Cool. Congratulations on taking the plunge. I'll get some champagne to celebrate." He started to rise, but Katherine put a hand on his arm to stop him.

"No, don't. We both have to drive, remember?"

He pouted. "See, if you'd let me drive you, you could have had champagne." Then he laughed, a little too highly pitched to be sincere. "Just teasing, of course."

Katherine forced a smile at his very unconvincing disclaimer.

"What's your novel about?" he asked after a few moments.

"I don't really know yet."

His eyebrows knitted into a puzzled frown. "How can you not know?"

"I just write what comes."

Jonathan chuckled. "That's mad. So you have no plot in mind, you just start writing?" He shook his head. "Mad."

Katherine grinned and relaxed a little. "I guess it does sound crazy, but that's about the extent of it."

Their meals arrived, and they tucked in. The trout was delicious, very fresh, and expertly pan-fried. Hand-cut chips nestled in a basket to one side of the fish. Jonathan's pie looked equally good; golden pastry with a rich, chunky filling, accompanied by a generous serving of creamy mashed potato and a small jug of gravy. A platter of vegetables for them to share completed the meal.

As they ate, Katherine talked more about her writing. Her father's encouragement, her mother's disdain. Jonathan listened attentively, prompting her with questions and comments.

By the time their plates were cleared away and they were sipping on cups of coffee, Katherine had done nearly all the talking. This was not what she wanted at all. She rarely talked about herself, but Jonathan had been easy to talk to.

"Jonathan, I'm sorry. I've just realized I've monopolized the conversation. All I've done is talk about me."

"Please don't apologize. I love to hear you talk." He reached across the table and took her hand, his eyes meeting hers. "And I want to know *everything* there is to know about you." His grip tightened on her fingers.

Twenty-One

Katherine snatched her hand away and scrunched up her napkin. "You're too kind, Jonathan. But tell me about you. You certainly don't have a local accent. In fact, I'd say you don't really have an accent at all. You speak what my mother would have said is BBC English."

Jonathan clapped his hands and smiled, then his voice took on the local burr as he said, "Aye, I got packed off ta boardin' school when I be just a lad." Then, in his normal voice, he added, "And being bullied for the way I spoke, I quickly learned to assimilate."

"That's awful. Children can be so unkind."

"Yes, they can, but none of it matters now." He reached across the table toward Katherine's hand as she still toyed with her napkin.

She made a show of looking at her watch, surprised to see that it was after ten-thirty. "Oh gosh, it's later than I thought. I'd better go."

"Do you have to?"

"Yes, I do," she said, getting to her feet. "Thank you for a lovely evening. It's certainly a nice place here." As they walked to the bar, she took out her wallet.

Jonathan put his hands up, palms facing her. "No, no. This is my treat."

"You don't have to do that."

"Of course I do. You're my date." Jonathan smiled, then handed his credit card to the barman.

Katherine gritted her teeth at Jonathan's smug, condescending tone. *Don't make a scene, not here.* But she'd have to find a way to let him know she wasn't interested in being 'his girl'.

Outside, the cool night air raised goosebumps on Katherine's arms, and she shivered as she unlocked her car and opened the door. "Thank you again, Jonathan."

"My pleasure. I'm so glad you came." He moved toward her, reaching as if to embrace her.

Katherine quickly climbed into her Land Rover, leaving Jonathan clutching an empty space. "Goodnight then," she said and pulled the door, giving him no option but to step back. The door closed with a resounding *thunk*, and she resisted the temptation to lock it.

"Um, well, goodnight, then." Jonathan's lip quivered, and his eyes shone. Was he about to cry? Surely not.

Katherine started the motor and reversed out of the car park. She glanced in the rearview mirror as she drove away. Jonathan stood in the circle of lamplight, shoulders slumped, head bowed. Forlorn and dejected. Another twinge of guilt gnawed at her conscience.

Katherine returned from her studio late afternoon the next day and put the kettle on. The sound of tires crunching on gravel alerted Katherine to a visitor, and she went to the door. The doors of a small, red hatchback opened, and two of her previous workmates got out. She ran to greet them, hugging them both in a three-way embrace. "Rebecca, Maddy, what on earth are you two doing here?"

Rebecca broke away and retrieved a bottle of champagne from the back seat. "Couldn't let you leave without at least some kind of farewell, so here we are." She thrust the bottle at Katherine. "It's already cool, but chuck it in the freezer for ten minutes and it will be perfect."

"And while that's chilling, you can show us around your new abode," Maddy said. "I know you wanted solitude, but really? Could you have got any more remote?"

Katherine led the others inside. After putting the champagne to chill, she led the girls on a tour of the house, leaving her bedroom till last.

"My God, that view! It's stunning," Maddy said. "I can see why you love it."

"I think it's what really made me decide on buying here," Katherine said. "That and the studio. Want to see it?"

"Of course," Rebecca said. "Lead on."

"Anybody home?" A male voice called from downstairs.

Katherine made a 'tut' sound. Jonathan. *What did he want now?* She trotted down the stairs, her friends following close behind her.

"I didn't know you had visitors. That's nice." Jonathan said, but his tone of voice was cold.

"Yes, Rebecca and Maddy are from work," Katherine said. "This is Jonathan, the estate agent who found my new home."

"Hello, Jonathan," Rebecca said, "You handled the sale of our flat, remember?"

Jonathan smiled. "Yes, of course."

"You found a lovely place for Katherine," Maddy said, "but too remote for me, I'm afraid."

Katherine said, "What can I do for you, Jonathan?"

"Just wondered how you were getting along, if there was anything I could do for you."

"No, things are fine. I'm settling in well, thanks."

Jonathan looked sheepish. "Any chance of a cup of tea?"

Katherine sighed. "I'll put the kettle on." She moved toward the kitchen and turned the kettle back on.

"Why don't we three go into the living room while Katherine makes the tea?" Jonathan extended his arms out as if to herd Rebecca and Maddy.

A few minutes later, Katherine brought tea into the living room to find her friends standing by the fireplace while Jonathan sat, his arms stretched out along the sofa back.

Rebecca glanced at Maddy, then said, "Look, we really should be going, shouldn't we, Maddy."

Maddy nodded emphatically. "Yes, definitely, we should."

"But what about the champagne?" Katherine asked.

Rebecca waved her hand in a dismissive gesture. "You enjoy it. We really have to go." The two girls started toward the door.

"Well, if you're sure," Katherine said, hugging each of her friends.

She waved goodbye as Rebecca drove away, then returned to Jonathan.

"You look worried," Jonathan said, putting his mug of tea down on the table.

"Not worried, just puzzled. The girls were so warm and friendly when they arrived, but they suddenly went very cool."

Jonathan shrugged. "Never mind, they're gone, now." He patted the seat beside him. "Come, sit, tell me what you've been doing."

"Well, since I saw you last night, not a lot. Spent the day writing, which is what I came here to do."

"Maybe your friends realized they were interrupting you."

"They didn't. I'd finished for the day before they got here. I hadn't even gotten to show them the studio when you arrived. You didn't say anything to them, did you?"

"Not a thing," Jonathan said, looking down at his hands.

Twenty-Two

JONATHAN

Jonathan finished his tea and decided it was time to leave. He hadn't expected Katherine to have visitors when he arrived, but even though they'd gone, she still seemed in an odd mood. And she'd practically accused him of being the reason the girls left so soon.

If only she knew.

As he drove back to town, he thought back over his handling of the situation. He'd manipulated it well. Got Katherine out of the way, while he'd got the girls on their own.

"Look, girls," he'd said, "I know you mean well and think Katherine is pleased to have you visit. Now she won't tell you, because she's too polite, but I took her for a drink the night she left work and she remarked how glad she was that she didn't have to see any of you again."

Rebecca had looked at Maddy, then back at him, her eyes wide. "She really said that?"

"Yes, she was quite vocal, in fact," he'd said.

Rebecca's expression had changed from disbelief to anger. "I'll give her a piece of my mind." She'd taken a step toward the kitchen.

Jonathan had grabbed her arm, terrified of what she might say to Katherine. He couldn't let her expose his lie. "No, stop. I'm sure she didn't mean it the way it sounds. I think what she really meant was that she just wanted to be left alone to write with no one interrupting her. Perhaps it would be best if you just left."

Maddy had nodded. "I agree. Let's just go."

He'd quickly sat down when he'd heard Katherine approaching with the tea.

Yes, he'd handled it well. No doubt those two would go back to the office and spread the word among their colleagues. So he could safely assume Katherine would have no more visits, which suited him just fine. Keep her isolated from everyone else but him.

It was all so easy.

Twenty-Three

KATHERINE

Katherine left the post office, threading the key to her new PO Box onto her key ring. She had rashly mentioned to Jonathan at dinner that she planned to be in Princetown and, predictably, he said he would be too, and could they meet for lunch? She'd told him no, she was only going to be there for an hour or so. Of course, she didn't mention her planned visit to the library, for fear he'd have wanted to help. But he'd insisted on coffee and she finally, reluctantly, agreed. God, he was persuasive.

As she struggled with her keys, the little TARDIS emblem dropped to the ground. She bent to retrieve it, but another hand reached it first, and she straightened to find herself face to face with The Stranger. The long, flowing coat and wide-brimmed hat were unmistakable. His dark, almost black eyes blazed at her, boring into her soul as he held out the little blue box. This close, she could see the lines around his eyes, and his weather-beaten face. She judged him to be in his late fifties. She tentatively reached out and took the TARDIS from him. "Thank you," she whispered, her voice not much more than a squeak. She started to walk past him, but he grasped her arm and held it firmly, whirling her around to face him. Too frightened to speak, Katherine stood facing The Stranger from the moor and her nightmares, the copper taste of fear flooding her mouth; her heart threatening to break her ribs with its jackhammering.

He leaned in toward her, his face inches from hers. "Ye'd best beware!" he hissed. "The cellar." Then his gaze flicked to something behind her, and he released her arm. As quickly as he'd appeared, he was gone.

Katherine's legs could no longer support her, and she stumbled back against the post office window.

"Hello, Katherine!" Jonathan called.

Katherine held a hand to her chest, trying to ease her thumping heart. She took a deep breath to calm her shattered nerves. "Jonathan. Boy, am I glad to see you."

Jonathan preened. His eyes sparkled and his smile stretched wider than she would have thought possible. He had misconstrued her greeting.

"I'm glad to see you, too." He moved close to her.

"Sorry, that came out wrong," she said.

"You're not glad to see me?" He sounded petulant.

"Stop it, Jonathan, stop joking around. I'm trying to tell you he was here. The man from the tor. He grabbed my arm and threatened me."

Jonathan clasped her shoulders, worry lines etching his face. "My God, are you okay? What did he say?"

"He told me to beware. Something about the cellar, but then he took off. Who is he, and why is he doing this to me? I'm frightened."

He gathered her into his arms and held her close, stroking her hair and cooing softly to her.

Against her better judgment, Katherine relaxed against him, relishing the softness of his caress on her back, his warmth, the safety of his arms. One hand stroked her hair, his fingers toying with her curls. She breathed in the scent of him, that same citrus-and-spice fragrance she'd detected at their first meeting, and turned her face up to him. His lips moved toward hers, his eyes half closed, his breath smelling faintly of mint and coffee. She parted her own lips, ready for his kiss.

No, this was wrong. She wrenched herself away, leaving him looking bewildered.

"Katherine?"

"I'm sorry. I don't know what came over me. Forgive me, it won't happen again."

"Don't say that, Katherine."

She shook her head. "Look, I'd better go. I'm feeling rather shaken."

"What about that coffee?"

"I'm sorry. I really just want to go home."

"Let me come with you, then," his tone verged on pleading.

"No. Thank you, but no. I'll be fine. Really."

"But I so looked forward to seeing you."

Feeling guilty again, she touched his arm. "Look, I've got to come into Tavistock later in the week, so we can meet up then if you're not busy."

"Yes, that would be great. I know this great little Italian place we can go to for lunch. My treat. You can tell me more about your book."

"Okay, I'll let you know which day, but you have to let me pay for lunch." Before Jonathan protested, she added, "After all, it's the least I can do for the man who found me such a wonderful house. You wouldn't deprive me of the opportunity to thank you, would you?"

"I guess not," he said, a touch of sadness in his voice, but then his face brightened and he smiled, somewhat smugly.

"I'll see you later in the week then," Katherine said. What was with the sudden change in Jonathan's demeanor? He was up to something. But what?

"I will count the hours until I see you again." Jonathan half bowed, a melodramatic gesture, the smug look still on his face.

Katherine turned to go, an uneasy feeling creeping over her.

Twenty-Four

Driving home, her mind returned to her encounter with The Stranger. Who was he? What did he want from her? Why did he threaten her like that? So many questions, but not enough answers.

Later that afternoon, Katherine made a thermos of tea and headed off to her studio, laptop under her arm. At the bridge, she stopped and looked into the water. There was Norman. “Hi, Norman; it’s me, Katherine.”

Norman said nothing, obviously not very talkative today.

At the studio, warm sunshine streamed in through the window. Katherine poured a cup of tea and set to work, lost in the world of her creation as the words flowed onto the screen.

Twenty-Five

JONATHAN

Jonathan knocked on Katherine's door and waited. No answer. Her Land Rover was parked outside, so she had to be home. Could she be at her studio? He knocked again, waited a few minutes, then walked around to the rear of the cottage and knocked on the conservatory door. Still no Katherine.

He opened the door and went inside, calling her name, and when no answer came, he wandered through the house, checking every room, but she wasn't in the house. The cellar door was closed, so he opened it and called her name, even though he doubted she would be there. She must be at the studio. Great. Time to do some snooping.

On the kitchen table, he found her phone. He picked it up and tapped the power button, expecting to find the handset locked and needing a pin, but to his surprise, when he swiped up, the phone unlocked. He chuckled. *This girl's got no idea about security.* The home screen displayed a calendar app, which opened to the current day. No entry for today, and he scrolled back. There was a note the day Rebecca and Maddy had visited, as well as the occasional mention of Jonathan. Scrolling further back, he noticed that every four weeks displayed 'X', the latest one being four days ago. His heart skipped a beat. *She* had put an 'X' in her diary when *her* period was due, so he knew when sex with *her* was a no-go. Maybe Katherine did the same. If that were the case, this was valuable information. Very valuable indeed.

He took a sheet of notepaper and made notes of the dates marked, then exited the app and put the phone back on the table. Perhaps there was a way to find out for sure. He headed upstairs.

In the bathroom, he checked the medicine cabinet and the cupboard beneath the hand basin, finding a box of tampons and a packet of pads. He took the lid off the small bin. Buried beneath cotton balls soiled with makeup and other unidentified substances was a used pad. So, his theory would appear to be correct. What a fantastic stroke of luck.

Now to see what treasures her bedroom would reveal. First, her bedside drawer. A well-thumbed paperback from the Tavistock library, a packet of tissues, and what's this? A small box of condoms. Was she seeing someone? She'd never mentioned a boyfriend. A wave of jealousy surged through him. No, Katherine was his and his alone. He wouldn't stand for her being with anyone but him. On examining the box carefully, he found the seal intact, and he breathed a sigh of relief. But then his pulse quickened and he felt a stirring in his groin. She'd obviously planned on having sex with him. What joy! He looked longingly at her bed, fighting an almost overwhelming urge to masturbate on her pillow. But he mustn't. Not here. Not yet. He reached down and, through his trousers, pinched the tip of his penis hard. So hard it brought tears to his eyes, and all thoughts of masturbation fled from his mind.

He found nothing else of interest in the bedside drawers, so moved on to the tallboy, where he found her underwear, pleased that they were not neatly folded; far less chance of her noticing anything out of place or perhaps missing. He picked up a pair of light blue cotton bikini pants and held them against his cheek, breathing deeply, savoring the faint scent of lavender. Lavender always reminded him of... no, he mustn't think of *her*. *She* was in the past. Katherine was the future. Katherine was the now.

He rummaged at the back of the drawer, and, as he'd expected, found a small drawstring bag smelling distinctly of lavender. Why did women feel the need to scent their underwear? He put the little bag to one side and sorted through the contents of the drawer, examining several pairs before finally picking out a black, lacy pair. They were so tiny, so delicate. He held them up, picturing Katherine wearing them, his penis stiffening at the image in his mind. Her beautiful body, clad only in these tiny briefs. Ha! No wonder they were called 'briefs'. These would make an excellent souvenir, so he stashed them in his pocket and closed the drawer. Next, he looked in her dressing-table drawers. The top one held makeup, hairstyling products, and a zippered case, which he opened. A manicure set. What on earth all those different gadgets were was anyone's guess. He put it back and closed the drawer.

It was time to head to the studio to find Katherine; she would need comforting after her ordeal with that horrid man this morning, and he intended to be the one to provide it. After all, that was the reason he'd come over in the first place. Being able to snoop was a bonus. He slipped his hand inside his pocket, fondling the lacy souvenir. Most definitely a bonus.

Twenty-Six

KATHERINE

The noise of the door opening startled Katherine, and she jumped up, her stomach lurching.

"Thought I'd find you here. How's the book going?" Jonathan wore the same pleased-with-himself smile from that morning.

Katherine's stomach relaxed, and her heart rate slowed; her emotions a mix of relief and anger. Certainly relieved it wasn't The Stranger come to threaten her again, or perhaps worse. Angry because it was now obvious why Jonathan had looked so smug earlier. He'd had every intention of coming over.

"What are you doing here?" She tried to keep her voice neutral, not to let him see he'd frightened her, nor how much another unannounced and uninvited visit from him annoyed her.

"I was worried about you and wanted to make sure you were okay."

"I'm fine. I told you that."

"I know, but you seemed so frightened. I just wanted to make sure you were really okay. You're angry with me." He sounded hurt.

Katherine let out a somewhat exasperated sigh. "I'm not angry with you; you just startled me."

"I'm sorry, I didn't mean to. I tried telephoning you, but there was no answer. I was worried."

"There's no phone in here. I don't like interruptions when I'm writing."

"You *are* angry with me. I'm sorry. I'll go." He walked out the door, closing it behind him.

Tempted as she was, Katherine couldn't let him go like that. She hurried after him. He'd only gone a few steps. "Jonathan, wait!"

He turned back toward her.

"Look, don't go. I'm sorry. I guess I'm more shaken up than I thought. Let's go back to the house, and I'll make some tea."

Jonathan's expression changed from sulky to triumphant in a flash. Why couldn't she be more ruthless? At this rate, she'd end up even more entangled with Jonathan and never get her novel written.

As they crossed the bridge together, Katherine called her usual greeting, "Hi, Norman; it's me, Katherine. And Jonathan"

Jonathan shook his head and rolled his eyes. "You're still talking to fish, I see."

"You bet. Norman and I are old friends. Aren't we, Norman?"

Norman said nothing.

"Not very talkative, your friend."

Katherine laughed and gave him a playful slap on the arm. "Stop teasing me."

Jonathan caught her hand and bent to kiss it. "I'll bet you Norman can't do this."

His lips were soft against the back of her hand, but Katherine squirmed in discomfort and withdrew her hand. "Jonathan..."

"Katherine, I'm sorry. I shouldn't have done that. Please forgive me."

He sounded so contrite, she said, "It's okay." Why, oh why, did she do that? Perfect opportunity to put him off, and she gave in because he made her feel guilty.

When they reached the house, Katherine led the way into the kitchen, where she filled the kettle and turned it on. As she waited for it to boil, she opened the fridge to get the bottle of milk, then gasped. Her normally sparse fridge was full of food. There were several packages of cheese, a chicken, a tray of sausages, some beans, carrots, a cabbage, salad vegetables, and a tray of fish fillets.

"What the..." She faced Jonathan, whose smile looked even more self-satisfied.

"I knew you wouldn't have had time to shop today, so I brought you some groceries. The chicken is for our dinner tonight."

"No, Jonathan, this is too much. You shouldn't have done this."

"But I *wanted* to, Katherine. I wanted to do something nice for you, to make up for that horrible man scaring you."

"That's thoughtful of you, but I really can't accept—"

"But you must! Anyway, it's done now."

"Then let me pay you for it."

"No, no. I wouldn't hear of it. Besides, as I said, the chicken is for our dinner tonight. I thought I would cook. If that's okay with you, of course."

Katherine was trapped. She couldn't turn Jonathan out now; it would be ungracious, so she did the only thing she could do; she said, "That's very kind of you, but you must let me help."

As they prepared dinner, they discussed some legends of Dartmoor.

"The story of Kitty Jay's Grave has always fascinated me," Katherine said, peeling a potato, "Although I've never seen it. Have you?"

"No, I haven't. We must go there one day, have a look for ourselves."

"It's quite sad, isn't it? To think that the poor girl killed herself when her lover betrayed her." Katherine peeled another potato.

Jonathan placed the chicken in the oven. "And mysterious. The fresh flowers on the grave. I wonder who does that. Oh, and what about Hairy Hands?"

"I don't know that one."

"Well, between Princetown and Postbridge, there's a bridge. The story is that several accidents have been caused by a pair of hairy hands taking control of the steering wheel."

"Heavens, has anyone been killed?"

"Apparently, yes. But enough of scary things. I put a bottle of wine in the fridge. Would you like a glass?"

"That would be nice. Shall we take them through to the living room?" Katherine put the peelings in the trash and rinsed her hands.

Jonathan poured the wine, putting on a silly French accent as he said, "*Oui, mademoiselle*. The wine, it is French. I hope you like it."

"*Merci, monsieur,*" Katherine said, also in a mock French accent. She still wasn't sure of Jonathan's motives, so she chose a seat in an armchair rather than the sofa. Less chance of him being able to make a move.

"So, have you explored the cellar yet?" Jonathan asked, taking a seat on the sofa, leaning toward her, elbows resting on his knees.

"I have, as a matter of fact. When I finished unpacking, I put all the empty boxes down there. Did you know that there was another cellar below that?"

"Really? I haven't been down there. When I looked over the house before listing it, I didn't have a torch with me and, well, I was alone and, well..."

"You were scared, weren't you?" Katherine teased.

"Well, not really..."

"Go on, admit it, you were." Katherine laughed.

Jonathan's face turned cold, his jaw clenched, and his lips pressed together.

Katherine put her glass on the coffee table and held out a hand to him. "Come on. I'll show you."

"What, now? You mean go down to the cellar?"

"Yes, come on."

"Okay, then." He grinned and took her hand.

Katherine unbolted the cellar door and opened it.

"I see you've put a bolt on the door."

"Yes, didn't matter what I did, the damned thing wouldn't stay shut, so I put a bolt on this side." She reached for the light switch and flicked it. Nothing happened.

"Damn, the bulb's gone again. That's the second one. Never mind, I'll get my trusty flashlight." She searched through the dresser drawers. "Here we are." The torch beam pierced the darkness in the cellar, and she started down the steps. "Come on."

Jonathan followed closely behind her. At the base of the steps, Katherine shone the light around and gasped. The packing boxes were no longer neatly stacked, but scattered all over the floor.

Twenty-Seven

"What is it? What's wrong?" Jonathan asked.

"The boxes. I stacked them on the shelf; now they're everywhere. Someone's been here."

"That's silly, Katherine. Who could have been here? Who would do that?"

"I don't know, but someone has. That man said something about the cellar."

"You mean the man who frightened you? What did he say?"

"He said to beware of the cellar. What do you think he meant?"

Jonathan shrugged. "No idea. Probably just a crank. I wouldn't worry about him. Now, you mentioned a cellar below this one. Want to show it to me, or would you prefer we go back?"

"Well, I..."

Jonathan put his arm around her shoulder and drew her to him. "It's okay, I'll protect you."

Katherine leaned against him, once again grateful for the comfort of his arm.

He took the flashlight from her trembling hands. "Which way?"

"At the end, to the left."

Jonathan removed his arm from her shoulders and took her hand in his. He squeezed it lightly. "Ready?"

"Not really, but okay." She squeezed his hand back, glad of the contact.

Jonathan led the way and shone the light down the stone steps. "Wow, this looks really old." He started down, Katherine following, her hand gripping his. When they reached the bottom and stood on the stone floor, Jonathan let go of Katherine's hand and shone the torch beam around.

"My God!" Katherine's voice verged on a scream.

Jonathan whirled around. "What?"

"Footsteps!"

"What footsteps? What are you talking about?"

She snatched the torch from him and shone it on the floor. The accumulated dust revealed several footprints. "See?"

"So there are footprints. You said yourself you've been down here before."

"But those aren't mine; they're too big." She placed her foot on one print. "See? Much too big for my foot."

Jonathan peered closely. "Hmm, yes, I see what you mean. But who else could get in here? You lock up when you go out, don't you? What about when you're in your studio?"

"Well, no, I don't..."

"You make sure you lock up properly from now on, then."

"Yes, I will. I hate the thought of someone being in here. It's like my home has been violated."

Jonathan put his arm around her and hugged her. "Come on, let's go back. Our dinner should be ready soon."

They returned to the kitchen and Jonathan bolted the cellar door, then refilled their wineglasses. Katherine set the table for dinner, toying with putting a kitchen chair against the cellar door, but deciding it was probably overkill.

After their meal, Jonathan cleared the table and stacked the dishwasher, refusing Katherine's offer to help.

"No, you just sit and enjoy your wine and tell me about your book."

"Damn. I left my laptop in the studio."

"Do you want me to get it for you?"

Katherine slumped back in her chair, shaking her head. "No, it's okay. I won't lose any work. It automatically saves and will just shut itself off when it's not used for a while. I'll get it in the morning."

"Are you sure? I don't mind."

"No, it's fine."

"Okay. Let's get comfortable then. Shall we adjourn to the living room?" He picked up their wine glasses without waiting for an answer.

Katherine followed. Jonathan put the glasses on the coffee table and picked the armchair, leaving her to sit on the sofa. She kicked off her shoes and curled her feet under her as she sat.

"Now, tell me about your book." Jonathan slipped off his own shoes and put his feet up on the coffee table. His socks sported a cartoon character with a large reddish mustache, wearing a sombrero and carrying two oversized pistols.

"It's about a woman who flees her abusive husband and settles in the country with her grandfather."

"Gosh, I hope you're not writing from experience."

Katherine laughed. "No, nothing like that. I know they say to write what you know, but if I limited myself to that, my book would be extremely boring." She took a sip of wine.

"Do you ever write about sex?"

Jonathan's question came totally unexpectedly, and Katherine almost spurted her mouthful of wine. She managed to swallow, but it went down the wrong way, and she started to cough.

Jonathan jumped up and started hammering her on the back.

When she had herself under control, she said, "Thanks, I'm fine now. Went down the wrong way."

"Would you like a glass of water?"

"Yes, thank you."

Jonathan hurried to the kitchen and returned a few moments later with a glass of water and more wine. He handed her the water, then refilled their glasses, giving Katherine most of what remained of the wine.

"So," he said, sitting down close beside her. "Do you ever write about sex?"

Katherine squirmed and looked away from his penetrating blue eyes, under the pretense of putting her water glass on the table.

"Well, yes, of course I do." She couldn't lie and say she didn't, but this was not a conversation she was comfortable having with Jonathan sitting so close, or at any other time, in fact. She could almost feel his breath on her neck.

Twenty-Eight

"Will you read some to me?"

"Good heavens, no!" Katherine laughed and moved away a tad, trying to lighten the mood of the conversation.

"Why not?" Jonathan asked. "Are you ashamed of what you write?"

How the hell did I get myself into this? "No, of course not."

"Then why won't you read some to me?"

"Because I haven't finished writing the first draft yet, and then I'll need to edit, rewrite, et cetera, before anyone sees it."

Jonathan smiled and sat back, arm stretched along the back of the sofa behind Katherine. "Well, you must promise to read it to me when you've finished it."

Katherine sensed his arm perilously close to resting on her shoulders, and she didn't want things to become awkward, so she leaned forward to pick up her wineglass and glanced at the clock. It was after ten. She turned to face him.

"Jonathan, it's been a lovely evening, but you really should think about going home."

"But..."

"No protests. It's getting late and I'm tired."

"I could stay, you know, to make sure you're safe." His voice had taken on that pleading tone that was becoming so familiar to Katherine.

"Jonathan, I'm fine. I will make sure I lock all the doors before I go to bed. I'll be perfectly all right!" She stood up and picked up the glasses, and headed for the kitchen.

"Well, I suppose, if you're sure." Jonathan stood and followed her.

"Thank you for all the groceries," Katherine said. "It was very kind of you." She glanced at Jonathan, who stood, shoulders slumped, looking very glum. "Cheer up, Jonathan, I really will be fine."

At the door, he stepped outside, but turned back. "It's been a wonderful evening, Katherine."

He leaned toward Katherine as if he was about to kiss her, but she retreated inside. "Goodnight, Jonathan, thank you again." She closed the door and leaned against it, exhausted. Once Jonathan drove away, she locked the door and walked through the entire house, checking every window, every door, ensuring everything that could be shut was shut and everything that could be locked was locked. She put the wine-glasses in the dishwasher and turned it on, then walked through the house again, just to make sure. All secured. She was halfway up the stairs when she changed her mind, returned to the kitchen, and wedged a chair under the handle of the cellar door.

Upstairs, she brushed her teeth and went into her bedroom, sliding a heavy chair in front of the door.

Satisfied that she was finally safe, she undressed for bed.

Twenty-Nine

JONATHAN

As Jonathan drove away from Katherine's, his anger rose. He wanted Katherine so desperately, but she constantly evaded his advances. How would he make her see that they were meant to be together? The day she walked into his life, he knew that she was the one. Obviously, he was going to have to try harder to win her. She'd already turned to him when she was scared. Perhaps if she were frightened enough...

When he was out of view of Katherine's house, he stopped the car and got out. From the trunk, he took a pair of hiking boots, a coat, and a hat. That man Katherine called 'The Stranger'. He'd seen him on the moor with his dog. He'd also seen him in Princetown that morning with Katherine. Her obvious fear of the man could be used to Jonathan's advantage.

Now dressed in the coat and hat purchased earlier that day, he locked his car and set off, grateful that the moon was rising and there was enough light for him to see without a torch.

He strode across the moor, not concerned with creeping in the shadows now. It would suit his purpose to have her see him. He reached the spot from where he'd watched before. His binoculars still lay where he'd dropped them, and he picked them up. He became aroused as he remembered the sight of her naked body. The image was indelibly burned into his mind.

The light in Katherine's bedroom came on. There she was, the object of his desire, and she was unbuttoning her shirt. His arousal grew, and his hand moved down and rubbed. She took off her bra, freeing her breasts. How he longed to touch them, to suck on her nipples. As she unzipped her jeans, he unzipped his own and masturbated.

He watched as Katherine turned her back, and as she pushed her jeans and underwear down, she leaned over. He almost came at the sight of her beautiful, round bottom, imagining his engorged penis rubbing against the cleft of her buttocks. Then she faced the window again, and he beheld her total nakedness, his eyes fixated on the dark triangle between her thighs. His hand moved faster and faster, his breath coming in quick gasps until he exploded, his semen spilling onto the heather. He cried out and fell to his knees, spent.

When he looked back at Katherine's window again, it was dark. His beloved had gone to bed. He got to his feet and zipped up his jeans, then made his way to the path. As he crossed the bridge, he said, "Hello Norman, you little fucking shit."

Thirty

KATHERINE

She stood, frozen in fear, as the cellar door slowly creaked open, the darkness spilling out as it did. Darkness that formed the shape of The Stranger and glided silently toward her. He reached out, catching her shirt in his claw-like hands, pulling her to him. She tried to scream, but her terror swallowed the sound. His arms snaked around her, pulling her back toward the blackness of the cellar. Down the stairs he dragged her, the cellar door slamming shut behind them. Then he laughed, and even in the absolute blackness, she sensed his face moving closer, his mouth opening. His teeth sinking into her neck. A horrible sucking sound ensued, and she felt her life draining away.

She screamed.

And woke.

Thank God.

Katherine got out of bed, her heart still thumping from the nightmare, and raced to the kitchen, making sure the cellar door remained shut. She tried to maneuver the dresser in front of the door, but it was too heavy, so she had to make do with a chair wedged underneath the door handle again.

She went back upstairs and showered, pleased that her period this month had been an easy one. Sometimes they were painful and lasted for six or seven days, but thankfully, this month it only lasted three days.

After drying her hair and dressing in her usual jeans and a blue and white check shirt, she made herself breakfast, comprising a cup of strong coffee and two pieces of Marmite toast. After she'd eaten, she made a thermos of lemongrass-and-ginger tea and went out through the conservatory, locking the door behind her. She hurried to the studio, eager to get to work. "Hi, Norman; it's me, Katherine," she called from the bridge, looking down into the water. Norman merely gave a flick of his tail and disappeared under a rock.

As she'd expected, her laptop had shut itself down, so she replaced the battery. While it was booting up, she scanned the tor, but thankfully saw no sign of The Stranger. Good, she was safe. She sat in her chair and opened her recent project, 'Charlotte's Shadow', reaching for a biscuit, but when she raised the biscuit to her mouth to take a bite, her hand stopped a few inches from her mouth, and her eyes widened in horror. The biscuit dropped from her hand, and she scooted her chair back so quickly that it fell, almost causing her to fall with it. She steadied herself and stared at her laptop. Centered in the middle of a blank page was one word: *BEWARE.*

She screamed and ran, not bothering to shut the door or even to speak to Norman. She thought of nothing but getting back to her house and safety.

Once inside, she sat in the kitchen, chewing on a fingernail. What should she do? Should she call the police? Yes. She reached for the phone, but hesitated. What would she tell the police? That someone had written on her laptop? Scattered boxes around her cellar? Left footprints far too big to be hers? They'd dismiss her as being some kind of crazy crackpot. She needed to talk to someone. Certainly not her mother. She could do without the inevitable lecture and remonstrations. Reluctantly, she picked up the phone and called the only person she could turn to who would understand: Jonathan. When she told him what had happened, he said he would rush right over, but not until he'd bought a decent lock for her cellar door and one for her studio as well. He'd fit them as soon as he arrived.

~

Katherine kept watch for Jonathan's car and rushed to the door, throwing it open and running to him, tears welling up in her eyes. He caught her in his arms and held her close.

"Jonathan, I'm sorry. I was so scared. Thank you. I'm sorry, but I didn't know what to do. I'm sorry." Tears cascaded down her face. She was blather-babbling but couldn't help it.

"Hey, come on, it's okay. I'm here now, and I'll take care of you."

His hand cupped her chin and tilted her head up. He wiped her tears away with his thumb, and then he kissed her. She kissed him back, knowing it was wrong, but desperately wanting to feel safe. His tongue caressed her lips, and she parted them, allowing him to kiss her deeply. He pressed against her, his arms enfolding her, his hands cupping her buttocks. Katherine put her arms around his neck, clinging to him as their kisses became hungrier. He lifted her and carried her inside, kicking the door closed behind him. Jonathan carried her up the stairs to her bedroom, where they fell on the bed, their lips locked, tongues entwined, hands touching, grasping, clutching.

Thirty-One

JONATHAN

At last, Jonathan had his hands on Katherine's body. That sensual, seductive, sinful body he'd desired from the second he saw it. He unbuttoned her shirt and unsnapped her bra. He moved his mouth down and sucked one nipple, enjoying the way it hardened. It was every bit as delicious as he'd expected. Katherine moaned at his touch, and he rejoiced. She was moaning for him.

He unzipped her jeans and slipped his hand inside her underwear, feeling the heat of her, her wetness. He pulled her jeans off and hurried to shed his own. But then she leaped off the bed and ran to her dresser. Returning, she thrust something into his hand.

"I'm not on the pill," she said, her breath coming in quick gasps as she lay back on the bed.

A condom. Damn. This wasn't part of his game plan, but he'd have to go along with it for now. Besides, if she'd only just finished her period, the timing wasn't right, anyway. He unwrapped the condom and rolled it down over his erect penis. Her legs were parted, and he plunged between them, guiding his erection into her.

As he moved inside her, she met his thrusts, and he smiled. At last, he possessed this woman. She had given herself to him. She was completely his. The thought tipped him over, and he climaxed, feeling

Katherine's nails digging into his shoulders. Her back arched, her body tensed, then shuddered. She called out his name, half screaming in the throes of her orgasm.

Their passion spent, he removed the condom and languished beside her, content, triumphant, exalted. Their future together stretched before him. She'd be waiting for him when he came home. He'd make love to her every night, explore every inch of her body with his tongue. He especially wanted to taste her and for her to taste him. Thinking of her taking him in her mouth got him aroused again, and he reached for her again.

"No," she said, pushing him away.

Yes, a condom. She would get another. He lay back, stroking himself, watching her. But what was this? She was getting dressed!

"What are you doing, Katherine?"

"This was a mistake. I'm sorry, I shouldn't have."

"But Katherine, I wanted to. I *still* want to." He moved toward her. "See?" He pointed at his erection.

She shook her head. "No, Jonathan. Look, I'm really sorry, this should never have happened."

"Didn't I satisfy you? Don't you like me?"

"It's not that. I do like you, but only as a friend. Not anything else. I'm really sorry."

"How can you say that after what we've just done? I love you! You're *mine*, now."

Thirty-Two

KATHERINE

Jonathan's petulant tone was back again, and Katherine fought to keep her own voice neutral.

"I'm sorry you think that way, but I'm not yours. You don't own me. I never should have let this happen, and I certainly didn't want to hurt you."

"But you enjoyed it too. I know you did!" Jonathan cried.

"Yes, I did, but it has to stop."

"But why?"

Any minute, he's going to stamp his foot in a tantrum. "I don't want a relationship, not with you or with any man. I want to bury myself in my writing for a while."

Jonathan scowled angrily and glared at her. He grabbed his clothes. "So." He snarled as he dressed. "You call me when you're scared, fuck me, and then throw me out when you're done. Is that about the size of it?"

"Look, I'm sorry. You're obviously angry with me, and you have a right to be. I didn't mean for this to happen, and I'm sorry you feel used. I don't know what else to say."

Jonathan finished dressing and faced her, fists clenched at his sides, eyes blazing, cheeks crimson. "I'm going, Katherine, before I say something I regret." He turned and ran down the stairs.

The front door slammed, and a moment later, his car started up and sped away. She stood at the window and looked out toward the studio, ashamed of her treatment of Jonathan, but at the same time relieved that it was over between them. With a sigh, she trudged downstairs and headed off along the path to retrieve her laptop.

She crossed the bridge, feeling very vulnerable again as she gave Norman her customary greeting. Everything was as she had left it, although the screen was dark. She moved the mouse, and the screen sprang to life. Quickly, she highlighted the word and hit the delete key. That done, she saved the project, erasing any trace of the warning.

Thirty-Three

JONATHAN

Jonathan sped away from Katherine's, his anger boiling. How dare she treat him like this? All he'd wanted to do was to love her, comfort her, take care of her, and this was the thanks he got. Used and then thrown away like a piece of garbage.

He drove in a fog of rage, narrowly missing a vehicle as he turned onto the main road. When the other driver blasted their horn, Jonathan raised two fingers and hurled abuse at the middle-aged woman and her companion. That he was in the wrong did not concern him at all. He was angry, and someone was going to pay. He slowed and pulled to the left to let the other driver pass, then sped up, getting closer and closer until his bumper almost touched the car in front. Then he honked his horn. One long, drawn-out blast. In the woman's rearview mirror, he saw her terrified eyes as she tried to get away, racing around bends, drifting onto the wrong side of the road.

Jonathan laughed. It would serve the silly bitch right if she crashed. At the next straight stretch of road, he zoomed past her, giving her the finger as he sped by.

By the time he reached his office, his rage had abated, and he realized he would have to make peace with Katherine or he'd lose her completely.

But he couldn't call her from the office. No, he'd let her stew for a while. He'd call her tonight and act all contrite and beg her forgiveness.

Thirty-Four

KATHERINE

The telephone on the table beside her rang, and Katherine jumped with a startled shriek, spilling her wine onto her white shirt. Dammit. Her nerves were shot. She'd checked all the doors and windows several times since it got dark and had been watching a romantic comedy to relax. She got up to retrieve her phone.

"Hello," she said in a timid voice.

"Darling, it's Mum. Just thought I'd call to see how you were settling in."

"Hi, Mum," Katherine said with a sigh as the tension left her shoulders.

"Well, don't sound so dejected to hear from your poor mother."

"I'm sorry, Mum. Of course, I'm glad to hear from you. It's been a crappy day, that's all."

"Oh dear. Do you want to talk about it?"

"Not really, Mum. How are you, anyway?"

"I'm fine, darling, just fine. Now, listen. I was playing bowls today with Mavis Thomas. You remember Mavis, she used to run the school canteen when you were little. Anyway, Mavis was asking if I'd seen your new cottage yet, and I felt awful having to admit to her I hadn't been invited yet."

"You knew I wanted to get everything in order first."

"Yes, dear, that's why I'm calling. To see if you're settled yet."

Katherine shouldn't put her mother off, and it might be good to have her around for a few days, particularly after what had happened with Jonathan.

"Pretty much, now. I was actually going to call you on the weekend." Katherine crossed her fingers that her mother wouldn't catch the lie. "Would you like to come and stay for a few days?"

"Darling, I'd love to. How about tomorrow? There's a train from Truro at about half-past nine, which gets in to Plymouth about a quarter to eleven. I think it's about half an hour from Tavistock to Plymouth. Are you far from Tavistock, darling?"

Katherine laughed. "You really have done your homework! Except I'm closer to Princetown than Tavistock."

"Princetown! Not that place with the prison. No, I don't like to think of you living near a prison, darling."

"Mum, I don't live near the prison; it's miles away, but Princetown is the closest town."

"If you say so, dear. Are you sure tomorrow is convenient?"

"Yes, Mum, it's fine. I'll meet you at Plymouth station."

"Okay, darling, I'll see you then. Love you. Bye."

Her mother hung up before she had a chance to say goodbye. Katherine put the phone down. Well, she'd see her tomorrow, anyway. Katherine went to the kitchen and poured herself another glass of wine before returning to the sofa and her movie.

The phone rang again, and Katherine hurried to answer it, sure it would be her mother having forgotten to tell her something.

"Hi," she said.

"Katherine, it's Jonathan. Look, I'm really sorry. I acted badly today and took advantage of you when you were vulnerable. I feel such a cad. Can you ever forgive me?"

Katherine groaned inwardly and remained silent.

"I understand completely about you not wanting a relationship and to concentrate on your writing. It was wrong of me to expect anything of you just because we... well, you know. Anyway, I've had some time to think now, and I wanted to say how sorry I was for the way I acted and the things I said. I hope we can still be friends. Is that possible, Katherine, do you think?"

Quite a speech; maybe he meant it, and they could still be just friends. He was not an awful man; he was quite sweet, really.

"Yes, I guess that's okay, Jonathan, but you have to promise not to try to take things further."

"You have my promise, Katherine. I would never do anything to hurt you; you should know that."

"Okay, then. I'm glad we have reached an understanding. I felt terrible about the way I treated you as well, so I'm pleased that you called and we can put things right between us."

"Good. I'm glad we're still friends. Look, I still have those locks for your doors. Would you like me to install them? I can come over tomorrow."

"I've got to pick my mother up tomorrow morning. She's catching the train from Truro and I'm meeting her in Plymouth."

"What time will you leave?"

"Her train gets in at about ten forty-five, so I'll leave here about ten."

"Okay, I can probably have it all fixed before you get back."

"That's kind of you, Jonathan. I really appreciate it, but I insist on paying you; otherwise, I won't let you do it."

Jonathan agreed, and they said goodbye. Katherine returned to her movie only to see the credits rolling. She sighed. At least she'd made up with Jonathan, and he seemed to understand that all they could ever be was friends.

Thirty-Five

"I'll start with the studio, if you like," Jonathan said when Katherine opened the door for him.

"Yes, okay, thank you," Katherine said. "I'll finish getting ready."

She ran upstairs and checked the room she'd prepared for her mother. It looked inviting despite being a little small, and it was next door to the bathroom, which her mother's aging bladder would appreciate. Satisfied that everything was in order, she went to her bedroom to get a jacket and take one last look in her mirror. Her dark-blue skirt suit and a pale blue shirt looked smart, the way her mother liked her to dress. Katherine would much rather dress in jeans and a casual shirt, but her mother described that look as being too common. It wouldn't do to get off on the wrong foot with her mother just because of the way she looked. She carefully styled her hair to control her curls. Her mother hated messy hair. Finally, she picked up her bag and slung its strap over her shoulder. Through the window, she watched Jonathan approach the bridge and smiled when he stopped and looked into the water. Perhaps he stopped to say hello to Norman. When he disappeared into the studio, she headed downstairs. It was time to go.

~

The train pulled in a few minutes late, and Katherine strained her neck to see her mother through the throng of people. She spotted her mother's trademark floppy straw hat with its peacock-blue band that matched her favorite pant-suit and called to her. Her mother waved, and Katherine ran to her, hugging her as she kissed her cheek.

"Hi, Mum. It's great to see you."

"Hello, darling. What a trip. There was this lady next to me, and she talked the whole way. I couldn't get a word in!"

Katherine picked up her mother's bright orange suitcase and started toward the exit.

"Hang on a moment, darling." Her mother looked around as people hurried past them. "Ah, here it is. Thank you, young man."

Katherine saw with dismay an even larger suitcase, this one pink with black trim, being deposited at her mother's feet. She picked it up, groaning at the weight.

"Would you like a hand with that, miss?" The young man who'd delivered the case asked.

"Would you? That's so kind. Thank you." Katherine gratefully put the case down.

The young man picked up the heavy case and also took the other from her. "Lead the way," he said.

She set off, weaving through the crowded entrance to the car park. With the suitcases safely deposited in the back of her Land Rover, Katherine turned to the young man, offering him a ten-pound note. "Thank you. You've been very helpful."

He brushed her hand aside. "I won't accept that. It was my pleasure. Your mother is delightful, and I was glad to help."

"Well, thank you again, then. Goodbye."

"What a nice young man," Katherine's mother said as he walked away. "You should find someone like him. It's time you settled down. I can't wait forever for grandchildren, you know. Your father would have loved to have some, but it's too late for him now."

Katherine wanted to scream, but stayed silent. Her mother had always made her feel inadequate and guilty for something. Seems that nothing had changed since her father's death. They got in the car and left the car park.

"When are you going home, Mum?"

"Gracious, Katherine. I've only just got here, and you're wanting me to leave already." She folded her arms and looked out of the window.

Katherine groaned. "Of course not, Mum. I was just thinking of all the things we can do together and wanted to prioritize them."

"Well, I haven't decided yet." Her mother sniffed, her tone indignant. "We'll just have to see, won't we?"

"That's fine. So, how about today I show you around the cottage? Then tomorrow, there are loads of apples to pick. Perhaps you can help me preserve them and maybe give me some of your secret recipes. Or perhaps you'd like to do some hiking on the moors."

"Don't be silly, darling. Why on earth would I want to go traipsing around the moors? No, you just go on with what you normally do, and I'll potter about." She made a dismissive, flapping motion with her hand.

"Well, I usually spend most of my time writing, but I want to spend time with you while you're here."

Her mother made a sound somewhere between a groan and a 'tsk'. "Oh, darling, you're not still on that writing malarkey, are you? Your father encouraged you far too much. Now you've shut yourself away in some desolate hole. You had a good job with that publishing firm. I don't see why you couldn't go back to it. You'll never meet a nice man stuck out in the wilderness on your own."

There was no point in arguing with her, so Katherine remained silent, but stole the occasional glance at her mother, who had at least unfolded her arms and was gazing around at the scenery.

As they passed over the cattle grate on the approach to Princetown, Katherine's mother gasped and fumbled with the door lock.

"What are you doing, Mum?"

"Locking the door, darling. You should, too. You can't be too careful, you know. What if one of those prisoners tries to car-jack us?"

Katherine sighed, but flicked the switch to lock all the doors. "There! Happy?" She'd tried to keep the annoyance out of her voice and knew she'd failed when her mother gave her a sharp look, folded her arms again, and stared straight ahead, a scowl on her face.

When Katherine caught sight of her cottage in the distance, she pointed it out. “That’s it. That’s my place.”

“You said it was remote, darling, but it’s in the middle of nowhere. You can’t possibly live there!”

“Sorry, Mum, but I do. That’s home.” Why did she always feel a need to apologize to her mother?

Her mother made an audible ‘harrumph’ sound. “Well, I never!”

Katherine turned into her driveway, disappointed to see Jonathan’s convertible still parked in front of the house.

Thirty-Six

"Have you bought a new car, darling? It's rather flash."

"It's not mine, it's Jonathan's." She caught her mother's smile of excitement. "And before you get the wrong idea, Mum, he's not my boyfriend. He's the Realtor who sold me the house."

"What's he doing here?"

"Putting new locks on the doors for me."

"Good idea, darling." She patted Katherine's knee. "You never know who has keys to a house when you buy it. I always say it's the first thing you do when you move into a new place. Change the locks."

Katherine pulled her car up alongside the Mercedes and switched off the motor. She unlocked her door just as Jonathan scurried out of the house and rushed to open her mother's door.

"Allow me, dear lady." He offered her his arm and then glanced across at Katherine. "I thought you were going to pick up your mother, but this lovely lady must surely be your sister."

Her mother laughed coquettishly and blushed. "Why, you dear man." She smoothed down the jacket of her suit and fluttered her eyelashes. "How lovely of you to say, but I really am her mother."

"I would never have guessed," Jonathan said, looking at Katherine and then her mother. "But I can see now where Katherine gets her beauty from."

Good grief. He's overdoing the charm in a big way, and Mum is just lapping it up.

"Now, Katherine, you take this lovely lady inside, and I'll bring in the luggage. I've made a pot of tea; I thought you might be tired after your journey."

"How did you...?"

Jonathan laughed and interrupted Katherine's question. "I kept watch, and when I saw your car in the distance, I made the tea." Jonathan turned back to Katherine's mother. "But where are my manners? I haven't introduced myself. I'm Jonathan Irving. And you are...?"

Despite her annoyance at Jonathan's still being here, Katherine almost burst out laughing as he made a little bow. She half expected him to click his heels.

"I'm Jacqueline Walters, but most people shorten it to Jacqui."

Jonathan took her hand and bent to kiss it. "I'm delighted to meet you. May I call you Jacqueline? A lady with your elegance and class should never shorten her name."

"Yes, of course you can, you dear man."

Katherine shook her head and rolled her eyes. *Get a room, you two.*

"Jacqueline, it is, then." Jonathan released her hand and hastened to retrieve the luggage.

Katherine led her mother to the kitchen. "This is the kitchen, of course. Have a seat and I'll pour the tea."

"Thank you, dear." Her mother pulled out a chair and sat. "What a charming man. Simply charming. I hope you're doing your best to attract him. He's good-looking and obviously wealthy. You could do a lot worse than Jonathan, you know."

Katherine groaned. This was the last thing she wanted. She handed a cup of tea to her mother and poured another for herself, then took the opposite seat.

Jonathan entered the kitchen. "I've put your bags in your room, Jacqueline."

“Thank you so much. You are very kind. Will you join us?” She indicated her cup of tea.

An expression of such sadness crossed his face; it must be feigned. “No, thank you. Perhaps next time. I need to get back to the office and make sure my partner isn’t too snowed under.”

Katharine rose. “I’ll see you out.”

At the door, Jonathan said, “I’ve put the locks on and I’ve left the keys on your dressing table.”

“My dressing table? You mean in my bedroom?”

Jonathan looked sheepish, his eyes downcast. “I just wanted to take one last look at where we... well, you know. It meant a lot to me, even though I know there will never be a next time for us.” He looked up at her, his sad puppy eyes pleading and remorseful, and he moved closer, reaching as if to embrace her. “Please don’t be angry with me, Katherine.”

Katherine stepped away from him and sighed. “It’s okay, Jonathan. I still feel guilty about what happened.”

Jonathan dropped his arms to his sides. “No, don’t be. At least I have a wonderful memory of you. Now I must be on my way. Take care, Katherine.”

“I will, and thank you, Jonathan. Goodbye.”

Katherine closed the door and returned to her mother.

“You took your time, dear. Anything you want to tell me?” Her mother’s voice bore a smug tone.

“No, there is absolutely nothing to tell you,” Katherine replied through clenched teeth.

Their tea finished, Katherine took her mother on a tour of the house, finishing in her bedroom.

“And this is my room.” Katherine threw open the door and stepped back for her mother to get the full effect of the view.

“Gracious! What beautiful roses!” her mother said, clapping her hands together.

"What?" Katherine pushed past her mother and stopped. On her dressing table was a vase filled with deep-red roses, their heady scent permeating the room.

Thirty-Seven

"Obviously, someone loves you very much, darling. Who are they from? You must tell me." Her mother hurried past Katherine and sniffed at the roses. "Gorgeous perfume. Look, there's a card." She snatched it up and read it. 'I'm so sorry, Katherine. All my love, Jonathan.' She read aloud, then hugged Katherine. "So you two *are* together. I'm so glad."

"Mum, we are *not* together." Katherine extricated herself from her mother's grasp. "It's all a misunderstanding."

"A misunderstanding? Now, darling, no man spends serious money on red roses on a misunderstanding. He obviously loves you very much. Why is he saying sorry?"

"Mum, just *leave it!* There is *nothing* between us, got that? *Nothing*!" Katherine's hands clenched into fists. Damn Jonathan. How dare he?

"All right, if you say so. But I think you're being silly, darling. He's a lovely man..."

"Just STOP!" Katherine yelled.

"No need to shout, dear, it's so common."

"Urgh!" Katherine growled and stormed out of the room. She

stomped back downstairs and poured herself another cup of tea, taking it into the conservatory to drink, wishing she could have a glass of wine instead.

When Katherine had finished her tea, her mother had still not come down, so she set about making lunch. She laid out some cold chicken, salad vegetables, sliced some bread, and set the table. Still no sign of her mother. *She's obviously sulking. I'd better go and make peace.*

She found her mother in the spare room, putting the last of her clothes in the wardrobe.

"Lunch is ready, Mum. I hope you don't mind cold chicken and salad."

"That will be lovely, dear, thank you."

The two women went downstairs together.

Lunch over, Katherine cleared the table and stacked the dishwasher. "Go into the living room if you like, Mum. Put your feet up."

"I will in a moment, dear, but I promised I'd call Mavis Thomas and tell her I'd got here safely. You remember Mavis, darling, she ran the school canteen when you were little."

"Yes, Mum, I remember." Every time her mother mentioned Mavis, she said the same thing. "There's a phone in the living room and another in the conservatory."

"Oooh, a conservatory. There's posh!" Her mother squealed in a mocking tone, then left the room, laughing.

Katherine smiled and relaxed a little. If the two of them stayed off the subject of Jonathan, or men in general, they might have a good time together.

The dishwasher stacked, the benches cleaned, she entered the living room. Her mother still talked on the phone, her back to Katherine.

"Yes, Mavis, it's gorgeous. She's got a conservatory, and all mod cons in the kitchen, an absolutely heavenly view out over the moors. And you'll never guess. She's got the most beautiful bouquet of roses from Jonathan— he's the lovely young man who sold her the house—and the card is signed 'all my love'. She denies it, of course, but he's obviously head over heels. If only she'd see sense and settle down. Jonathan would be perfect. He's handsome and so charming, not to mention well-off. You should see the car he drives. One of those classic Mercedes-Benz. Must be worth a fortune."

Katherine sighed and quietly left the room.

Thirty-Eight

JONATHAN

Jonathan didn't return to the office as he'd told Katherine. Instead, he parked at a pull-off to think.

Katherine's mother had obviously taken a shine to him. Could he use her somehow? Perhaps get her on side to help him achieve his desires? His charm hadn't yet worked on the daughter, but her mother had obviously relished it. Probably more chance of getting Jacqueline to spread her legs for him than to seduce Katherine again.

An image of Jacqueline Walters naked sprang to mind, all saggy tits, flabby stomach, and cellulite thighs. Revulsion shuddered through him, and he forced the image away, calling to mind Katherine's naked body, the smoothness of her skin, the firmness of her breasts, and the wetness between her thighs. His groin stirred, and he let his hand rest in his lap, his fingertips brushing along his hardness.

A motorhome pulled in, parking in front of him, and a family piled out. Father, mother, twin boys about seven years of age, and a girl who appeared to be mid-teens, judging from her sullen expression and the exaggerated open-mouth gum chewing. What a cheap-looking tart. Skirt so short she may as well not have it on, short, cropped jet-black hair, a stud through her lower lip, and some kind of animal skull, perhaps a wolf, tattooed on her upper arm. She leaned against the side of the vehicle, holding her phone in front of her, her lips moving as if singing along to the tinny music emanating from the phone. For a moment, her eyes met Jonathan's before her lip curled in a sneer, and she extended her middle finger with its long, pointed black fingernail in an upward jabbing motion.

Jonathan bristled. How dare she? He reached to open the car door, intending to give her a piece of his mind, but at that moment, the girl's father strode toward her and slapped her hard across the face. The girl's head snapped back against the side of the motorhome with an audible thud. Her phone flew out of her grasp, coming to rest several feet away, and the girl burst into tears, holding one hand to the back of her head while the red print of her father's hand blossomed on her cheek.

Jonathan started his car. If he were quick, he might still get his revenge. He put the car into gear and gradually let out the clutch, inching forward, carefully lining up. A little to the left, a little further...

Crunch. Got it.

He sped away, watching in his rear-view mirror as the girl ran to pick up the mangled mess that had once been her phone. That'll teach the little cunt.

Thirty-Nine

KATHERINE

Katherine and her mother chatted amiably as they walked through the orchard.

"I see what you mean about apples, darling. This lot will keep us going for ages. Whatever will you do with them all?"

"I'm not sure, really, Mum. I'd like to make some jelly, apple sauce, and preserve some for pies and crumbles. I'm open to suggestions."

"We'll make a start tomorrow, then." Her mother plucked an apple. "These are certainly ready."

"How can you tell when they're ready? I ate one a few days ago and it seemed okay, but I wasn't really sure."

"Well, you cup one in your hand and sort of lift and twist. If the stem breaks away from the branch easily, it's ready. Like so." She twisted an apple, then held it out to Katherine. "See?"

"That's easy enough. Thanks, Mum." Katherine took the apple from her mother and bit into it. Juice dribbled down her chin, and she wiped it away.

At the stone bridge, Katherine stopped and peered over the side. "Hi, Norman; it's me, Katherine. And my mum, Jacqui." She glanced across at her mother, who was looking at her as if she'd lost her mind. "It's Norman. He's a fish."

Her mother rolled her eyes and shook her head. "You've named a fish after your father. Whatever next."

"Look, there he is!" Katherine pointed, and her mother looked into the water. Norman gave a flick of his tail and was gone. "Probably not used to strangers."

They walked on to the studio, and Katherine opened the door. "Here we are. This is where I write."

Her mother stepped inside and looked around. "Well, I must say, it's a lovely spot; but, darling, it's so isolated! Don't you get worried about being here all on your own?"

"Not in the least." The lie came easily to her lips. "Never see a soul, and that's the way I like it."

"So who's that, then?" Her mother pointed out the window.

Katherine looked, and her blood ran cold. The Stranger stood on the tor, his long coat fluttering in the wind, watching them. If she told her mother the truth, well, the consequences didn't bear thinking about. Instead, she brushed her mother off by saying, "He's a farmer who lives around here. I've seen him a few times out on the moor, but I don't know his name."

"He looks rather sinister, doesn't he?"

"Hmm, I suppose he does, but I've never really thought about it." Katherine lied again.

Her mother strode to the window and waved.

Forty

Katherine rushed to her mother and pulled her back from the window. "My God, Mum, don't do that!" Her heart skipped a couple of beats before settling into a canter.

"Why ever not? He knows we've seen him; it would be impolite not to wave."

Katherine's heart slowed a little as The Stranger disappeared from view, descending the far side of the tor. "Well... because I'd just rather keep my distance."

Her mother peered at her from beneath her frown. "Really, darling, you're behaving very oddly. What with that business about the flowers from Jonathan and now this. What on earth's got into you?"

"Nothing, Mum. I came here for the solitude, so I can finally write my novel. I don't want people dropping in all the time."

"Is that why I needed to prompt you for an invite? You didn't want me interrupting your solitude?" Her words oozed with sarcasm.

"No, not at all. I didn't mean you. Why do you always twist things around? I just want to keep my distance from other people."

Her mother gave her a sly smile. "Except Jonathan, of course."

Katherine groaned. *Oh, what's the point? She never listens.*

~

"We need a wheelbarrow." Katherine's mother suggested after they'd carried two buckets of apples back to the cottage. "Might make harvesting a little easier."

"Good idea. I have one; hang on, and I'll get it." Katherine had purchased a new wheelbarrow on her last trip to Princetown. All she'd used it for so far was to take a load of firewood to the studio.

Katherine and her mother soon filled the barrow with apples and made their way back to the kitchen. The rest of the morning and most of the afternoon were spent peeling, coring, and cooking apples. By the end of the day, the kitchen table was crowded with jars of pie apple, apple sauce, and several of her mother's apple pies. Katherine had tried time and time again, but could never make apple pie the way her mother did.

"It's all in the pastry, darling," her mother said, but didn't offer to divulge her secret pastry recipe.

Katherine had her hands in a sink full of soap suds when the telephone rang in the living room.

"Do you want me to get that, dear?" her mother asked.

"Yes, please, Mum."

Her mother returned a few minutes later as Katherine dried her hands.

"Who was it, Mum?"

"It was Jonathan, darling. He's invited us both to lunch tomorrow."

Katherine groaned. "So what did you say?"

"Well, of course, I said we'd love to. We're to meet him at twelve-thirty at The Coachman's Rest in Merrivale. He said you know it."

"Mum, why didn't you ask me before you said yes? I don't *want* to have lunch with Jonathan!" Katherine threw the towel onto the bench, not bothering to stifle her anger.

"Good gracious, Katherine, don't be so churlish. I don't know what's got into you." She stomped back to the living room, leaving Katherine seething.

Bloody Jonathan. Bloody mother.

Forty-One

Jonathan was leaning against his convertible when Katherine pulled into the parking area of The Coachman's Rest, but rushed over as soon as she'd stopped.

"Jacqueline. How lovely to see you," he said as he opened the car door and gave her his hand, helping her out of the car. He kissed her hand, then bent so that her mother could kiss his cheek. His eyes met Katherine's, and he smiled, a smug look of triumph on his face. She turned away.

Jonathan was attentive throughout the meal, chatting animatedly with her mother, complimenting her on her pretty pink dress, touching her arm, laughing at her jokes, almost ignoring Katherine. Not that she minded; it was a relief that he wasn't flirting with her, but his flattery seemed so false. Why couldn't her mother see that?

Katherine put her napkin on the table. "Back in a few minutes." She picked up her handbag, pushed her chair back, and headed for the ladies' room. She took her time re-applying lipstick and fussing with her hair. One curl just wouldn't sit right, and it annoyed her. She didn't want to be rude, but seeing Jonathan fawn over her mother was sickening. It was so fake. And why was he doing it? Was he trying to make Katherine jealous by captivating her mother? Would he stoop that low?

No, he'd promised not to pursue her, although she feared her mother would do whatever possible to get Jonathan and her together. She groaned. *Why do I let myself get into these situations? Why? Why?*

Reluctantly, she opened the ladies' room door to see Jonathan and her mother leaning across the table, their heads close, in animated conversation. As Katherine walked toward the table, her mother glanced her way, then patted Jonathan's hand. They sat back in a hurry, like guilty schoolchildren caught out by their teacher, before Jonathan looked toward Katherine, giving her a self-satisfied smirk.

"What have you two been gossiping about, then?" Katherine sat down, looking from her mother to Jonathan and back.

Her mother laughed nervously, avoiding eye contact with Katherine. "Nothing much. This and that."

Jonathan cleared his throat and looked at Katherine. "Actually, Katherine, I was just telling Jacqueline that we came here on our first date together."

Katherine stared at him. "You said what?"

"Our first date. Surely you remember, it was only last week."

"Jonathan, it was NOT a date. We had dinner together, that was all."

"Of course it was a date. I invited you to dinner, you accepted, and I paid. Ergo, it was a date."

Katherine's jaw clenched, and her hands curled into fists. She forced her fingers to spread and pressed her hands flat on her thighs. "No, Jonathan, it was definitely not a date."

Katherine's mother patted her arm. "Come on, darling. Don't be ungracious."

"I'm not being ungracious, Mum," she said through gritted teeth. "Now, will you please stop meddling!" She looked back at Jonathan. "Jonathan, this has to stop. I'm sorry if I've given you the wrong impression; if you think there is something between us. There isn't. There never was and there never will be." She stood up and signaled to the barman for the bill.

"It certainly seemed like it when you screamed my name in bed."

Forty-Two

Jonathan's words stopped her in her tracks. She turned back to face him, the heat of her anger flooding into her face, her neck. This time, she didn't stop her hands from clenching into fists.

"How dare you!" she hissed at him. "I told you then it was a mistake. I'm even more sure of it now." She looked at her mother, ignoring the shocked look on her face. "Come on, Mum, we're leaving."

She stopped long enough to pay the bill and stormed out, her mother following in her wake.

"Darling, I really think..." her mother said, but Katherine glared at her, and she quickly closed her mouth.

They drove back to the cottage in silence, Katherine livid at Jonathan. He had no right to say those things in front of her mother. Not only did he divulge what Katherine had assumed would remain a secret between the two of them, but he'd also embarrassed her. God knows what her mother must think of her now.

Katherine parked in front of her cottage and went inside, her mother trailing behind her. She grabbed her laptop. "I'm going to the studio to write." She left without giving her mother a chance to reply.

Forty-Three

JONATHAN

Jonathan watched them go. Perhaps he'd overplayed things a little with that last comment about Katherine screaming his name. Might have to work a bit harder to undo the damage. Still, it had been a very productive lunch, and her mother was on his side now. She'd help him win Katherine. After all, she thought he was charming; she'd told him so more than once. Sure, she'd been shocked when he'd said that about them in bed, but while Katherine was paying the bill, she'd caught his eye and mouthed the words 'call me' to him. Yes, she was on his side, alright. It was only a matter of time.

He walked to the bar and ordered another beer. The barman served him politely, but his friendly chatter from the previous visit was absent. Had he overheard their conversation? Maybe, but Jonathan didn't care. He didn't care what anyone thought. Well, anyone except Katherine.

With the barman giving him the cold shoulder, Jonathan wandered over to the fireplace, sipping his beer. The black-and-white cat lay curled up asleep in one chair. Jonathan could easily sit in the other chair, but why should he? He put his beer on the mantel, picked the cat up by its scruff, and threw it on the floor. The cat yowled and took off like its tail was on fire. Jonathan laughed and turned back to the mantel to pick up his beer.

"Hey! You!" the barman shouted, striding toward Jonathan. "Get out."

Jonathan sneered. "What's the problem?"

"I may not be able to throw you out for treating your girlfriend like you did, although you richly deserve it, but I can throw you out for mistreating my cat. Now get out before I call the police."

"It's just a fucking cat!"

The barman grabbed Jonathan by the collar and frog-marched him to the entrance, giving him a final shove through the door. Jonathan staggered and almost fell, but managed to keep upright. He turned to face the barman to continue his tirade, only to see the barman close the door.

Jonathan made a very noisy exit from the car park, a plume of gravel spewing from his wheels, clattering against the windows of the inn, hopefully smashing a few.

"Take that, you prick."

Forty-Four

KATHERINE

Katherine strode down the path, her thoughts in turmoil. What was she going to do about Jonathan? What was she going to do about her mother? Hopefully, today had given him a convincing message, and he'd leave her alone.

When she reached the bridge, she stopped and looked down into the water. There was Norman in his usual place near the overhanging rock. "Hi, Norman; it's me, Katherine." She spent a few moments gazing into the water, watching her fishy friend, then walked on to her studio and unlocked the door.

She sat down and turned on her laptop, wishing she'd brought a flask of tea with her. Her packet of chocolate digestives still sat on the desk, and she took two before scrunching the packet closed again. Taking a bite out of her biscuit, she opened her project and soon all thoughts of Jonathan and her mother vanished, and in their place, the perils of Charlotte, Owen, and Tom.

Katherine looked up at the sound of a scratching noise at the door and went to open it, her mind still half on her writing. She looked down and saw Felan. His tail wagged as if happy to see her. She reached out to pat him. "Hello, boy."

A hand shot out and grabbed her arm. The Stranger! She let out a startled cry and tried to pull away. He was strong, and he held on to her, his face close to hers, dark eyes blazing. "Ye need to beware!" he said. "Beware of the cellar."

Katherine struggled to free herself. Fear gripped her. What did he want? What would he do to her? And what was this about the cellar?

"Are you there, Katherine?" her mother's voice called.

The Stranger released his grip on Katherine, and she staggered back, a hand on her chest over her racing heart, knees on the point of collapse. She mustn't let her mother see her like this. She took several deep breaths and looked around. No sign of The Stranger now, nor his dog.

"Ah, there you are, darling," her mother said, rounding the corner. "I was wondering whether you'd like a cup of tea. You've been here for hours."

"Yes, thank you, Mum. That would be lovely."

"Goodness, girl, you look all flustered. Is anything the matter?"

"No. Not at all. Give me a moment to shut down my laptop."

As Katherine packed up her laptop, her mother looked out of the window. "There's that man again." She turned back toward Katherine. "You know, darling, I could have sworn I saw him near your door when I came over the bridge."

Katherine tried to still her trembling knees, sure her mother would hear them knocking. "I didn't see him, but he often walks the moors with Felan."

"Is that the dog's name? How do you know that?" Her mother eyed her with suspicion.

"I was out on the moors one day, and the dog came up to me. He called out 'Felan' and the dog ran to him."

"I see. Not an admirer you've thrown Jonathan over for."

"Mum, I haven't thrown Jonathan over. We were never together."

"But, darling, you *slept* with him. In my book, that means you're together."

"Yes, well, that was a mistake. One that I deeply regret." Katherine gathered her things and led her mother from the studio, securely locking the door behind them.

"Don't be silly, darling. Jonathan obviously adores you. He told me he would do anything to win you back."

"Did he now? And when was this?" Katherine looked at her mother, pleased to see the guilty look on her face.

"Oh, I..."

"Was this what you were discussing when I came out of the ladies' at the inn? You were as thick as thieves, you two. Now I understand why you both looked so guilty."

"But darling, he *loves* you. He's such a nice young man, and you're not getting any younger, you know."

"Oh, for fuck's sake. Stop your bloody meddling, mother!" Katherine shouted.

"Well, you don't have to shout, dear. And you certainly don't need to swear. Really, you've become quite common."

"Look, Mum. I've had just about enough. If you mention Jonathan's name again, you'll be on the train home so fast you won't know what's hit you."

"Well, I'm only trying to help, darling."

"I don't want your help. I don't *need* your help. It is none of your business. Do I make myself clear?"

"Perfectly." Her mother said in a snarky, clipped tone, and strode away. Katherine followed a discreet distance behind, stopping to greet Norman as she crossed the bridge.

Dinner that evening was a tense affair, both being polite but not engaging in conversation beyond 'would you pass the salt please'. Katherine cleared the table and her mother took her glass of wine in to the living room.

When Katherine joined her, her own wine glass refilled, she sat in the armchair.

"I think I'll catch the train home tomorrow," her mother said, a haughty tone in her voice.

Katherine sighed. "Mum, you don't have to go."

"Yes, I think I do, darling. I don't think you're as settled as we thought."

"Look, Mum. I'm sorry we fought, but I'd like you to stay a little longer. I was really looking forward to a shopping trip with you. It's always so much fun." Katherine reached across and grasped her mother's hand. "Go on, Mum, please stay," Katherine pleaded, a whine in her voice so reminiscent of Jonathan when he didn't get his own way.

"Hmm, well, if you're sure. I don't want to be a nuisance."

"You're not a nuisance, Mum," Katherine said, thinking exactly the opposite.

"All right then, I'll stay a couple more days." Her mother's voice held a hint of smug satisfaction.

"Fancy a trip to Princetown, shopping?" Katherine asked her mother over breakfast.

"No, dear, not Princetown. How can you bear to shop there with all those criminals about?"

Katherine laughed. "Mum, the criminals are all in prison. It's fine!"

"No, dear, let's go to Tavistock instead. Much nicer."

Katherine sighed, defeated. "Okay, Mum, we'll go to Tavistock." *Let's just hope we don't run into Jonathan.*

"Splendid, darling. I'll buy lunch. Where's a good place? A pub, not a cafe."

"Well, The Cornish Arms always does a lovely lunch."

Her mother nodded emphatically. "Cornish Arms it is, then."

They strolled along the high street, browsing in shop windows, popping into one when something caught their eye.

"Hello, you two," Jonathan's voice called from behind.

Katherine groaned inwardly. This was what she'd feared; another awkward encounter with Jonathan. "Hello." She kept her voice cool and polite and didn't return his smile.

Her mother, however, was far more exuberant. "Hello, Jonathan dear, lovely to see you."

"And you too, Jacqueline." He bent to kiss her hand. "I really must apologize for my behavior yesterday, ladies. Some of the things I said were completely out of line. Can you possibly forgive me?"

"Yes, of course we can." Her mother patted his arm reassuringly.

"Can't we, darling?" She elbowed Katherine as if prompting her to agree. Katherine remained silent.

"Thank you, Jacqueline, that means a lot to me." Jonathan clasped her mother's hand and then turned his attention to Katherine.

"What about you, Katherine? Can you find it in your heart to forgive me?" He held up a hand, palm toward Katherine in a signal to stop, as if she had been about to speak. A redundant gesture. She hadn't been going to say anything.

"I understand," he said. "I promised before that I'd not try to take things further, and I broke that promise."

"Yes. You did," Katherine said, her voice chilly.

"I know I did, and I'm very sorry. I felt awful when you left yesterday. You were so angry with me. I didn't get any sleep last night worrying about you, how I'd hurt you. Please, Katherine, please forgive me. I can't bear the thought of you being angry with me. Please let us be friends."

"Well, I…," Katherine began.

Jonathan clasped her hands in his, his pleading eyes searching hers. He looked as if he was about to drop to one knee, or worse, start crying. Perhaps he really was contrite. She thawed a little toward him.

"Okay, Jonathan, I guess we can still be friends, but this is your last warning." She spoke sternly, putting a lot of emphasis on the word 'friends', for there to be no mistaking that's all it would ever be. Friendship. She regretted their fight, almost as much as she regretted going to bed with him. She liked him. He was good company when he wasn't making her squirm with his directness, but she wasn't interested in him romantically. She'd lay some ground rules once her mother left. Now wasn't the time.

"Thank you, Katherine. You can't imagine what this means to me. I promise I'll not let you down." He threw his arms around her and hugged her before releasing her.

"We're just off for lunch," her mother said, "The Cornish Arms."

"How lovely. I envy you." Jonathan glanced at his watch. "Well, I must get back to the office. You two enjoy yourselves. Goodbye, ladies."

They watched him stroll away up the street.

"Well, I'm glad you two are at least talking again," her mother said.

Katherine sighed. “I guess I am, too. Jonathan can be infuriating, but I still value his friendship, and I hate fighting with anyone. I hope he can stick to being just friends.”

Her mother hooked her arm through Katherine’s. “Come on, darling, let’s have some lunch, and then I want to go back to that shop where I saw that gorgeous blue dress. It will be perfect for the bowling club end-of-year party.”

“Darling, I promised Jonathan I’d take him some apples. I hope you don’t mind,” Katherine’s mother said at breakfast. “You don’t need to come if you don’t want to. It will give you a chance to do some writing, if you’d prefer.”

“Will you be alright to drive the Land Rover? It’s a bit bigger than your little hatchback.”

“Yes, of course, dear. You forget your father used to have a Range Rover, and I’ve driven that before. I’ll be fine.”

“Okay, Mum. I’ll help you pick the apples, though.” Katherine pushed back her chair and cleared away the breakfast dishes.

Katherine couldn’t concentrate on her writing. Her thoughts kept drifting back to her mother. Her mother had never encouraged her writing before— quite the opposite— and yet she’d seemed very keen to go off on her own. Was her mother up to something? She hoped not; she couldn’t face another round of squabbling, not with Mum or with Jonathan.

She read back over her output from the last hour. Only a couple of paragraphs, and they were crap. May as well do something else. Make some apple jelly, for instance.

No sign of The Stranger on the tor, or the surrounding moor, so Katherine returned her laptop to the conservatory and headed to the orchard with three enormous shopping bags, where she selected apples for her jelly.

Her mother was not home at midday, so Katherine ate lunch alone and then returned to her apple processing. By mid-afternoon, Katherine was a little worried. She considered telephoning Jonathan, but decided she'd wait a while longer.

Not long before four p.m., Katherine heard the crunch of gravel. *Thank goodness.* She hurried outside to meet her mother.

"There you are, Mum. I was worried about you."

"Don't be silly, darling, you needn't have. Jonathan ended up taking me to this wonderful little Italian place for lunch. We got chatting and time just flew." She laughed, a silly, high-pitched, girlish laugh.

Had she been drinking? "I'm just glad you're alright. Come on, I'll make some tea."

Sipping her tea, Katherine looked at her mother, who kept shifting around in her seat, picking her cup up, putting it down without drinking, twirling it around in her saucer. "Okay, what's going on, Mum? What's wrong?"

Forty-Five

Her mother's face bore an expression that Katherine could only interpret as fake innocence as she looked anywhere but at Katherine. "Nothing, dear. What makes you think something is wrong?"

"Just the way you're acting. You're all... fidgety."

Katherine's mother laughed, a nervous titter. "Darling, you really are being quite silly."

"Come on, Mum. What have you done? I know that look. You're up to something."

"Well, if you must know, dear, I've booked my train ticket for the day after tomorrow."

"Oh, is that all?" Katherine laughed. "That's fine. I'll miss you, of course."

"I'll miss you too, dear." She still fidgeted.

"And?" Katherine prompted, her eyes narrowing suspiciously. "What else?"

"Look, dear, I know you'll be angry, but I've invited Jonathan to dinner tomorrow night. Now, before you say anything." She held her hand up as Katherine opened her mouth to protest. "Jonathan's been very kind to me, and he was telling me about how apple pie is his favorite pudding, and I said I'd make him one."

Katherine waited a moment to ensure her mother had finished speaking and then said, "You know he's buttering you up, don't you? He told *me* his favorite pudding was apple crumble."

"I'm not a fool, Katherine, but believe it or not, your mother is not immune to the attentions of a charming young man, even if you are. Anyway, I've invited him and that's that."

Katherine smiled and reached across the table to take her mother's hand. "I'm not objecting, Mum. As long as both of you understand, I don't want a relationship with Jonathan. I'm quite content to be friends with him."

Katherine spent the next day finishing the apple jelly she'd started, then watched her mother make the finishing touches to a pie. She decorated it with little pastry leaves, crimping the edges evenly, studying it from every angle before announcing it finished.

"What time is Jonathan coming, Mum?"

"He said he'd be here about six-thirty." Her mother looked up at the clock. "Gosh, it's almost five now. I'll take these jars down to the cellar while you get the roast in the oven."

"Be careful on the steps, Mum."

"Yes, dear," her mother replied, an exasperated tone to her voice.

Katherine made little slits in the lamb and inserted garlic cloves and sprigs of rosemary. From the cellar came a startled cry, followed by a series of thumps.

"Mum?" she called.

Only silence answered her.

Forty-Six

She rushed to the cellar door. Her mother lay in a crumpled heap at the bottom of the steps. "Mum?" Katherine hurried down and knelt beside her mother. "Mum?" She shook her mother's shoulder, but her mother didn't stir, and her head lay at an odd angle. Katherine held her mother's wrist, hoping for a pulse, but found nothing. She put her ear to her mother's chest, silently praying for the sound of a heartbeat, but again, there was nothing.

No. This couldn't be happening. Not her mother. Perhaps she was just unconscious. Katherine checked her mother's pulse again, but again, it was absent. She stumbled up the stairs to phone for an ambulance, and then sat on the top step to wait, her gaze locked on her mother lying at the bottom. The bottles of apple jelly, remarkably unbroken, lay a short distance away from where her mother must have dropped them when she fell.

The approaching siren stirred her, and she ran to open the front door. One ambulance officer hurried in while the other opened the rear of their wagon. Katherine led the officer, who introduced himself as Anthony, through the kitchen to the cellar door, where she stopped and pointed down the stairs. Anthony hurried down the steps.

Katherine turned away. Her mother hadn't moved in over half an hour and, deep in her soul, Katherine had known the moment she saw her mother lying at the base of the stairs that she was dead. She didn't want to watch strangers do whatever they needed to do to reach the same conclusion.

Anthony came to where she paced the living room floor. She stopped and faced him.

He shook his head. "I'm sorry, there was nothing we could do."

Having her mother's death confirmed removed any small glimmer of hope that she'd clung to. Her throat tightened, and she covered her face with her hands, tears coursing down her face, her heart once again breaking. She still mourned the loss of her father. It wasn't fair that fate would deal her a second blow.

Anthony knelt beside her and put his hand on her shoulder. "Is there someone we can call? Someone who can sit with you?"

Katherine shook her head.

Jonathan crashed through the door. "Katherine, are you alright? I saw the ambulance." He crouched by Katherine and scooped her into his arms as Anthony stood to make way for him.

She clung to him, sobbing. "It's Mum. She's dead!"

"Oh my God, no. What happened?"

"She fell down the cellar stairs. I think she broke her neck."

"Is that what happened?" Jonathan asked, looking up at the ambulance officer.

"It appears so, sir," Anthony said, "But the coroner will issue an official cause of death."

"Poor Jacqueline." He stroked Katherine's hair and wiped her tears away. "My poor Katherine."

"We've called the police, Ms. Walters. They'll be here shortly." The other ambulance officer entered the room.

Jonathan shot to his feet. "Police? We don't need the police. The poor woman fell down the stairs."

"It's routine in cases of accidental death, sir," Anthony said.

Katherine tugged at Jonathan's sleeve. "It's alright. They have to do their job."

~

Katherine related the events to the questioning police officer while he took notes. Only when he asked how Katherine got on with her mother did Jonathan interject.

"Are you accusing Katherine of pushing her mother down those stairs? That's ridiculous. Katherine loved her mother." His tone was angry as he spoke to the police officer, then became indulgent as he turned to Katherine, saying, "Didn't you, darling?"

"Of course I loved my mother." Katherine addressed the police officer. "It's true we didn't always get along, but I certainly had no wish to harm her."

"What about you, Mr. Irving? What was your relationship like with the deceased? Er, I mean Mrs. Walters."

"Now you're accusing me? This is too much."

"Jonathan, please!" Katherine protested. "Let them do their job." To the police officer, she said, "Jonathan wasn't here when... it happened."

"I see." The police officer closed his notebook. "That will be all for now."

"What happens now?" Katherine asked.

"There'll be a postmortem, which is routine. Then we'll release your mother's body. You can start arrangements if you wish. Shouldn't take too long."

"Thank you," Katherine said.

Jonathan slipped an arm around Katherine's waist and led her to the sofa. "Yes, thank you, officer. I'll take care of Katherine now, won't I, darling?" They sat, Katherine's head resting on Jonathan's shoulder, his arm around her.

A metallic rattle came from the hallway, and Katherine looked up as the ambulance officers wheeled a sheet-draped stretcher through the opposite doorway. She buried her face in Jonathan's chest, fresh tears soaking his shirt.

"I can't believe she's gone."

"There, there, sweetheart." Jonathan stroked her hair and kissed the top of her head. "Your mother was a lovely woman. Let's just remember her the way she was."

"I know, but I feel so guilty. If it wasn't for that stupid apple jelly, she wouldn't have gone down to the cellar, and she'd still be alive." Katherine pulled away and sat forward, taking a tissue from the box on the table.

"It's not your fault, Katherine, you know that."

Katherine didn't reply. He didn't understand. How could he? Her mother *always* made her feel guilty. As in life, so in death. Despite that, she loved her mother dearly. Now she was alone. Both parents gone in the same year. She had no one left.

Forty-Seven

Jonathan patted her shoulder and rose. "I'll make you a hot drink."

He returned a few minutes later and handed her a cup. "Here, this might help."

She took it from him, savoring the warmth of the cup in her hands for a few moments before taking a sip. Hot, sweet, and potent. "My goodness, what is this?"

"It's hot chocolate à la Jonathan." He sat beside her again. "It's laced with brandy. I found some in the kitchen."

"It's very good, thank you."

She sipped the chocolate, her thoughts turning again to her mother.

"I hope you don't mind, but I turned your oven off and put the lamb and things in the fridge. I didn't think you'd want a roast tonight." Jonathan said.

"Thank you. You're very thoughtful." Katherine's eyes brimmed with tears again, and she blinked, trying to keep them at bay. She yawned; suddenly very tired. Gosh, how much brandy did he put in that drink?

She got up from the couch and staggered. Jonathan caught her as she started to topple, and she slumped against him. She was vaguely aware of being lifted, her mind foggy and disjointed. Jonathan's voice came from far away, and the world around her receded as if she was falling down a well, her consciousness getting smaller and smaller until...

Forty-Eight

Katherine clawed her way back to consciousness. She shook her head, trying to clear the fog. Awareness crept back into her senses. She was in bed. She was not alone.

Jonathan lay beside her, still sleeping. What? Then the events of the previous evening crashed back into her mind. Her mother was dead, Jonathan had come over, and she'd had brandy. She must have passed out.

Panicked, she lifted the sheet, then let it drop. She was wearing her pajamas. But how? Did Jonathan undress her?

"Good morning, Katherine."

Katherine looked at him but said nothing.

He threw back the covers and got out of bed, fully clothed in blue jeans and a red T-shirt.

"How did I get here?" she asked.

"Don't you remember? You were rather drunk. I think I overdid the brandy." Jonathan smiled guiltily at her. "Sorry about that."

"Who undressed me?"

"You did, of course. How else... oh, you think I undressed you? No, I can assure you I'm not responsible."

"Then what are you doing in my bed?"

Jonathan hung his head. "I'm sorry, Katherine, I couldn't sleep where your mother..."

How could she have been so thoughtless? "Gosh, I'm sorry, of course not. I never thought. Forgive me."

Jonathan sat on the edge of the bed and took Katherine's hand. "Of course, I forgive you. Now you get dressed, and I'll make breakfast."

Katherine waited until Jonathan left before getting out of bed. Dust motes danced in the light streaming in through the window, promising a warm sunny day. Days like this usually filled Katherine with joy, but not today. Today, she faced the task of preparing to bury her mother.

She trudged to the bathroom and turned on the shower, waiting until it was hot before stepping underneath.

"Ouch." She flinched as the hot water hit her skin. Gingerly, she touched her breasts. Her nipples were a little swollen, her breasts tender. She cooled the water a fraction and soaped herself. Washing between her legs, she encountered tenderness there, too. Sometimes she got rather tender before a painful period. Usually, periods didn't bother her, but every so often, a bad one would lay her low with cramping pain that left her curled in a fetal position, clutching a hot-water bottle. She groaned. Her period wasn't due for a couple of weeks, but the tenderness in her body bore the hallmark of a debilitating one.

Once dressed in a pair of loose-fitting slacks and an oversized jumper, she made her way downstairs and into the kitchen; her gaze drawn to the cellar door. Her eyes welled with tears. Jonathan put his arm around her and steered her to a seat at the table, her back to the cellar.

"Come on, I've made you some breakfast."

Katherine slumped in the chair. "I'm not hungry, just coffee will do."

"You've got to eat. You missed dinner last night. I've made scrambled eggs; please have some."

"Alright then, but just a little." Eating was the last thing Katherine wanted to do, but Jonathan insisted.

He placed a plate in front of her. Two rashers of bacon, scrambled eggs, grilled tomato, and mushrooms. Two slices of buttered toast on the side.

"No, this is too much."

"Just eat what you fancy."

She ate methodically; put a forkful of food into her mouth, chew, swallow, repeat, her thoughts not on the food, but on her mother, and the image of her at the bottom of the stairs. Her heart ached, breaking into a thousand jagged shards, and tears trickled down her cheeks, dripping onto her partly eaten breakfast. She pushed her plate away.

"Good girl, you've done better than I thought you would." Jonathan handed her a steaming cup of coffee.

"Thank you." She wrapped her hands around it, the warmth of the cup doing little to eradicate the chill in her body.

"My pleasure. Now, what would you like to do today? Maybe go for a drive, find a pleasant spot for lunch. It's a lovely day."

Katherine looked at him, incredulously. He was smiling! How could he look so pleased? Had he forgotten? "Jonathan, I need to start organizing my mother's... funeral."

"Oh, that. Yes. Alright."

Jonathan's sunny enthusiasm vanished in a flash, replaced with what? Annoyance? No, it couldn't be; he'd been so kind and caring. And he'd genuinely liked her mother. No, she must have misread his tone. She finished her coffee, sighed, and got up from the table. May as well make a start. First task, though, was to get rid of Jonathan, otherwise he'd just fuss around her like a mother hen.

"Jonathan, I need to make some calls."

"You go right ahead. I'll start making some soup for lunch."

"No, Jonathan. You've been very kind and I appreciate it a lot, but I need some time alone now."

His body stiffened. His lips pressed together, and his eyes narrowed. "Are you saying you want me to go?"

"Yes, I suppose I am. Today is going to be hard for me, but I need to do it and I'd prefer to do it alone."

"So you're throwing me out again? Just like last time. You use me when you want and then throw me out."

"Jonathan, please." She put a hand on his arm. "It's not like that. I'm not throwing you out at all. Please try to understand. I've just lost my mother."

Jonathan's face softened, and he smiled again, taking Katherine in his arms. "I know, sweetheart, and I'm sorry. I wasn't thinking, please forgive me."

"Of course. I know you liked Mum too, and she liked you. Said you were 'charming'."

"Did she really?"

Katherine pulled back a little and looked up at Jonathan. He preened, a self-satisfied grin on his face.

"Look, tell you what, I'll leave you alone to do what you need to. I'll come back about six and take you out to dinner. Then we'll come back here..."

"No, Jonathan." Katherine extricated herself from his arms and moved away from him, leaning against the kitchen bench.

"You'd prefer we eat here?"

This was getting exasperating. "I mean that I'm okay. I can look after myself. You don't need to take me out or cook me dinner."

"But you need me. You can't stay here on your own."

Forty-Nine

Katherine sighed. Jonathan was whining again. She didn't want another fight with him, but she needed to make a stand or he'd walk all over her. "Of course I can stay here on my own. I'm sad, but I'm not helpless."

"But... but... what if that man comes back?"

"What man?"

"That man on the moor."

How could she have forgotten about The Stranger? Should she change her mind? Accept Jonathan's protection? No. She must stand firm. Live her own life.

"I'll be fine, Jonathan. He's had ample opportunity to attack me if he was going to and hasn't done so, so I can't see why he will now." Katherine spoke quickly, yet firmly, her confident tone countering her inward trepidation. "No, you go. You'll have your own things to do. I'll call you in a couple of days and let you know what arrangements I've made."

"A couple of days! No! I've got to take care of you! You need me!"

Katherine stood erect, summoning all her courage. "Jonathan, I've tried to be nice. I've tried to be polite. I'm very grateful for everything you've done, but now it's time for you to go."

He stared at her. His clenched fists, his set jaw, his downturned mouth, left little doubt he was angry.

"Please go, Jonathan," Katherine said again, her tone stern and commanding.

He left without a word.

The front door slammed. A few moments later, his car engine roared as he sped away.

Fifty

JONATHAN

Jonathan drove away from Katherine's at speed, missing the courtyard wall by a whisker as his car slewed on the gravel. How dare she treat him like this? He'd gone out of his way to be kind, caring, considerate, not to mention loving and attentive, while she grieved over her poor departed mother. But was she grateful? No bloody way. She had the gall to ask him to leave. Bitch.

Different story last night when she'd clung to him, sobbing, his shirt soaked with her tears. For God's sake, it's not as if the woman had been Katherine's best friend. From what he'd seen, the two didn't get on that well together, but the way Katherine carried on, you'd think she'd lost her firstborn, rather than a woman who only seemed to annoy her.

Still, the hot chocolate shut her up, thankfully. He couldn't have stood much more of her wailing. He'd slipped more than brandy in her hot chocolate, intending for her to pass out if only to stop her blubbing. Of course, when she asked him this morning who undressed her, he had to lie.

He smiled ruefully, remembering laying Katherine on the bed and then undressing her; finally having her naked again. Kissing, touching, fondling, caressing, sucking, nibbling, and squeezing, ravaging her body several times. He'd been none too gentle, either. Oh, the things he'd done to her. Not like the first time when he needed to consider her pleasure. This was all about him and his needs, his wants, his satisfaction, and he'd taken it all and then some, until he'd collapsed, utterly spent, and thoroughly satiated.

Then, after he'd recovered a little, he'd dressed her in pajamas; a task not unlike trying to get a sweater on an octopus. By the time he'd finished, he'd been thoroughly exhausted.

His smile faded, turning his mouth down into a scowl. Last night, he'd thought he'd achieved his goal of possessing Katherine. Then this morning, she got all assertive and wanted to be alone, despite his protestations that she needed him. Even reminding her of the threat from the man she called The Stranger didn't sway her, although he'd seen a quick flicker of fear cross her face.

Why couldn't she stop this cat-and-mouse game she played? Why couldn't she accept they were meant to be together? Why couldn't she just love him?

Soon, Katherine. Soon, you will have no choice. The timing had been perfect.

Fifty-One

KATHERINE

The day of her mother's funeral, Katherine was standing at the entrance of St George the Martyr church in Truro, thanking each of the mourners for coming, when a woman who looked vaguely familiar approached her.

"Katherine, dear, you may not remember me. I'm Mavis Thomas..."

Tears prickled Katherine's eyes, but she forced a smile. She could hear her mother's voice now. 'You remember Mavis, darling, she ran the school canteen when you were little.'

"Yes, I remember you, Mavis. Mum spoke of you often."

"I just wanted to say how sorry I am. Your poor mother. I'll miss her terribly. We had such fun at bowls, her and I. She was my best friend." Mavis broke into sobs on that last word, and Katherine's tears, never far away over the past week, made their way down her cheeks. Katherine and Mavis clung to each other and cried until Jonathan put his arms around Katherine and turned her away from Mavis.

From the church, the funeral procession made its way to the Truro Public Cemetery, where, after a brief graveside prayer, the coffin was lowered into the ground beside her father's grave.

"Together again," Katherine said, dissolving into tears. "I never dreamed I'd be burying Mum so soon after Dad. It's just not fair."

Jonathan held her while she cried, muttering soothing sounds for a few moments before leading her away from the grave.

The ladies' bowling club put on a splendid feast in honor of their teammate. Cakes, scones, slices, sandwiches, bite-sized quiches, and all manner of savories. Over cups of tea and coffee, everyone chatted amiably, reminiscing on their memories of 'Jacqui'. Of course, Jonathan made a great show of being attentive and caring toward Katherine. While grateful for his kindness, she secretly wished he wouldn't fuss so much. He was being quite possessive.

Katherine stayed on at her mother's house for a few days to sort through things. Jonathan, predictably, wanted to stay with her, whining and pleading, telling Katherine how much she needed him. She'd had enough of him being so possessive and said so. Predictably, this led to another argument, and Jonathan left, but not before extracting a promise from Katherine that she would call him the moment she returned home.

Most of her mother's clothes, linen, crockery, and such, Katherine donated to Oxfam, along with the pieces of furniture that she didn't want to keep. Her mother's jewelry and more personal items, along with what remained of her father's things, were packed in boxes and brought back with her. Mavis offered her husband's services to bring the heavier items up in his van the following Saturday.

All that remained was to put the house on the market. Katherine left keys with Mavis so that the local realtors could view the property and prepare a valuation and marketing plan. Katherine initially thought about asking Jonathan for his opinion, but then decided against it. He'd just want to take control, and she didn't want to give him any more opportunity to insert himself into her life.

Now back at home, after dinner, she sat watching reruns of *Red Dwarf*; something light-hearted to help her relax before bed.

The phone rang. She picked up the remote control, meaning to mute the sound, but hesitated. It would have to be Jonathan. She'd promised to ring him when she got home, but all she wanted right now was some time alone. If he knew she was home, he'd insist on coming over, she'd say no, and they'd fight again. She put the remote back on the coffee table and ignored the ringing phone. Eventually, it stopped.

When her eyes refused to stay open, she turned off the television and did her rounds of the house, checking and double-checking all the door locks and ensuring all the windows were firmly closed. Satisfied that everything was in order, she put out the lights and climbed the stairs.

Fifty-Two

JONATHAN

Out on the moor, Jonathan watched from his usual vantage point. Katherine hadn't answered when he'd phoned earlier, but some inner sense told him she was home. Sure enough, her lights were on, and he settled down to wait for the show to begin.

Finally, the lights on the ground floor went out, and after a few minutes, the bedroom light came on. There she was.

His pulse beat faster, anticipating what lay ahead, and his hand moved down to the bulge growing in his pants. Katherine moved toward the window, and he unzipped, extracting his erect penis. So many days since she'd been here for him to watch, he knew he would come within seconds. *Come on, Katherine, undress.* He held his breath and stroked his erection. What was she waiting for?

"No. No. NO! You can't do that!" He shook his head, crying out in frustration as Katherine closed the curtains. There would be no show tonight, no pleasure for him. His erection dwindled. How could she betray him like this?

Fifty-Three

KATHERINE

Katherine stood at the window, looking out. Her own reflection looked back at her. She shivered, and the hairs on the back of her neck prickled. She sensed eyes on her, watching her. It was silly, of course. No one in their right mind would be out on the moors after dark. But despite that, the feeling stayed. She hurriedly closed the curtains.

On Friday morning, she finally called Jonathan to let him know she was back. He sounded cool, distant. She mentioned that Mavis and Jack would bring the rest of her mother's furniture up the following day, half expecting him to offer to help with the furniture, but he didn't. Maybe he was still angry with her, or maybe he'd at last understood she didn't want a relationship. Then again, he might just be busy. Whatever the reason, Katherine didn't prolong the conversation, merely wished him a pleasant weekend, and said goodbye.

Fifty-Four

JONATHAN

Jonathan hung up the phone. So, she finally got around to telling him she was home. Well, he'd show her. She'd spurned him once too often. The last straw was when she'd told him to go home after her mother's funeral and promised to call him as soon as she returned. Now she rings two fucking days later! Katherine needed him, and he'd gone down to Truro for her sake, not her damned mother.

He'd felt physically sick buttering up the old duck in order to get her on side to help him win Katherine, but it hadn't worked. When he thought back to how he'd fawned over her, he shuddered. The silly bitch had lapped it up, though. When he'd met her on her own that day, he'd flattered her, told her how beautiful she was, and that he would love to have her as his mother-in-law. She had agreed to help him one final time.

He'd played her so well, quite proud of his stage-managing of the whole scenario. She'd believed him! When he'd gotten her to invite him for dinner the next evening, he told her he wanted to surprise Katherine with a proposal of marriage. He'd hidden some champagne in the cellar, he'd told her. Would she be good enough to go down and get it at precisely five? He would arrive early and propose to Katherine, and then they would celebrate with the champagne.

The silly old bitch fell for it. Sure enough, at five, the light came on in the cellar, and she came down the steps. It was so very easy. Her neck snapped like a twig in his hands.

Fifty-Five

KATHERINE

At eleven-thirty on Saturday morning, a van lumbered into the courtyard, and Katherine ran to welcome Mavis and Jack. Mavis carried a basket of flowers.

"From your mother's garden," Mavis said, handing the basket to Katherine, her eyes sparkling with unshed tears.

Katherine hugged the woman, fighting back her own tears. "Thank you, Mavis. How thoughtful." After a moment, she drew back and smiled at her mother's friend. "Come in, have some tea. You must be parched after the drive."

Over cups of tea and slices of Battenberg cake, they shared reminiscences about Katherine's mother, the latest happenings in Truro, and the solitude of Katherine's new home.

Jack pushed back his chair and rose. "I'd better get started."

It took them almost two hours to unload and place the furniture. Her mother's favorite recliner went beside the fireplace in the living room, and the crystal cabinet in one corner. The bed ensemble and suite replaced the rather tired old spare bed Katherine had bought in a jumble sale many years before.

"What do you want to do with the old one, Katherine?" Jack asked.

"I don't know; I haven't thought about it. Just leave it in the hall for now, and I'll get rid of it later."

"I can take it with me, if you like," Jack said. "We can drop it at the waste disposal center on the way home."

"That's so kind of you, thank you."

They stacked the boxes in the hall alongside those Katherine had brought back with her. After another cup of tea and some hastily made sandwiches, Mavis and Jack set off home.

"Thank you so much, Mavis, Jack," Katherine said, giving each of them a hug. "You've been very kind."

"You're welcome, my dear," Mavis said, a tear in her eye again. "Your mum was a good friend."

Katherine watched them drive away and waved till they were out of sight, then scurried back inside, locking the door behind her.

Ever since Jonathan mentioned The Stranger coming back for her, she didn't feel safe unless the doors were locked. She'd even taken to closing the curtains since she'd gotten back from Truro and sensed someone watching her. Now, as soon as dusk fell, she closed them all and double-checked every lock.

For the rest of the afternoon, she unpacked boxes, sitting on the floor surrounded by a growing pile of paper as she unpacked each memory. The little sundial her father bought at The Lizard, the Venetian glass gondola her mother brought back from Italy when she'd gone with the ladies' bowling club. So many memories. That was all she had of her parents now. Just memories.

With the last piece carefully placed, Katherine gathered up the packaging paper and sat in her mother's recliner, feeding the fire until all the paper was gone. Then she flattened the boxes and picked them up, remembering another time she'd taken boxes to the cellar.

They say that if you fall off a horse, the best thing to do is get straight back on. This was much the same. She could avoid the cellar today, but if she did, who knows when she would have the courage to venture down there. Or she could face the demon of her fear head-on and get on with her life. Before her bravery deserted her, she picked up the key and unlocked the cellar door. The darkness and the chill seemed to reach out for her, and she hesitated. Then, swallowing the lump in her throat, she flicked the light switch. The darkness vanished in an instant, and she stood at the top of the stairs, looking down. The last time she'd been in the cellar, her mother's lifeless body lay at the bottom of the stairs. Now there was just the cellar floor.

Taking a deep breath and mustering what remained of her courage, she descended the steps; boxes tucked under one arm, her free hand gripping the handrail. It wouldn't do to fall and break her neck, too. She stacked the boxes in the corner and looked at the jars of apple jelly she'd made the day her mother died. Someone had gathered them up and put them to one side. Who would have done that? Maybe the police, or even Jonathan. She shouldn't blame herself, but couldn't help thinking she was responsible for her mother's death. If she hadn't made the jelly, her mother wouldn't have needed to go down to the cellar and would probably still be alive.

She left the jars untouched, but made a mental note to dump the jelly. No way could she ever eat it. Every taste would remind her that the jelly had cost her mother her life. She went deeper into the cellar to get a couple of bottles of wine. She chose a bottle of Brown Brothers Shiraz and a Ninth Island Sauvignon Blanc, both from a case of Australian wines she'd picked up at a wine and food fair in Exeter a few months back. It was cool in the cellar, and the white would only need a short time in the fridge before being the right temperature.

Satisfied with her wine choice, she started back.

Suddenly, the light went out, plunging the cellar and Katherine into darkness. She let out a cry, which morphed into a nervous laugh. That blasted bulb again. Obviously, something was wrong with the wiring, and she'd have to call an electrician to check it out. A rectangle of thin watery light emanated from the open kitchen door, and she shuffled forward carefully, sliding each foot across the floor rather than stepping. Once she found the bottom step, she'd be okay.

The rectangle of light changed, getting thinner. Her eyes widened in horror as the door swung closed, leaving her in darkness.

Fifty-Six

"No!" She rushed forward, kicked the bottom step hard, and fell, wine bottles clattering to the floor. Carefully making her way up the steps, she tried to swallow her rising panic. It would just be that draft that seemed to swirl around the cellar. That's all. The door would just have swung shut on the breeze. Finally, she reached the top and pushed the door. It wouldn't open. She shoved harder, then put her shoulder to it and pushed with every ounce of strength, but it was no use. The door remained firmly shut. She was trapped.

The darkness was absolute. She held a hand up in front of her face, less than an inch away from her eyes, but she couldn't see it. If she had her phone, she'd use its torch. But it was still sitting on the coffee table in the living room.

Somehow, she'd have to break the lock or the door. But how? She needed something robust to bash the door until it, or the lock, broke. Perhaps one of the stone flagons in the lower part of the cellar. One of those must be strong enough. If only it wasn't so dark! Gripping the handrail with every ounce of strength, she started back down the stairs, ever mindful of how her mother met her end. Every single step took several moments to navigate. Slowly move her right foot until she could feel the edge of the step with her toe, and then shuffle her left foot forward. Then her right foot over the edge and down. Only when it was firmly on the step would she bring her left down to join it.

Right foot forward, slowly. Her hand slipped on the rail, and she lurched and almost fell. Panic exploded through her—heart racing, gut doing somersaults, gasping for breath. She grabbed the rail with both hands and held it in a viselike grip until she recovered her balance. When her panic subsided and her breathing slowed to some semblance of normal, she rubbed one sweat-slick palm on her jeans and then the other. Slowly, she continued down, pausing every few steps to wipe the palms of her hands. Was that what caused her mother to fall? Sweaty hands?

By the time she reached the floor—and she only knew it was the floor because the handrail stopped—she was exhausted. Not just her palms now, her whole body was slick with sweat.

After allowing herself a few moments' rest, Katherine edged her way along, arms stretched out in front of her, until she felt the edge of a shelf. The clink of bottles told her she had found her preserves. At least she wouldn't starve to death.

She worked her way along the shelf, knowing that at the far end there was a small table and beyond that, the steps to the lower cellar. She bumped the table and felt her way around it, trying to picture in her mind how far it was to the end. Again, she moved slowly, inching forward. Her outstretched fingertips found a corner. Was this the start of the steps? Why hadn't she paid more attention when she'd been down here before? With her heart in her mouth, she inched her foot forward until it, too, found an edge. She'd found the steps.

There was no handrail here, and the stone steps weren't even. She could easily trip if she didn't concentrate fully on the task ahead. Pressing her hands against the walls on either side of the steps to steady herself, she carefully inched her way down. Shuffle forward to the edge, brace herself, then step down. No, she couldn't do this. Without a handrail, the risk of falling increased dramatically. The only way to do this was on her bottom. She sat and put her hands in her lap, rolling her shoulders forward, backward, and then stretching her neck.

She started back down, feeling for the edge of the step with her hands and then shuffling her bottom forward until she plopped down on the next step. This was much easier. If she'd thought of this back at the other steps, she might have been out of here by now.

At the bottom, she got up and stood for a moment, picturing the layout of the cellar in her mind. The flagons were on a shelf to the left, so she headed in that direction.

A chill draft curled around her body, and she shivered. She caught a sound. What was that? A rat? She turned in the direction she thought it came from, listening intently in case the sound came again. An evil laugh emanated from the darkness in front of her. Katherine shrieked and fled for the steps, but in her panic crashed into a wall. She turned her back to the wall, pressing her body against it. Which way to run?

Fifty-Seven

She listened for movement. There! She ran the opposite way. Strong arms caught her and held her captive. Katherine struggled to free herself, but something cold closed around her wrist. A rattle of chains, and then her other wrist was fettered.

"Please let me go," she pleaded as she struggled against the chains that held her captive. She sensed her captor walk away from her. "Who are you? Please don't hurt me."

A match flickered, and the light, as bright as the sun, stung Katherine's eyes. The light became a million suns as a candle flame glowed in the darkness. Gigantic shadows loomed, and the figure faced her, holding the candle in one hand, a pair of night-vision goggles in the other. So that's how he'd seen her in the darkness.

Katherine recognized her attacker instantly. She had seen him many times, out on the moors, his long black coat fluttering in the wind. He wore a black scarf of some kind over his nose and mouth, his black hat pulled down, shadowing his eyes. The Stranger! Her heart pounded, its sledgehammer blows threatening to smash her ribs in its attempt to escape the terror engulfing her, drowning her in its blackness. She pulled against the chains holding her wrists, twisting her body away from the horror that stood in front of her. Her screams bounced off the walls, echoing back to her as though a dozen unseen voices screamed along with her.

He laughed. A chilling laugh. An evil laugh. A laugh with madness at its core.

He lumbered menacingly toward her, his boot heels scuffing the floor as he got closer, closer.

She pulled away as far as her shackles would allow. “No. No. No.” Her head shook, but her gaze never left The Stranger’s shadowed face.

His hand reached out toward her, and Katherine shrank back, but to no avail. He touched her cheek in a soft caress, and Katherine shuddered as horror rushed through her veins, spreading its chill throughout her body.

The Stranger leaned in, his face close to hers. “Beware,” he whispered, his voice a low and sinister hiss. Then, with a flurry of his long coat, he turned and blew out the candle. The shadows pounced, swallowing Katherine in the darkness. Only The Stranger’s laughter remained, fading, fading, fading. An icy breeze snaked around Katherine’s ankles, whispering its way up her legs as the last vestiges of The Stranger’s laughter died away, leaving only a shroud of silence.

Katherine pulled against her restraints. First with her right arm, then her left, grunting with the strain of exertion, the cuffs around her wrists biting into her flesh. She cried out for help, despite knowing the chances of being heard were a million to one. Her cottage was so far away from any roadway, and she was deep underground. In the short time she’d lived here, she’d seen nobody except Jonathan and The Stranger. No hikers, no cyclists, no letter-boxers, not even a lost tourist.

Her cries for help became wails of despair, and she slumped against the shackles that held her. Helpless. Trapped and chained like a dog. Jonathan had warned her. Even The Stranger himself had warned her, but despite her fear, she hadn’t really taken the threats seriously. Now here she was. Alone and at the mercy of The Stranger.

Fifty-Eight

What did he want with her? Why would he want to keep her prisoner? And why would he even warn her? Still so many questions. And still no answers.

How long before anyone noticed her missing? Then again, who would even notice her missing? If she hadn't given Jonathan such a monumental brush-off, he might have come looking for her and maybe would have found her. But, judging by his coolness toward her in their last conversation, that wasn't likely now.

She might die down here. Would the cold, thirst, or starvation get to her first? It was ironic; only a short time ago she'd been thinking she wouldn't starve because of her preserves, but now... Thank God there was no evidence of rats down here. She shuddered at the thought of being eaten alive by rats.

Time passed. Was it an hour? Two? Half a day? In the absolute darkness and with no frame of reference, she had no concept of time, of how long she'd been trapped. Eventually, she dozed, but each time her body relaxed and slumped, the shackles bit into her wrists, and she woke.

Time passed.

An icy breeze caressed her, rousing her from her half-slumber. A beam of light blinded her, and she scrunched her eyes closed and turned her head. The light dropped away, and she turned back to face The Stranger.

"Who are you? What do you want with me?" She tried to quell the tremor in her voice. Better to sound indignant, not let him see her terror.

The Stranger remained silent, looking at her as though studying her, perhaps wondering what to do now that she was his captive. He dipped his hand into the pocket of his coat. He brought out a foil-wrapped package, unwrapped it, and held it out to her. A sandwich. Puzzled, Katherine looked from the sandwich to The Stranger and back. Her stomach gurgled. He thrust the sandwich closer to her face. All she had to do was bite it. She leaned forward a little, then hesitated. What if it was poisoned?

She turned her head away. The Stranger grasped her chin in his hand and held it fast, his thumb and fingers pressing hard against each cheek, forcing her mouth open. He pushed the sandwich toward her. She dutifully took a bite, and he let go, seemingly satisfied. She spat the food into his face.

In an instant, his hands were around her throat, squeezing. She struggled to breathe, but nothing came. Her heart thumped faster, harder, louder, and she tried to twist her body, her head, anything to loosen his grip, but he held her fast. Pinpricks of light exploded in her darkening vision as her consciousness receded down a tunnel. Her struggles became weaker.

As quickly as the attack happened, it was over. His hands were gone from around her neck. She took in deep, whooping breaths, ignoring the searing pain in her throat, relishing the oxygen again coursing through her body. Her heart continued to hammer in her chest, and she concentrated on breathing deeply, calmly, visualizing her blood cells changing from blue to red as they engorged with oxygen and whizzed around her body, delivering their payload to her furthest extremities.

Finally, her breathing and her heartbeat slowed. Partially recovered, but for the pain in her throat, she looked around for The Stranger. He was nowhere in sight, but a candle still burned. Katherine savored the light. After so long in the dark, a single candle flame was a shining beacon of hope.

She stared at the flame, watching it burn lower, the small stub of wax getting shorter with every passing minute. How long before she was again plunged into darkness?

All too soon, the flame weakened, sputtered, and died. Darkness again shrouded her.

"No! Oh, please, help me, somebody."

She shivered as an icy chill passed over her skin, and she opened her eyes. Had she dozed again? The flicker of a match and then that wonderful glow of another candle. The Stranger was back.

He came to her and held a cup to her lips. She drank, hesitantly at first, but as the water cooled the fire in her throat, she gulped greedily. This time, when he offered her a sandwich, she bit into it and ate, not daring to challenge him again. She savored the taste of cheese, tomato, and some kind of relish. When she finished the sandwich, he gave her more water.

"Please let me go." The bravado that she'd endeavored to display earlier had long since departed, leaving her a mewling, whining creature begging for its freedom.

The Stranger said nothing, merely walked away and blew out the candle. A cool breeze brushed her face. He had left.

How does he come and go? She hadn't explored this cellar; she had no need to. But she was sure she'd locked all her doors, so maybe there was a hidden passage somewhere. No, surely that was silly. Why would there be? And where would it lead to? It didn't make sense. There was nothing around for miles, only the old railway and the quarry, both long ago abandoned.

Katherine yawned; weariness took over her body. If only her chains would allow her to lie down or at least sit down, she might manage to sleep. This fitful dozing hanging from her shackles wasn't restful. She needed a proper sleep. Some time back, she'd read an article about a man who died after going without sleep for about ten or eleven days. She couldn't conceive of going without sleep for a day, let alone over a week. Even at university, when she'd gone out partying with her friends, she was always home and in bed before midnight. How they used to tease her. On one occasion, to appease her friends, she had stayed out, ignoring her body's cry for sleep. By the time she'd got home, it was after three a.m., and she fell into bed, utterly exhausted. Next morning, when the alarm woke her, she'd crawled out of bed, still shattered, and dragged herself through the day. Sluggish, unable to concentrate. Never again.

Or so she'd thought until now.

Again and again she dropped off, only to wake at the pain in her wrists and shoulders, until finally, her body's demand for rest overwhelmed her and she eventually slumped and slept.

She woke and struggled back to her feet. Her wrists hurt where the shackles bit into them as she hung from the chains, and her shoulders felt stretched to the point of being about to pop out of their sockets. Her hands tingled as she rotated her shoulders and flexed her fingers, pumping blood back to them.

As always, when she woke, her bladder was full, and she needed to pee. How would she manage that? She couldn't reach her jeans, let alone be able to unbutton them. Heat flushed her face. She would have to ask The Stranger. If he arrived in time, that was. It better be soon, or she might not be able to hold on.

God, hurry up. She squeezed her legs together, then crossed them, her bladder begging for relief. She was desperate. This was torture.

He didn't come.

Fifty-Nine

Finally, her full-to-bursting bladder won and purged its contents. As urine ran down her legs, soaking her jeans, shame flushed hot on her cheeks. She hung her head and sobbed, partly with shame, but mostly with relief.

Katherine stirred from her half slumber as the icy breeze curled around her wet jeans, emphasizing its chill. The Stranger had arrived. A flash as a match struck, then a candle blinded her with its light. He walked toward her, but stopped and sniffed the air.

She bowed her head and blinked back tears, ashamed that she'd soiled herself.

His long coat made a swishing sound as he spun around and hurried away from her. Then the cellar was again plunged into darkness, and the chilling breeze swirled against Katherine's hot cheeks. The Stranger was gone.

"No!" Katherine cried. "Come back!"

She struggled against her bonds, screaming for The Stranger to return. She screamed until something gave way in her throat, and she feared she had damaged her vocal cords. But what did it matter, anyway? She would die in here.

~

He was back! A mixture of fear and relief rushed through Katherine as the candle flame came to life. The Stranger approached her, wearing blue rubber gloves. He reached toward her waist, but Katherine twisted her body, trying to get away, not wanting him to touch her. A sharp slap stung her face, and she stopped struggling immediately, lest his hands again found their way to her throat.

She stood still and compliant as he removed her shoes, socks, and jeans. He hooked his thumbs into her underwear, and she instinctively kicked a leg out, her foot connecting with his shin. Again, he slapped her, this time on the bare thigh, then returned to his task of removing her underwear. She had no choice but to let him.

Was that his intention, after all? To rape her? He would keep her here and use her body for gratification, and there was nothing she could do about it. She swallowed hard, took a deep breath, let it out slowly, then took another, mentally preparing herself for the violation to come.

But The Stranger stepped away, bundled up her soiled clothes and stuffed them into a bag, walking back toward the candle. Katherine's hope that he was about to leave turned to dismay as he returned to her, carrying a bucket and a towel.

Her face flushed hot, and she looked away. But her embarrassment soon turned to elation. He'd have to unchain her so that she could wash herself. This was her chance. She must get away. Her mind whirled with possibilities. She must decide. Quickly!

Sixty

Her excitement—and any hope of escape—faded as he withdrew a sponge from the bucket and washed her. Humiliated, she had to stand there and let him sponge her. When he washed between her legs, she dropped her head, shame flaring not just in her cheeks but in her whole body.

His fingers touched her intimately, stroking her as if trying to arouse her. Revulsion shuddered through her while his breathing quickened. She steeled herself for the inevitable. He'd merely wanted her clean before he raped her.

He withdrew his hand and then dried her, the roughness of the towel scratching her skin.

"Please, let me go," Katherine pleaded. "What do you want from me?"

Without a word of reply, The Stranger turned away, taking the bucket and towel with him. He stooped to blow out the candle, and then darkness enveloped her again.

The breeze that accompanied his leaving chilled her half-naked body, raising goosebumps on her skin. At least she would be able to half squat to pee, now, so she wouldn't soil herself.

When The Stranger returned, he carried a folding chair. He set it up near her, and while she longed to sit, the chair was out of reach. He moved behind her; the chains rattled, and her arms dropped. She cried out in pain as the change in position caused blood to course through her shoulders, down her arms, and into her hands.

"Sit." The word was delivered in a deep, thunderous command.

Katherine sank into the chair, lay her head back, and sighed in comfort. After so long on her feet, her legs twitched and jumped like spitting firecrackers. She thrust them straight out, rotating her ankles, trying to still their trembling.

Time passed. It might have been hours, it might have been days, but not months. Not yet, anyway. At least she could sit or stand when she wanted. When she needed the toilet, she stretched as far away from her chair as her chains would allow. The Stranger washed her and cleaned up the mess she made. She was like a helpless child, dependent on a parent to wipe her bottom. It was this, more than anything, that humiliated her.

The Stranger brought her sandwiches, which she ate ravenously. He gave her water and sometimes juice. How would he react if she requested something specific from him? Would he attack her again? She took a deep breath. "Um, would it be possible to have something else to eat, do you think? I mean, sandwiches are great..." She trailed off as he turned to look at her.

"What you be wantin'?"

This was the first time he'd responded to her since she'd been held captive. Their conversation, if you could call it that, had been limited to single-word commands from him. Now she heard the distinct burr and drawl of the West Country in his deep, gruff voice.

"Well, it's cold here, and it would be nice to have something warm. Some soup, perhaps? Maybe a blanket?"

"Orright, then." He turned away again, and soon he was gone, leaving Katherine alone in the dark.

How long had she been here? Katherine lost hope of ever being rescued or escaping. This place would become her tomb. What would he do with her body when she died? Would he leave her here, still chained? Would some future archaeologist discover her bones and form a theory of who she was and why she had been kept here? Or would The Stranger bury her somewhere, in an unmarked grave? She'd once read a novel where a murderer disposed of his victims' bodies by chopping them up and feeding the remains to his pigs. Would that be her fate? Did The Stranger even keep pigs?

Why was he keeping her prisoner? Did he think she'd stumbled onto a secret so terrible he needed to ensure her silence? But then why not just kill her and be done with it? He didn't appear to want her for sex. He could have had her on several occasions, but after that first time he'd washed her, he'd been careful not to touch her intimately again.

So, what did he want? For that matter, who was he? He lived nearby, but she didn't know exactly where.

She shuddered. The chilly gust that heralded The Stranger's arrival swished around her legs. Her heart beat kicked up a notch, and she waited, hardly breathing. The flare of a match and the flame of a candle hurt her eyes, and she scrunched them shut, then opened them the tiniest slit, then a little more, until her eyes adjusted to the light.

The Stranger came toward her, his face covered except for his eyes; although why he'd bother, Katherine didn't understand. It's not as if she didn't know who he was. But what was this? Her nose wrinkled at a hint of something fragrant. Was that soup? Whatever it was, it smelled amazing. She stood, straining at her chains as the scent of tomatoes, herbs, and onions assailed her nostrils. Saliva flooded her mouth. This was heaven. Surely nothing on earth could smell so deliciously wonderful.

He held a cup to her lips. "Careful, it be 'ot."

She sipped and tasted and breathed a contented sigh. It was indeed nectar, and she had guessed right. Tomato soup. She tried to gulp great mouthfuls, but The Stranger moved the cup away, allowing her only a few little sips.

"No! Please, some more, please."

"Yer'll burn yer'self if yer go too fast." He walked away and put the cup down on the table, next to a thermos. Katherine groaned. He'd taunted her with a taste of heaven, only to take it away again. But what was this? Another smell, even more delicious than the soup, drifted toward her. Hot roast chicken. She drooled.

The Stranger tore pieces of meat off the carcass and popped each morsel into her mouth one by one. She ate ravenously, juices running down her chin and dripping onto her shirt.

All too soon, the chicken was finished. The Stranger again brought her the soup; this time it was cooler, and he allowed her to drink it all down.

When the cup was empty, she licked her lips, savoring every drop of flavor.

He took the cup back to the table and returned, holding up a pair of greenish-blue fluffy slippers.

"Brought these. I 'ope they be yer size."

He placed them on the ground, and Katherine slipped her feet into them. After the hard, cold stone of the cellar floor, the soft, warm, cozy slippers were heaven.

"Thank you," Katherine said, tears of gratitude blurring her vision.

"Orright." He turned and began to walk away.

"No, please don't go."

Sixty-One

He stopped, but didn't turn back.

"I'm lonely down here on my own. Would you stay and talk to me for a while?"

The Stranger remained silent.

"I'm Katherine, but I guess you know that."

"Aye."

"What's your name?"

He didn't answer.

Frustrated at his silence, Katherine spoke more sharply than she intended, her quiet conversational tone replaced by one of demand. "Look, why are you keeping me here?"

He whirled back toward her, covering the distance in two strides, shaking his clenched fist in front of her face. He growled. "Don't ye be askin' questions o'me."

He glared at her, his steely blue eyes cold with anger. She recoiled in horror.

Suddenly, he turned and was gone, snuffing the candle as he went, leaving Katherine once again in the darkness.

Hunger gnawed at Katherine's stomach, its growl loud in the silent stillness of the cellar. She tried to lick her parched, dry lips, but her tongue had no moisture to share. She desperately needed water. When had she last eaten or had something to drink?

Going by the number of times she'd had to squat, several days had passed. She should never have questioned him. No doubt he was punishing her for it. But was that it? Was that all it took? Would he now just leave her here to die?

She slumped in her chair, not caring if she died. Death would be better than this existence. Surely. She just didn't want it to hurt. Does it hurt when you die of thirst? That would probably be the thing that got her first.

Her thoughts turned to her mother. She, too, had died in this cellar, but at least Katherine had been able to bury her mother properly. Who would do the same for her? How long before she was found? And who would find her?

When Jonathan had first shown her the cottage, she'd fallen in love with it immediately. She'd been so full of excitement and hope when she moved in. How eagerly she'd begun her novel. She had grasped the world with both hands; it was hers for the taking.

But it all turned sour. Her novel would never be finished, let alone published. Tears tumbled down her cheeks as her father's face surfaced in her mind. How disappointed he would be for her. The cottage she fell in love with would become her tomb.

Grief overwhelmed her, and she sobbed. She didn't want to die. Not here. Not like this.

"Please, God, save me." She prayed.

Sixty-Two

Eventually, she slept. And dreamed. She dreamed of The Stranger as she'd last seen him, his eyes like cold blue steel.

Katherine woke with a start; the dream whisked away like smoke in the wind. Something wasn't right, and it niggled her. Something about... oh, it was no use. She racked her brain, but nothing came. Whatever it was, it had vanished with the dream.

She stood and stretched her limbs as much as her shackles allowed.

A chill stirred around her ankles. Was he coming back, after all? She cried, relieved that maybe she would not die just yet. She waited. And waited.

He didn't come.

She wailed, her voice ripped from her throat in a howl of despair.

As she got weaker, standing became almost impossible. Her lips had become thick and dry, and there seemed to be too little room in her mouth for her tongue.

How much longer did she have to live? Perhaps a couple of days. She read somewhere that a person could survive for eight days without water. Was that right? She didn't know. Anyway, she didn't know how long since her last drink, so it was a moot point. At least she didn't have to pee. It seemed like it had been days since she'd last felt any pressure on her bladder.

She dozed fitfully, muttering in her dreams. Dreams of running blindly in the near darkness, chased by the hollow laughter of The Stranger as he pursued her in a labyrinth. She rounded a corner, and ahead of her a tiny point of light beckoned at the end of a long tunnel. Katherine ran faster. If she could only reach that light, she would be safe.

The chill around her ankles stirred her into half-wakefulness. Eons ago, she'd believed the chill heralded The Stranger's arrival, but it must have been a coincidence. She had felt that breeze many times, but he hadn't come.

Resting her head back, she turned toward the tunnel.

Must. Reach. The. Light.

Light stabbed her eyes, and she twisted her face away, scrunching her eyes closed.

"Katherine. My God, are you alright?"

Jonathan's voice. Was she still dreaming? Something, someone, touched her knee, then started shaking it.

"Katherine, wake up. It's Jonathan."

She half-opened her eyes, only to clamp them shut again as the light from a torch blinded her.

"-ight." Her tongue was too dry to form the 'l' and the word came out slow and thick and slurred as if spoken through treacle.

"Sorry." Jonathan's voice again. Was he really here? The light moved away, and Katherine gingerly opened her eyes a sliver. It was true. Jonathan knelt before her.

"ona-an?" She sobbed with relief, but no tears fell. Her body held too little fluid to squander on something as wasteful as tears.

"My dear Katherine." Jonathan touched her cheek.

"-irs-y."

"What? I don't understand."

"-irs-y, -a-er."

He studied her, his brow furrowed in concentration. Then he clapped his hands. "Oh, you're thirsty. Yes, water. Be right back."

Katherine opened her eyes a little more, squinting against the light emanating from a flashlight on the floor. She was alone again.

Her eyelids drooped. So tired.

A hand cradled her head, and cool liquid dribbled on her parched lips, rousing her from her doze. She opened her mouth, and water trickled over her parched tongue. Swallowing was difficult, but she managed it, then took another drink, rolling it around in her mouth before swallowing again. She drank eagerly, her gaze locked on the bottle in Jonathan's hands. A bottle that contained not just water, but hope. Hope and salvation and life.

"Easy, Katherine, small sips or you'll be sick." He allowed her a few more swallows before putting the bottle down on the floor.

"Come on, let's get you out of here." He picked up a pair of bolt cutters and set to work on the cuffs circling her wrists. He strained and grunted as he squeezed the cutters closed, snapping through first one cuff and then the other.

Free of their shackles, her arms dropped to her sides, sensation rushing back as if a thousand hot needles were being plunged into her wasted muscles. Her arms and legs dangled uselessly as she slumped in the chair. She didn't even have the strength to sit upright, so there was no way she would be able to walk out of her prison. She looked pleadingly at Jonathan, her bottom lip trembling.

Sixty-Three

"Let me give you a hand." He lifted her effortlessly in his arms and carried her.

Up the stone steps, his flashlight digging into her ribs, but it didn't matter. Nothing mattered except each step. Each step that took her further from the darkness, her prison, her tomb, up toward the light, her freedom, her life.

After the blackness of the cellar, the brightness of the kitchen was unbearable, and Katherine closed her eyes, burying her face against Jonathan's chest.

"Here, I'll lay you on the sofa and draw the curtains to shut some of the light out till you get used to it. Better tuck this round you, as well. Should keep you warm."

She was aware of Jonathan tucking a soft blanket around her, but kept her eyes shut until the light through her closed lids dimmed, then she opened them a little and watched him. Never had she been as glad to see someone as she was right now. She'd given up all hope, but Jonathan came and rescued her. Her savior.

"Who did this to you?" Jonathan asked.

"The Stranger." She sobbed; her shoulders shaking, tears cascading.

"Really? Are you sure it was him?"

Katherine nodded. “His coat, hat.”

Jonathan growled. “That man. I warned you he was dangerous.”

Katherine hung her head. “I know. I didn’t listen. I’m sorry.”

“Well, never mind that now. We need to get you well. How about some more water and perhaps some soup?” Jonathan crouched beside her, smiling, his blue eyes full of concern for her. Concern and love.

She sipped more water, forcing herself to remember not to gulp.

Jonathan flitted away to the kitchen, but kept appearing in the doorway to check on her before disappearing again.

Finally, he returned to her. “It’s only tinned, I’m afraid. I found it in your pantry. Cream of mushroom. I hope that’s okay.” He set a bowl and spoon on the coffee table in front of her and helped her to sit up, propping cushions behind her back. She reached for the spoon, but her fingers wouldn’t work. She couldn’t pick it up.

“Let me.” Jonathan picked up the spoon. He knelt on the floor beside her, dipped the spoon in the soup, and offered it to her.

Shame burned inside Katherine. Her face crumpled, and she cried.

Jonathan put the spoon down and gathered her up in his arms, rocking her, stroking her hair, whispering soothing sounds until she quieted.

He again offered her soup, and this time she accepted. She ate about half the bowl and then shook her head.

“No more.”

Jonathan took the tray out to the kitchen. When he returned, Katherine asked if he would call the police.

“Plenty of time for that. You’re in no fit state to be subjected to a barrage of questions from them.”

“But what if The Stranger comes back?”

Jonathan again knelt in front of her and took her hands in his, cradling them as if they were precious and fragile. “I’ll take care of you. I’ll be with you constantly, and I won’t let anything or anyone hurt you.”

“But—“

Jonathan pressed a finger to her lips. “No buts. We’ll see how you are in a day or so. Now, would you like me to bathe you? Wash your hair for you?”

Katherine looked at him, her emotions raw and ragged. How could she have been so awful to this man? He was thoughtful, gentle, and caring, while she'd been mean and cruel.

She lowered her gaze, another wave of shame flushing her cheeks. He'd washed her, The Stranger, and a shudder again ran through her at the memory of when he'd touched her intimately. She longed to wash away the memory of his touch, of her prison. To feel clean again. But she was too weak. She couldn't stand; she couldn't manage without Jonathan. She nodded, her tears dropping onto their clasped hands. He reached a hand up and wiped away her tears with his thumb.

"Hey, don't cry. You're safe now. I'll run a bath for you." He got up. "You sit tight and don't worry about a thing. I'll look after you."

Katherine looked around the room. She'd thought she'd never see her cottage again. It looked somehow foreign, as though she was seeing it for the first time.

Jonathan returned after a few minutes. "Right. Bath's run. Let's get you cleaned up."

He picked her up and carried her up the stairs. He'd taken off his jumper and rolled up his shirt sleeves, exposing the plaited leather bracelet and the tattoo on his arm. The Southern Cross. A tribute to his lost mate. She smiled up at her hero.

Jonathan sat Katherine on the closed toilet lid while he took off her shirt and bra, then picked her up and lowered her into the bath.

She sank down, letting the warm, fragrant water cover her body. This was paradise. She closed her eyes, letting Jonathan sponge her body, feeling as if she might melt or float away.

"I'm going to freshen the water," Jonathan said, and as the water drained, she opened her eyes a crack. The bath water had turned a dirty, yellowy-brown. Humiliation flushed hot in her cheeks, and she turned her face away from Jonathan.

"Hey, don't worry, Katherine. We'll have you fresh and clean in no time."

"I'm sorry," she mumbled.

"No need for you to be sorry; it wasn't your fault."

While the tub filled with fresh water, Jonathan said, "I need to wash your hair. Do you have one of those hand-held spray things?"

"Under the basin."

Jonathan sorted out the spray and turned it on. Katherine tilted her head back, letting the water run through her hair. Bliss! How long since her hair had been clean? Jonathan worked shampoo through her hair and rinsed it, then repeated the process. A third shampoo and rinse, and the water was murky again.

He drained the bath, using the spray to rinse Katherine's body as well. While the tub was refilling, he added some bubble bath. A sea of foam rose around her, enveloping her. How she wished she could just drift away on its perfumed cloud.

Jonathan put conditioner in Katherine's hair and combed it, easing out the tangles and knots. By the time he'd finished and rinsed her hair, Katherine was struggling to stay awake. Exhaustion engulfed her.

Jonathan drained the water and lifted her from the bath, dried her, then wrapped her robe around her and carried her into the bedroom. He sat her at her dressing table and turned on her hair dryer.

"Finished. You can wake up now."

Katherine opened her eyes, unaware that she'd slept. In the mirror before her, she hardly recognized herself. Her now dry hair stuck out in all directions, making her look like a cartoon character who'd got hold of a live electric wire. Jonathan's reflection smiled apologetically at her.

"Yeah, okay, I'm not the world's best hair stylist." He leaned forward and put the dryer back on the dressing table.

Katherine's returned smile morphed into a yawn.

"Time for bed, sleepyhead." Jonathan scooped her up and carried her to the bed. "Pajamas?"

"Bottom drawer." Katherine pointed to a tallboy, and Jonathan pulled open the drawer.

"These okay?" He held up a pair of light blue pajamas covered with little white clouds.

"Fine." Katherine stifled another yawn.

Once in her pajamas, Katherine lay back on the bed, sighing gratefully as her head sank onto her pillow. Jonathan pulled the duvet up, covering her shoulders, then brushed her cheek with his hand.

"Sleep well," he whispered.

Katherine closed her eyes and drifted.

Katherine woke, panicked, heart racing, panting. Where was she? What happened? Slowly her memory returned, her panic subsided, and her heartbeat returned to more-or-less normal. She was no longer captive, but lying in her own bed. Jonathan had saved her.

Thirsty, needing water, Katherine pushed back the duvet and tried to get out of bed. She got her legs over the edge of the bed and sat up. Even this small task demanded a Herculean effort. Beads of sweat formed on her forehead, and she sat a moment, working up the courage to stand.

With a deep breath, she pushed herself off the bed and stood. Immediately, her head spun, her legs buckled, and she crumpled to the floor.

Sixty-Four

Running footsteps and Jonathan's voice. "Katherine, what on earth?" She opened her eyes and found herself looking at a pair of scuffed trainers. Jonathan crouched beside her, scooped his hands beneath her, and helped her up. She sat on the bed, Jonathan beside her.

"You shouldn't be trying to get out of bed yet. What were you doing?" Jonathan said, his tone sympathetic and indulgent.

"I'm thirsty," Katherine said, again close to tears.

"Okay, I'll get some water. You stay there. Promise?"

"Promise." Katherine remained seated on the bed, still dizzy, but if she kept her head down, it wasn't bad. It was when she looked up too fast that her brain did a quick spin to the left, throwing her out of kilter. She kept her gaze steady as she very slowly raised her head, concentrating on breathing normally. This time, instead of her brain acting like a spin dryer, it acted more like a lazy, manageable carousel.

She looked toward the doorway. The rectangle of light spilling in from the hallway still hurt her eyes, but not as much as when Jonathan first brought her up from the cellar.

Jonathan returned with a glass of water, and she reached for it, but her hand trembled, and she couldn't grasp it. He put the glass to her lips and held it steady while allowing her to drink. She drained half before turning away.

"Thank you," she said, her lip quivering. She cried; tears of relief, frustration, anguish, and salvation cascaded down her cheeks, her body shaking with each sob. Jonathan's arms folded around her shoulders, and she leaned against him, taking comfort in the strength of his arms. Gradually, her sobs diminished, and her tears subsided. He wiped her remaining tears away and kissed her forehead, his lips lingering.

"You're safe, Katherine," he murmured. "Nothing can hurt you now. Just let me take care of you and get you well again."

She tried to speak, but her breath hitched, so she took a few slow, deep breaths to calm herself and tried again. "How did you find me? Why did you even look for me? I'd been so awful to you."

"I just felt something was wrong. I had this dream. Everything was dark, and yet I heard your voice calling me. I ignored it at first, but it came again. Then the third time I heard it, your voice had grown weaker and distant. I got frightened for you, so I telephoned, but there was no answer. At first, I thought you were still mad at me, but after trying to call you a dozen times, I decided to come over to check if you were alright."

Katherine's eyes filled with tears again. "Oh, Jonathan, I'm so glad you did. I can never repay you."

"Don't be silly, Katherine. I'm just happy that I found you before... well, you know."

Katherine shivered. She had been close to death; of that, she was certain. If not for Jonathan, she would surely be dead by now.

"But how did you get in? I'm sure I locked up."

Jonathan looked away. "The conservatory wasn't locked."

Katherine frowned. She'd been so careful about locking up, she could swear she had locked it. Obviously, she needed to be even more meticulous in the future.

"How did you come to look in the cellar?"

Jonathan gave a half-hearted laugh. "I think we have your dear mother to thank for that."

Katherine drew back and looked up at him. "Mum? How?"

He pulled her head back down to rest on his shoulder again. "I checked the house; I knew you weren't far because your car was outside. Then I checked the studio, and you weren't there. I came back here and was about to leave when I sensed a tug on my arm. When I turned around, I swear I saw Jacqueline standing in the kitchen, pointing toward the cellar. So I came down and found you. How long were you down there?"

Katherine shrugged. "I don't know. The light went out, and the door shut. I tried to open it, but it wouldn't budge. I thought if I got one of those stone flagons, maybe I could break the lock, but he grabbed me." Her voice trembled on the last words, and she bit her bottom lip to hold back the flood of emotion threatening to engulf her.

"You must have been petrified." He wrapped his arms around her and held her close to him. "So, you rang me on the Friday when you got home from Cornwall, and we haven't spoken since. What happened after that?"

"Mavis and Jack brought Mum's things over the day after I rang you. The Saturday. I unpacked the boxes that afternoon and took them down to the cellar that evening. That's..." Her mouth trembled, and her voice quavered. She cleared her throat, steeling herself. "That's when he grabbed me."

"Are you saying you've been there since then?" Jonathan's hushed tone of incredulity caused Katherine to look at him again; her brow creased in puzzlement.

She nodded.

"Katherine, that was almost four weeks ago."

Sixty-Five

Four weeks? No wonder Jonathan sounded so doubtful. Katherine couldn't get her head around it either. Although in one sense it seemed like forever, it felt surreal now.

Jonathan patted her hand. "If I'd stayed in Truro with you, perhaps none of this would have happened."

Katherine slumped back on the bed, shaking her head. "I shouldn't have pushed you away."

Jonathan didn't answer for a while, then he rose. "I'll get you something to eat," he said and left the room.

Katherine wriggled around, pulling the duvet over her and resting her head on the pillow. In minutes, she was asleep, but dreams of the cold, the dark, and The Stranger haunted her sleep.

Jonathan woke her some time later and helped her to sit up. She sniffed, trying to place the wonderful aroma that seemed to emanate from a bowl on the dressing table.

"What can I smell?"

Jonathan smiled. “I made you some dinner. It’s called Chicken à la Jonathan.”

Katherine rolled her eyes. “Well, I hope there’s not too much ‘à la Jonathan’, like your hot chocolate.”

A puzzled frown crossed his face, then he paled and quickly turned away. “Um, no. Nothing like that.”

Katherine swung her legs over the side of the bed, aware that she needed to empty her bladder. She was trying to stand when Jonathan rushed over and caught her shoulders, easing her back down.

“What on earth are you doing? You can’t stand.”

“Jonathan, I need the toilet.”

His face flushed scarlet. “Um… ah… Yes. Okay.”

“Can you help me?”

Jonathan’s hands flapped about nervously, then he stepped forward and scooped her up and almost ran to the bathroom with her. He put her down in front of the toilet, holding her hands in support until she regained her balance.

“What now?” he asked, lifting the lid of the toilet.

“Now you can wait outside, if you don’t mind.”

“Yes, of course.” Jonathan rushed out, closing the door. “I’m just here if you need me.”

Katherine got her pajama pants down without falling in a heap and plopped her bottom on the toilet seat. She sighed with relief as her bladder emptied. After enduring the discomfort and humiliation of squatting in the dark like an animal to urinate, the pleasure of being able to sit comfortably on a toilet seat was heaven.

When she’d finished, she pulled up her pajamas and flushed the toilet. Would she be able to walk the couple of steps to the washbasin? Only one way to find out. She placed a hand on the wall for support and shuffled one foot forward, just a little, then the other. So far, so good. Another few shuffles and she reached the basin. She washed her hands, dried them, and studied herself in the mirror.

She’d lost weight; she already knew that from the looseness of her pajamas, but seeing how gaunt her face was, how pale her skin, how sunken her eyes had become, confirmed just how much she had lost and how ill she looked. Her pajama top hung off one shoulder, and she pushed it further, gasping at the protruding bones of her shoulder and clavicle. While she'd always thought she could lose a pound or two, she was way beyond even skinny. She looked emaciated, like one of those advertisements that tugged at your heartstrings to help the starving in Africa. Tears filled her eyes, and she swiped them away angrily.

"Everything alright?" Jonathan called from outside the door.

"Yes, just washing my hands." She called back, turning away from her reflection and shuffling her way back to the door.

When she opened the door, Jonathan moved to pick her up, but she put a hand on his arm. "I'd like to try to walk."

He straightened up, a worried frown creasing his brow. "No, it's too soon. You're too weak. Let me carry you."

"Please, even if it's only a few steps. Hold my hand and walk beside me."

"Well, alright, if you insist." Jonathan sounded doubtful, but he stood beside her and gripped her hand.

She took a step forward, gripping Jonathan's hand, then another step. By the third step, beads of sweat covered her brow. By the fourth step, the beads trickled into her eyes. By the fifth step, every muscle in her legs screamed out at the torture being inflicted on them. She leaned against the wall, panting with the exertion. When she had recovered a little, she looked ahead. Her shoulders slumped, and she let out an anguished cry. She'd not even made it halfway. Reluctantly, she turned to Jonathan, shaking her head, tears filling her eyes. "I can't."

Without a word, he picked her up and carried her effortlessly the rest of the way and set her down by the dressing table.

"Ready to eat now?" He indicated the bowl in front of her.

She looked at the contents of the bowl. Bite-sized pieces of chicken and various vegetables in a sauce that bore a hint of something fragrant. Tarragon perhaps. Her stomach made a very audible growl.

Jonathan laughed. "I guess that answers the question." He pulled the chair out for her to sit and, with a flourish, tucked a napkin on her lap and handed her a fork.

She got a piece of chicken onto the fork and brought it to her mouth. Food never tasted so delicious, and she ate greedily. At least as greedily as her impaired coordination would allow. Finally, unable to eat any more, she pushed the rest away and patted her stomach. "Thank you, Jonathan. That was wonderful." His reflection in the mirror beamed with pleasure and pride.

Katherine smiled at him, then stifled a yawn. "I think I might go back to bed. I'm so tired."

"Of course, you've been through quite an ordeal." Jonathan picked her up and carried her the few steps to the bed. "Would you like a hot chocolate to help you sleep?"

"Gosh, no. No more 'à la Jonathan' tonight." She expected him to laugh at her tease, but he looked away, almost guiltily, busying himself fluffing the pillow, straightening the duvet. *How odd.*

Sixty-Six

The next morning, Jonathan carried Katherine downstairs to the kitchen.

"Now you sit there and let me make you breakfast. I thought maybe some poached eggs on toast."

Katherine's eyes darted to the cellar door. It was shut, but it still gave her the creeps. The cellar had claimed her mother's life and almost her own. A chill shivered through her body.

"Katherine?"

"I'm sorry, Jonathan. Eggs would be wonderful, thank you." She hesitated. Something wasn't right. "No! After four weeks, anything in my fridge will be off. You'll have to chuck it all out." Last night's dinner. What did he make that with? Would that make her sick?

Jonathan's jaw clenched, and his eyes blazed, then in a second his face relaxed, and he laughed. "Don't worry. As luck would have it, I'd done some grocery shopping before I came over to find you. The bags were still in my car." He laughed again. "Now let me get you those eggs."

Katherine watched as he prepared breakfast, whizzing around her kitchen, humming to himself.

He slid a plate before her. Two poached eggs sat on a slice of buttered toast, four small triangles of toast on one side.

"This looks great." Katherine picked up a toast triangle and stabbed one egg with it, dipping the toast into the runny yolk before conveying it to her mouth.

"Okay?" Jonathan asked.

"Perfect." She picked up her knife and fork and ate while Jonathan stood across the table, watching her.

"Um, Katherine, I don't really know how to broach this, but I need to get some things done at the office. Would you consider staying at my place for a while, until you're well? It would make it easier."

Katherine looked up, tears filling her eyes. "That would be good. I need to go to the police, anyway."

"Yes, yes. Of course. We'll get you settled at my place first. Now, you finish your breakfast, and I'll get us organized."

Once Katherine finished eating, Jonathan loaded the dishwasher and turned it on.

"Right, let's get some clothes for you." He carried Katherine back up the stairs to the bedroom. "Now, where will I find a case or something?"

"Under the bed. It shouldn't be too dusty." She'd last used it when she'd gone down to Cornwall for her mother's funeral. Her heart ached with sorrow for her mother, her father. Perhaps in a few days, she would ask Jonathan if he'd take her to visit their graves.

Jonathan put the case on the bed and opened it. "Now, you tell me where to find things, and I'll pack."

She directed Jonathan to the various drawers for jeans, shirts, laughing as he blushed scarlet when it came to choosing underwear.

When the case was full, Jonathan zipped it closed. "I'll take this out to the car and come back for you."

Katherine looked around her bedroom. It was too soon to decide what to do with the cottage. Her emotions were still too raw after her ordeal. She needed to get her strength back before making any life-changing decisions.

Jonathan came bounding back in. "Ready?"

Katherine stood. "Yes," she said with determination in her voice. "Let's get out of here."

~

After unpacking her case, Jonathan made soup for lunch and then left for his office, leaving Katherine alone, but with strict instructions to call him at any time if she was worried or frightened.

She thought back over the weeks she had been held prisoner. She still had no idea why The Stranger held her. Did he ever come back? Did he know she'd escaped, or had he left her there to die?

Katherine dozed.

The dream came again. The same one as in the cellar, but again, it vanished, leaving her with the same tiny niggle. She couldn't place it. Her mind was playing tricks, and not much wonder after what she'd been through.

If it wasn't for Jonathan...

Sixty-Seven

She must report her capture to the police and do it now. She looked around for her cell phone, but couldn't find it anywhere. Had she left it back at her cottage? No, she remembered having it in the car on the way to Jonathan's. Damn, she must have left it in the car. Jonathan didn't have a landline line so her police report would have to wait. She'd ask Jonathan to take her when he got back.

Katherine waited until they had both settled in front of the television with a bottle of merlot—a thank-you gift from a client whose house Jonathan sold. She took a sip, rolling the wine around her mouth before swallowing it. It was smooth, not too dry. The bottle promised flavors of raspberry, cherry, plum, and vanilla, but the only flavor she detected was wine.

She set her glass down and faced Jonathan. "Would you take me to the police station tomorrow, please?"

Jonathan put his glass on the coffee table, a frown furrowing his brow. "Whatever for?"

"Well, I haven't reported it yet. I've got to make sure he's arrested."

He slid his arm around her shoulders and drew her close. “You don’t need to worry about all that. I’ve already done it for you.”

“Really? When?”

“Earlier today, on my way to the office. I called in at the police station and made a statement on your behalf.”

“That’s wonderful. Thank you.” She snuggled closer to him, relieved that she was free of the burden of talking to the police.

Jonathan held her and kissed the top of her head. “So it’s all over, darling, and you don’t have to worry any more.”

“Thank you, Jonathan, for everything. I don’t know what I’d have done without you.”

In the ensuing days, the two of them settled into a routine. Jonathan would make breakfast, then go to his office for a couple of hours. Katherine, meanwhile, would nap, read, watch television, slowly getting her strength back.

One evening after dinner, they sat on the couch together, watching a romantic movie where the hero had rescued the heroine from the clutches of a villain, and when the two finally kissed, and the scene faded to the credits, Katherine turned to Jonathan and said, “They’re like us. You’re my hero. You’ve been so kind, so caring. I’m so grateful for everything. I don’t deserve it.”

“But you do. I swore to protect you and take care of you, and I intend to.” He cupped her chin and turned her face up so their eyes met. “You must know how much I love you, Katherine.”

Katherine’s eyes brimmed with tears. “I know, Jonathan and I never intended to, but I think I love you too.”

Jonathan kissed her tears away. “My beautiful Katherine, you can’t know how I’ve longed to hear those words from you.”

Their eyes locked on each other, their lips moved closer, meeting in a slow, tender kiss. Katherine’s eyes closed, welcoming his kiss, realizing that she’d meant what she said. She really did love this man. How could she not after everything he had done for her? She owed him her life.

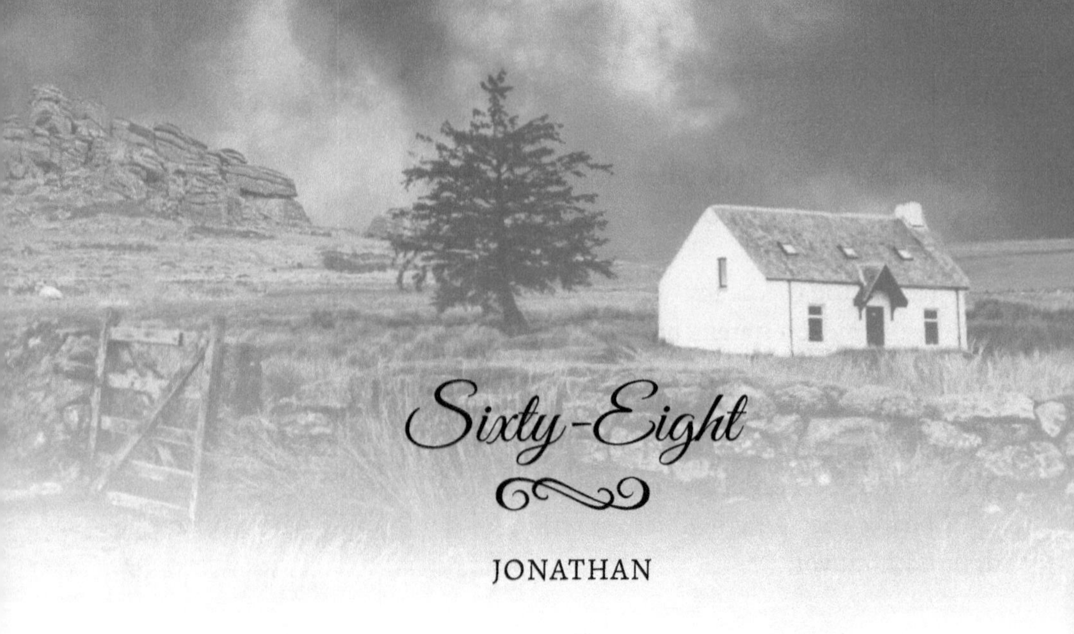

Sixty-Eight

JONATHAN

Jonathan had won. Finally, Katherine loved him. He'd tried wooing her with flowers and kindness and charm, to no avail. But save her life, and she was like putty in his hands.

Since he'd rescued her, they'd shared a bed, but other than a cuddle and a goodnight kiss, he hadn't touched her. He'd lain awake at night, his erection throbbing, his balls aching. When he was sure she slept, he'd creep from the room and go downstairs, out to the garage, where he wouldn't be disturbed. Or heard. He'd taken a photograph of Katherine lying naked on her bed the night he'd dispatched her mother. That photograph remained hidden beneath a pile of old paint-spattered drop sheets. He'd stare at it, masturbating furiously, remembering how it felt to be inside Katherine, to control her, to possess her, to own her.

And now Katherine loved him.

He kissed her; softly at first, their lips barely touching, but her arms slipped around his neck, and she lay back on the couch, pulling him down with her, her kisses hungry, urgent. He could take her right here, but held back. No way was he risking her changing her mind this time. He'd tease her, tantalize her, play with her until she begged.

So he reached behind his head, unclasped her hands, and pulled away from her.

There'd be no backing out soon, anyway. He'd taken care of that.

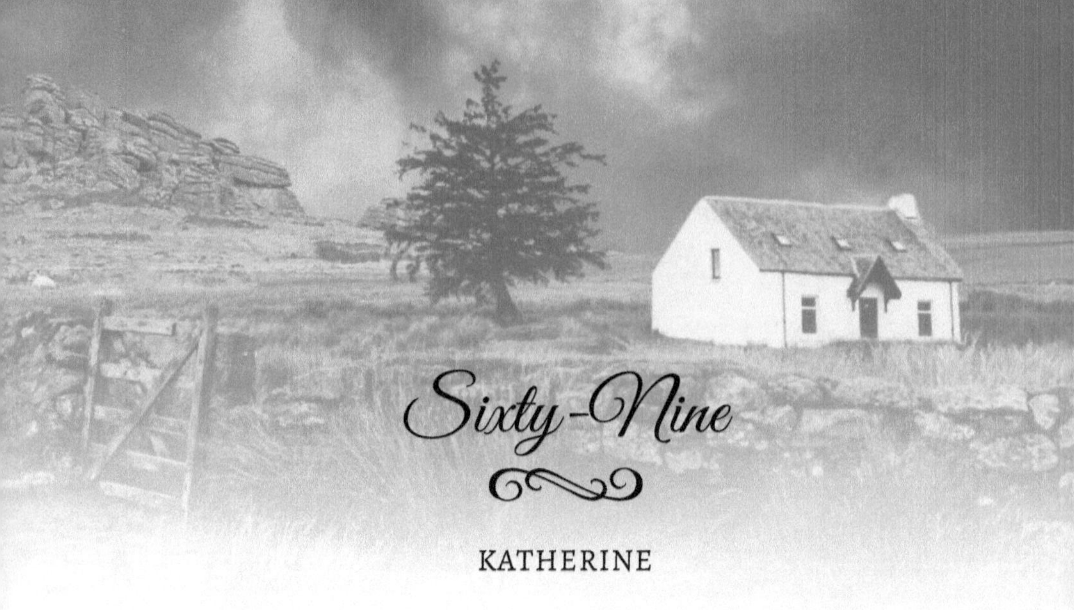

Sixty-Nine

KATHERINE

Katherine itched to get on with her life. It was all very well trying out new exotic recipes for dinner just to keep herself occupied, but she wanted some sort of independence; some relief from the boredom of domesticity. So she suggested to Jonathan that they go to pick up her car.

"I don't see why you need it, darling."

"I can't live off you forever, Jonathan. I need to think about getting on with things. Get my life back in order."

"But I want to take care of you, remember?"

"I know. I'm not leaving you, Jonathan. I enjoy living with you, but I need to get some things from home and think about getting a job."

"You don't need a job. I can provide everything you want," Jonathan said, the familiar petulant tone creeping into his voice. She decided not to push it further.

"That's very good of you. I'd still like my car, though, and my laptop, so I can finish my novel."

Jonathan relented, but reluctantly. Still, it was a small win. Little steps. Getting her car and laptop at least would give her a little freedom and something to do, give her life some purpose again. Jonathan was going out of his way to be gentle, kind, and supportive, but as much as she appreciated his caring for her, his protectiveness was a little stifling.

When she'd first told him she loved him, she'd expected him to make love to her. She'd wanted him to, but he'd pulled away. They still hadn't made love. In fact, he'd not made any moves toward her, other than an occasional kiss and cuddle. She'd tried several times to make love, but he'd only go so far before backing away. She'd even placed his hand between her legs and guided him to touch her, and he'd seemed willing enough, but when her orgasm was close, he'd stopped, given her a quick kiss, and said goodnight.

Well, she was tired of their weird platonic relationship. Tired of resorting to masturbation to relieve her sexual tension. Tired of waiting. She wanted an actual relationship with him; to be a proper couple. To marry him, have children with him. A splinter of sadness pierced her heart; her mum would have been so pleased that she'd finally got together with Jonathan. Tears pooled in her eyes and overflowed, trickling down her cheeks.

Jonathan put a hand on her shoulder. "What's up?"

Katherine shook her head and managed a half-smile. "I'm okay. Just thinking of Mum."

Jonathan's hand dropped from her shoulder, and he turned away from her. "Oh."

"I think we'll leave the roof up today," Jonathan said the next morning. The weather had turned cool, and the gray clouds held the promise of rain. Before they'd even left Tavistock, Katherine turned the car heater on, glad of the warmth around her knees. Tension crept into her body as they drew closer to her cottage. She looked down at her hands, which were trying to clench themselves into fists, and she flexed them, fingers spread wide, forcing them to relax.

Jonathan parked in front of the house, then came around and opened her door. "Come on, sweetheart, let's get your stuff."

She climbed out of the car and held his hand as they made their way to the door. Inside, still holding Jonathan's hand, Katherine headed straight up the stairs, giving him no option but to follow.

She turned toward him, sliding her arms around his neck and pulling his head down to hers, kissing him, tenderly at first and then more greedily. He tried to pull back, but she held on to him, pressing her body against him.

She thrust a thigh between his legs; he was rock hard. One of his arms encircled her waist, and the other was in her hair, pulling her head back, his mouth finding her throat, nibbling, licking, sucking, his breath hot on her skin. She was on fire, and she would not let him back out this time.

"I want you, Jonathan," she whispered, her voice husky with desire.

He pulled away, letting her go.

Seventy

She stood there, emotions see-sawing through her. She couldn't take this any longer. "Look, Jonathan. What's wrong? Why do you keep stopping? Pulling away from me. What do I have to do? Beg you to make love to me?"

Jonathan remained silent.

Katherine slid open the drawer of her dressing table and removed a condom. She held it out to him. "Make love to me, Jonathan, please. I'm begging you. Make love to me."

Without a word, he unbuttoned her blouse and unsnapped her bra. She dropped her head back as he again kissed her throat before moving down to her breasts. He flicked his tongue across her nipples and sucked each one.

They undressed each other in between kissing and fondling, and when they were both naked, Katherine lay back on the bed and held her hand out to him. He kneeled above her, then his mouth was on her, his tongue tickling, his teeth nibbling as he moved down her body. He pinched one nipple with a thumb and finger, rolling it around, pulling at it, then suckled with his mouth, scraping his teeth lightly over the nub. She laced her fingers behind his head and pushed him down. He flicked her belly button with his tongue and moved further down. She moaned, spreading her legs wide. His fingers parted her lips, his tongue teased her clitoris, then he blew gently, the coolness of the air contrasting with the heat of her arousal. His tongue again, then cool. This was such exquisite pleasure. She craved the release of orgasm.

Her head whipped side to side, her body on fire. Still, he teased her. She wanted to feel him inside her, to reach orgasm with him. "Please, Jonathan, please. I want you inside me."

He drew back, kneeling between her thighs, and she watched him roll the condom over his erection, and then his weight shifted on her, and he entered her, plunging and thrusting deep inside her, grinding her clitoris with his pubic bone. Her orgasm started rushing toward her, a freight train barreling through a tunnel and filling her body. She screamed and clung to Jonathan as she climaxed, wave after wave of ecstasy flowing through her.

As her climax faded, Jonathan still moved inside her, and she kissed him hungrily, encouraging him. His thrusting became more urgent, his breathing rapid, his hands holding her hips as he plunged into her.

With one last thrust, his body tensed, shuddered, and, a few moments later, relaxed.

"Katherine, my darling. I've waited so long for you. I love you so much."

Their eyes met, and inexplicably, Katherine sensed that odd niggle again. The one from her dream. What on earth? Why now?

As Jonathan gazed at her, his love for her clear in his eyes, her mind flicked between her first encounter with The Stranger in Princetown and the last time she'd seen him in the cellar. Slowly, the niggle flared into a dawning horror.

It was not the black eyes of The Stranger that she'd looked into that last time in the cellar, but the steely blue eyes of Jonathan Irving.

Seventy-One

JONATHAN

Jonathan gazed into Katherine's eyes. She was his now, and soon he would share his little secret with her. She'd be shocked at first, but when she got used to the idea, he knew she'd be thrilled.

But what was this? Katherine was screaming and scrambling off the bed.

"Katherine?"

"It was you!" She was off the bed and glaring at him, her face full of thunder. "All the time. In the cellar. It was you!"

Shit. She wasn't meant to figure it out. How on earth? "What in heaven's name makes you think it was me?" Jonathan needed to play for time, to see if he could talk her down.

"Your eyes are blue."

"What are you talking about, darling? Come back to bed."

"When The Stranger grabbed me in Princetown, I saw his eyes; they were almost black. But the eyes I saw in the cellar were blue. Your eyes."

Jonathan noticed the trembling in Katherine's voice; perhaps he could still turn this around.

"Don't be silly, darling. Lots of people have blue eyes. Come on, come back to bed." He patted the bed beside him.

"You bastard. You kept me chained up." Spittle flew from her mouth as she screamed. "I nearly died!"

The game was up. Jonathan's lip curled into a sneer, and he chuckled. "Don't be so bloody melodramatic, Katherine. You were never in any real danger."

"How can you say that? You left me there for weeks without food, without water."

"I checked on you every couple of days."

"I thought you loved me."

"Of course I love you; you're mine."

Jonathan lunged for her, but she spun out of reach and ran. He sprang off the bed and followed her. Down the stairs, out the front door. She ran to her car and wrenched the door handle, but it didn't open. Like a good little girl, she'd kept everything locked up tight in case The Stranger should happen by.

"You'll never escape from me, Katherine. You're mine. You've always been mine. Do you think after all I've done for you, I'll just let you go?"

Jonathan stepped closer to Katherine, but she backed away, scooting around behind his car.

"Why, Jonathan? Why did you do it?"

"Why do you think? You turned me away. You were supposed to love me. I had to make you want me as much as I wanted you!" Jonathan edged around the car as he spoke. "It worked. You told me you loved me. You do love me, Katherine, I know you do."

"How can I love you after what you did to me? You kept me prisoner!" Katherine moved away, maintaining the distance and the barrier between them.

"I used to watch you, you know. There's a lovely view of your bedroom from the moor. I used to watch you undress. I fantasized about possessing you."

He edged his way around the car, Katherine moving too, the game of cat and mouse still being played out.

He laughed. "You were so scared, simply because of some footsteps and scattered boxes. You should have seen your face." He sprang to grab

Katherine, but she darted away again. "Remember the words on your laptop, the night we had dinner here?"

"That was you?"

Jonathan nodded. "When you called me, I nearly died of happiness. You were scared, and you needed me. When we made love that first time, I thought my prayers were answered, but then you spurned me."

The cat crept closer; the mouse scurried away.

He sneered. "Then there was your dear old mother."

"What about my mother?"

"Can you imagine how sick I felt having to pander to that old bitch, to get her on my side, to make you see sense?"

"How dare you!" Katherine's voice cracked.

"She was so damned gullible. I told her I'd hidden champagne in the cellar and arranged for her to get it while I arrived early and proposed marriage to you."

Katherine had stopped moving, as though mesmerized.

"Have you ever snapped a person's neck, Katherine? Hmm? Just like breaking a twig."

"You killed my mother?" Katherine's anguished scream echoed off the stone walls.

"I certainly did, and it gave me the greatest pleasure. The night I dispatched the pathetic old bitch, I thought I'd won you. You were helpless. You needed me. But you changed again and threw me out."

Again, he made a grab for Katherine, and almost caught her, his fingers brushing her arm before she twisted away from him.

"That man you call The Stranger. He told you to beware of the cellar. You never understood, did you?"

"Understood what?"

"There's a tunnel that runs from your cellar to the old railway halt. Smugglers used it in days gone by. Those flagons in the cellar. They weren't cider flagons but illicit brandy. Stolen from French ships lured to their fate on the rocks, taken across the moor in the dead of night, then stored in your cellar until they could be sold. The tunnel was how I could come and go as I pleased."

"That chilly breeze in the cellar, a few moments before you arrived."

"Clever of me, don't you think?" He edged closer. Soon she'd be in reach.

Seventy-Two

KATHERINE

Katherine moved toward the driver's side door of the Mercedes and prayed Jonathan hadn't locked it. If he had... She gingerly tried the door handle and almost collapsed with relief when it opened. She dived into the car and jabbed the door locks just as Jonathan rushed forward and pulled on the door handle. For the moment, she was safe, but how the hell would she get out of this? Had she sealed her own fate by getting into the car? Maybe she should have run across the moors. But where would she have gone? Jonathan's longer stride meant he would catch her before too long. Then what? Would he drag her back to the cellar and chain her again? No, he would kill her. No way he'd let her walk away from this. If she didn't escape, she would certainly die.

Jonathan hammered on the window, then pulled on the door handle again. "Come on, Katherine, open the door. Let's talk about this. I love you. You know that." His voice had taken on the syrupy, whining, pleading tone so familiar when he didn't get his own way.

Katherine shook her head. "How can you say that after what you did to me, to my mother? I hate you."

Jonathan walked away, gravel crunching under his bare feet, and rested his hands on the stone wall, his head bowed. Katherine watched him for a moment, his shoulders heaving. Was he crying? She reached to open her door, her hand hovering over the handle. Perhaps she should make a run for it. Get back to the house and call the police. She looked toward the front door, mentally measuring the distance, calculating the time it would take to reach it. Could she make it in time and lock the door before Jonathan reached her?

She looked back at Jonathan, mentally preparing herself to run, but before she could open the car door, Jonathan sprinted to her cottage and returned in mere seconds, brandishing Katherine's largest chef's knife. With a snarl of pure rage, he rushed toward the car and buried the knife through the car's soft top, its blade inches from Katherine's face. She screamed and frantically scanned the car for something to defend herself. What could she use? A twinkle of silver caught her attention. She stared, eyes wide, hardly daring to believe. The three-pointed star. Jonathan's keys. *Oh, thank you.*

The car started easily, and she slammed it into reverse and sped backward, knocking Jonathan to the ground, the knife still protruding through the roof, but he raced after her and sprang onto the hood. She stomped on the accelerator pedal, but somehow Jonathan clung on to the windscreen wipers. She braked and put the car into first gear, accelerating and swerving in an attempt to throw him off. The car clipped the back of her Land Rover, crumpling the corner of the Mercedes' hood. She backed away, relishing the look of shocked dismay on Jonathan's face at the screech of torn metal. The front left bumper peeled back, its jagged edge visible above the damaged hood. Again, she accelerated and then braked suddenly. Jonathan slid forward, the windscreen wiper snapping in his hand as he fell in front of the car.

Katherine backed away and stopped. Jonathan got to his feet, bloodied and covered with dirt. He grinned and shook a finger at her as if admonishing a naughty child. He stood between her and the courtyard exit.

Katherine's terror subsided, replaced with ice-cold fury. This man had not only kept her chained like a wild animal for weeks, he'd also killed her mother. She stared at Jonathan, overwhelmed with hatred as she selected first gear. Her left foot kept the clutch pedal depressed while her right hovered above the accelerator. Her knuckles turned white as she gripped the steering wheel. She sent up a silent prayer. *Please don't let me stall.*

She waited.

He didn't move.

Her right foot pressed down on the accelerator, her left still on the clutch. The motor's whine became a howl.

She waited.

Still, he didn't move.

She floored the accelerator, the scream of the motor mingling with her own.

Now! She released the clutch and the car shot forward. Jonathan turned to run, but the Mercedes covered the distance in a heartbeat, its momentum knocking him to the ground before he disappeared beneath the car.

Above the roar of the motor, Katherine heard a faint scream, but she didn't stop, didn't look. She didn't want to see him lying there, broken and bleeding. All she wanted was to get away.

A thump, thump sound emanated from the front wheel. What a time to get a flat tire. She paid it no heed. She must get to Princetown, to the police. Jonathan would find the keys to her Land Rover and come after her. There was no time to lose.

She sped around a bend and swerved as a pony stepped into her path, the front of the car bouncing over the verge into the ditch. Damn it. She rammed the gear lever in reverse and pressed the accelerator, but the car wouldn't budge. Again and again she tried, to no avail. She slammed her fists on the steering wheel in frustration.

Seventy-Three

Her door opened. "Are ye alright, girl?"

Katherine turned toward the voice, and she clapped a hand over her mouth, stifling a scream. The hat and coat made The Stranger instantly recognizable. His black eyes, full of concern, met hers, and she burst into fresh tears. She reached her hand out and touched his arm. "Help me, please. I need to get to the police."

The Stranger crouched beside her. "I saw...what happened. You're safe, now."

"But he'll come after me. He won't let me get away. He'll kill me!"

The Stranger stood and looked away, shaking his head. "He's in no condition to come after you."

She must have hurt him, perhaps broken his leg. He'd need an ambulance, and she'd sort it when she got to the police. She relaxed a little, rested her head on the steering wheel, and closed her eyes.

Something cool and wet nuzzled her cheek, and she opened her eyes to see Felan's paws on her leg, his tongue hanging loosely as he panted. Her face flushed as the realization of her nakedness filtered into her brain. She reached for the dog and hugged him close, using him to shield her naked body. She ruffled his ears. "Hello Felan, who's a good boy?" Felan promptly licked her face. Katherine looked across at The Stranger. "Who are you?"

"I live yonder." He pointed toward a distant farmhouse. "Name's Jim. Jim Woodman."

Katherine thrust out her hand, smiling at him through a fresh crop of tears. "Hello, Jim. I'm very pleased to meet you. I'm Katherine Walters."

He hesitantly took her hand and shook it before taking off his coat and offering it to Katherine. "Here, you be wanting this."

Gratefully, she grabbed the proffered coat and, while Jim discreetly turned away, calling Felan to his side as he did so, slipped it on as she got out of the car. "Thank you," she murmured. Jim's body heat, retained in the coat, warmed her, and she wrapped it tightly around herself. It smelled of the farm, a mix of sheep, dog, pipe tobacco, and sweat.

"We'd better call the police, lass. Can you walk?"

"I think so. But if you help me change my flat tire, I can drive." She started toward the passenger side to survey the flat tire, but Jim stopped her.

"Best not." He shook his head, his hand on Katherine's shoulder, but she shrugged him off and moved toward the front of the car.

She looked.

She saw.

She screamed.

Arms enfolded her, turning her away, and she buried her face in Jim's chest, her eyes closed, wishing she could unsee. Burned into her mind like a firebrand was a vision that would haunt her. A vision of a twisted, broken grill and, caught around it, a bracelet of plaited leather still encircling the wrist of the bloodied, broken, very dead body of what had once been Jonathan Irving.

Seventy-Four

Katherine, now fully dressed, sat in the conservatory, her legs curled up underneath her, holding a hot cup of tea in a viselike grip. Jim sat across from her, his coat thrown over the arm of the sofa, his own cup of tea resting on the coffee table between them. Felan slept at his feet.

The police had finally left, having examined every inch of her house, the cellar, and the tunnel, asking Katherine the same questions, time and time again. Both she and Jim had been requested to visit the police station to make formal statements within the next forty-eight hours.

"What will ye do now?" Jim asked.

Katherine shrugged. "I don't know, Jim. I think I'm still in shock."

"Course ye be. It's been a terrible ordeal for ye. I hate to leave ye alone, but I can't stay wi' ye. The wife, well, she ain't too good, you see. I need to go home."

Katherine uncurled her legs and put her cup down. "Of course. I'm very grateful for everything you've done for me. I hope your wife will be better soon."

Jim shook his head. "Nay, she won't, but thank you for your thoughtfulness," Jim spoke with such sadness in his voice that Katherine was moved to tears.

She put a hand on his arm. "Jim?"

He patted her hand. "She's got MS. She'd been relatively good until a few months back. Now she needs help to get from the bed to a chair." Tears filled Jim's eyes, and a sob racked his body.

"Jim, I'm so sorry." She clasped his hand in hers. "You must go to her."

"Aye. But will ye be alright? Here, on your own?"

Katherine had no answer for him and simply shrugged.

He put his hand on her shoulder. "There be nothing here that can hurt ye now. Ye know that."

She nodded, although she couldn't yet believe his words. "When I first moved in, there was a storm. Was that you on the orchard path?"

"Aye, it were me. I didn't know the place was occupied. A couple of my sheep got through into your orchard. Me and Felan were getting them back. Near scared me half to death when I saw you at the window." He chuckled.

"You tried to warn me, that time in Princetown. How did you know?"

"I'd seen him. Out on the moor at night. I didn't know at first what he was doing there, but night after night I saw him." Jim scratched Felan's head absently as he spoke. "One night, I crept close to him to see what he was doing. He was watching your bedroom. He was..." Jim trailed off, averting his eyes.

"He was what?" Katherine asked.

Jim's voice dropped to a murmur. "He was, you know, playing with his-self."

Disgust, revulsion, hatred boiled through Katherine. All those times she'd not bothered pulling her curtains at night, those times she'd stood naked before the darkness outside, and he'd been watching, masturbating. Jonathan's image rose into her mind, sweat slicking his hair, his mouth hanging slack, eyes closed at the point of orgasm. She gagged, swallowing down the vomit threatening to spew from her roiling stomach. She had thought nothing more could disturb her about Jonathan, but this - this betrayal violated her, humiliated her all over again.

Jim continued. "In Princetown, I warned you, but then I saw him approaching you. When I saw you in his arms, I thought I'd got it wrong, but then I saw he was using the tunnel. So I tried to warn you again at your studio, but a woman interrupted."

"That was my mother. God, I feel so stupid. I thought you were *threatening* me. I was scared of *you*, but all the while you've been trying to warn me, to protect me."

"Aye. But ye be safe now, so all's well." Jim stood. "All's well."

"Thank you, Jim." Katherine got up and kissed him lightly on the cheek. "Now you go home to your wife and take care of her. What's her name?"

"Monica."

"Give Monica my regards."

"Aye, I'll do that. C'mon, Felan, time we was making tracks. We'll head back through your orchard. It's quicker."

He pulled on his coat, and Katherine opened the door for him. She watched him walk away for a few moments, then ran after him and caught his arm. He stopped and turned to her, his eyebrows raised, questioning.

"Jim, would it be okay if I came to visit Monica, do you think? Perhaps read her some of my novel? Do you think she'd like that?"

Jim's eyes sparkled, and he nodded. "Aye, I reckon she'll be thrilled. Be nice for her to have some female company. All she sees all day is this ugly old mug." He pointed to his own face.

She wrapped her arms around him and hugged him tightly. "I don't think you're ugly, Jim. I think you're the most wonderful man in the world."

Jim laughed hard, a good, deep belly laugh. "Ah, go on with ye, before I have to buy a bigger hat."

"Right. Well, I'll come over in the next couple of days to meet Monica."

Jim nodded. "I'll tell her to expect you."

"Thank you, Jim. For everything."

Jim nodded again and patted his leg to call Felan to his side, then turned and walked away.

Katherine watched Jim until he disappeared from view in the orchard. She ran back to the house, up to her bedroom, and stood watching for him to appear out on the moor. When she saw Felan running, his thick, silky coat flowing in the wind, she felt a great uplifting of joy. Jim, no longer The Stranger, strode into view, each long, swift stride carrying him away to his home.

Katherine was safe. She knew that now, and that thought had her whooping for joy and running down the stairs.

Pulling on a jacket, she thrust her laptop under her arm and ran out the door, down the path, and through the orchard, pausing by the bridge for a moment.

"Hi, Norman; it's me, Katherine. I'm back, and I'm here to stay!"

Part Two

Seventy-Five

When news broke of Jonathan's death, Katherine found herself the center of attention for a few days. News reporters camped outside her home, clamoring for an interview, which she refused to give. But then a particularly gruesome murder involving three children and the family pet saw them hurry away. At last, Katherine could return to a normal life without fear of being hounded any time she stepped outside her door.

Katherine liked Monica instantly and visited every few days. She would make tea for them and they'd sit beside the fire, chatting. Katherine would read her latest chapters aloud, while Monica listened and knitted. The click-clack rhythm of her needles varied with the mood of the scene, and Katherine knew immediately whether she had created the right atmosphere. If a passage was suspenseful, the speed of the click-clack increased along with the tension, but at more sedate scenes, Monica's needles lapsed into a lazy rhythm.

The click-clack became the soundtrack of Katherine's writing. As her own fingers tapped out the words on her laptop, she would hear the rhythm of knitting needles in her mind.

Monica would ask Katherine to go over the occasional passage, questioning when something didn't quite work, and suggesting how to improve it. As a result, Katherine's writing became sharper, clearer and more focused.

She looked forward to their time together. Her only niggle was that she'd been getting the odd bout of nausea the last few weeks. Much to her embarrassment, she had to excuse herself to Monica several mornings and rush to the toilet where she had thrown up her breakfast. After she'd returned from her latest bout of vomiting, she slumped down in her chair with a groan.

Monica laid her knitting in her lap. "How far gone are ye, lass?"

Katherine looked across at her friend, puzzled. "I'm sorry. What did you say?"

"I asked how far gone ye are." Monica nodded toward Katherine's abdomen.

"I'm not pregnant, if that's what you mean. Nothing like that, just haven't been well lately."

The older woman raised an eyebrow but said nothing.

"Anyway, I can't possibly be, I've had a period since Jonathan... we..." She laughed. A high-pitched, nervous, humorless titter. "No, just some bug, I suspect."

Monica picked up her knitting. "I guess it must be, then."

Katherine continued to be unwell for another week. Maybe she should see her doctor. If she wasn't any better by the following week, she'd make an appointment. Gradually, though, the symptoms tapered off, and she began to feel her old self again.

When she mentioned this to Monica, seated in her customary place by the fire, the older woman nodded and said, "That's good, dear."

"I'm so much better now. I can eat properly again. Maybe a bit too much." She patted her stomach. "My skirts and pants are getting a bit tight around the middle."

Monica smiled, but said nothing.

Christmas shopping wasn't enjoyable for Katherine this year. With her mother gone, she had no one with whom to celebrate the festive season. She would buy a present for Monica and Jim, but no one else. There *was* no one else. Christmas Day for her would be very quiet indeed. No point cooking a turkey or ham just for herself; she'd still be eating the blasted thing by Easter. No, she might roast a chicken or even splurge on a duck. She considered the possibility of snow, although it wasn't usual to have snow until January. Still, a light dusting would be nice.

Her isolation and the thought of being snowed in turned on Katherine's squirreling instinct. She needed to stock up on essentials. One good fall of snow may have her unable to get out for several weeks. She remembered one winter when she was a young girl, it had snowed so heavily that you could walk across the fields and be on the same level as the tops of hedges. If that were to happen now, she'd be stranded. Even her trusty Land Rover could not navigate that kind of snow.

Wandering down the health and beauty aisle in the supermarket in Princetown, pushing a trolley laden with groceries, she reached for a packet of tampons and then stopped, her hand inches from the box. Something was wrong. She should have had a period last week. Or maybe even the week before.

Confused, she took out her phone and opened the calendar. Today was the sixteenth. Her last period was... she counted back... nearly seven weeks ago? *No, that can't be right. Try it the other way around. Let's see.* She'd had a period a day or two after Jonathan died, which was here. She put her finger on the calendar and counted forward. There was no mistake. It had been seven weeks.

She stepped back from the display of sanitary products, her brow furrowed, staring at the calendar. Seven weeks! Something was definitely not right. Her last period had been late and extremely light, almost to the point of non-existent.

What if something was wrong? What if she'd caught something from Jonathan? Or worse still, that she was pregnant? They'd used condoms, but it was still possible. She must see her doctor. Katherine hurried through the rest of her shopping and drove home, still trying to fathom what was going on. Those seven weeks haunted her.

At home, she left her groceries in the car and rushed inside to ring her doctor.

The doctor's receptionist was apologetic. "I'm sorry, Miss Walters, but Doctor Marsden is fully booked until the new year. Would you like to make an appointment for then?"

"No, that's too long. Is there anyone else I can see?"

"I'm afraid there isn't. Sorry."

Katherine's stomach knotted up. "Look, this is really urgent. Can you please see if you can fit me in somewhere?"

"I'll certainly put your name down on a waiting list, and if it's possible, I'll call you. That's about the best I can do, I'm afraid."

"But it's urgent. What do I do?"

"All I can suggest is that you ring the urgent care service in Plymouth. Do you want the number?"

Katherine groaned. "Yes, I suppose so. Thank you."

Katherine lay on an examination table, a sheet draped over her lower body as Dr. Sharma performed an internal examination.

"Just relax, now, Miss Walters," the doctor said.

"Easy for you to say," Katherine muttered, enduring Dr. Sharma's poking and prodding.

Finally, the examination over, Dr. Sharma peeled off her examination gloves and dropped them in the waste. "Okay, you can get dressed now, then come and take a seat."

A plump woman with a thick plait of black hair down her back, Dr. Sharma looked to be in her early forties, and she spoke with a hint of an accent from her native India. Her white coat over a colorful sari accentuated the deep brown of her skin.

She smiled broadly as Katherine sat across the desk. "Well, Miss Walters, I'd say you're definitely pregnant."

"But I can't be! I haven't been with anyone since my last period and even before I'd ensured we used a condom." Tears pricked Katherine's eyes. This couldn't be happening. There must be some other explanation.

"Miss Walters, there are certain changes a woman's body goes through when she becomes pregnant. You are exhibiting those signs. Have you done a pregnancy test, such as you buy from the pharmacy?"

Katherine's jaw clenched in frustration. "I'm not PREGNANT! Why won't anyone believe me?" She stood and paced the room.

"Please, Miss Walters, sit down."

Katherine faced Dr. Sharma, who smiled at her the way a mother would placate a child having a tantrum. Reluctantly, Katherine sat.

"I'll get an ultrasound scheduled for you. That will give us a better picture of what's going on. When that's done, come back to see me and we'll take it from there. Okay?"

Katherine nodded and sighed with relief. "Yes. Thank you." At last, the doctor was going to do something.

The following week, Katherine again lay on an examination table, but this time her abdomen had been liberally coated with gel by the technician, Caitlin. A woman in her twenties with a closely cropped head, save for a stripe of hot pink hair running from her forehead to her crown that made her look like Marvin the Martian's sister. She wore heavy eye makeup, false eyelashes and a ring through her eyebrow from which dangled a tiny skull. She chatted animatedly while she spread the goop over Katherine's stomach with a probe. Today was Caitlin's last day before she was off on a three-week holiday. Her boyfriend, Adam, was taking her on a cruise around the Caribbean for Christmas.

"I was supposed to work tomorrow and Christmas Eve, but I've swapped with Laura so that I can have a facial and get all my waxing and a spray tan done before the cruise. I think Adam's going to pop the question." Caitlin's excitement was evident in her broad smile and her jiggling in her seat. She clicked buttons and moved the probe, pressing down occasionally.

"Don't press too hard, or I'll pee myself." Katherine giggled nervously. "Why do I have to have a full bladder for this, anyway? It's so uncomfortable."

Caitlin chuckled. "If your bladder's full, it pushes your uterus up, and we can get a better look at your little one, but hang in there, we're nearly done. Want to see?" Without waiting for a response, she flicked a button and a screen set into the ceiling flickered to life.

Katherine stared at the image. A terrifying dread took hold of her heart, spreading ice through her veins. Time stood still, and Caitlin's chatter echoed through the void between them as if from another world. There was no mistaking what she saw on the screen—the tiny form of her unborn baby sucking its thumb. As if on cue, the baby removed its thumb and raised its hand, fingers splayed as if waving.

Katherine screamed.

Seventy-Six

Katherine drove back to Tavistock like an automaton, her mind turning over her conversation with Dr. Sharma, who she'd been lucky to see straight after her ultrasound. Probably screaming her head off and having to be restrained by two nurses helped ensure she received urgent attention. She still didn't believe that she was actually pregnant. She'd been so careful, or so she'd thought. Jonathan had used a condom both times they'd had sex. How could this have happened? Dr. Sharma had explained that some women can still have what appears to be a mini period while pregnant, which obviously was what happened, but she was around eighteen weeks pregnant. That didn't make any sense. Eighteen weeks! If it had happened when she and Jonathan first had sex, then she should have been much further along, and if it was the second time, then she'd only be a couple of months.

She parked her car and took out her phone, hoping to sort out her confusion with the aid of her calendar. Today was December 22nd. Katherine counted back. Eighteen weeks would put her conception date around...

"You fucking bastard!" Katherine growled. More pieces of the puzzle fell into place as she recalled when her mother had died. Eighteen weeks ago. She'd awoken the next morning with no memory of the previous evening after she'd drunk the hot chocolate Jonathan made for her. Her nipples and vagina were tender, and she'd assumed she was due for a painful period. Since she'd been trapped in the cellar when it was due, and had no concept of time, she hadn't thought about it. Jonathan must have drugged her the night her mother died and then raped her when she passed out.

She thumped her hand on the steering wheel. What was she going to do? Dr. Sharma had suggested there were three possible options. First, Katherine could have the baby and raise it herself. Second was to have the baby and give it up for adoption, or her third was to terminate the pregnancy. Katherine considered the options, none of them ideal, and none of them pleasant. Bringing up a child was the last thing she wanted to do, particularly the child of a man she hated. According to Dr. Sharma, terminating the pregnancy at this late stage was still possible, albeit not as straightforward as much earlier in a pregnancy. But as much as Katherine hated Jonathan, she couldn't face the thought of actually killing the baby. Which really left her with the alternative of giving the baby up for adoption. But that meant she had to go through with the pregnancy and childbirth anyway, distasteful as that thought was.

Dr. Sharma told her that nothing could be done until after Christmas anyway, so she had a few days to mull it over and decide. She had been given the number of a social worker if she wanted someone to talk to. She didn't.

Katherine checked her reflection in the rearview mirror. Her pale face stared back at her, dark circles under her eyes. She got out of the car and walked to the post office to check her mailbox. Despite renting a postbox in Princetown, she still hadn't got around to advising everyone of her change of address from Tavistock, something she made a mental note to do in the new year. As she walked back to her car, looking through the small pile of envelopes, a voice called out to her.

"Miss Walters!"

Katherine stopped and turned around to see a man she vaguely recognized rushing toward her. He carried a briefcase and looked as though he was out of breath.

"Miss Walters, thank you for stopping." He panted rapidly and heavily, taking in gulps of air. "Phew, not as fit as I once was." He patted a hand on his chest.

Katherine waited for him to catch his breath. She'd seen him before, but couldn't work out where. Why would he want to talk to her?

"I wanted to tell you how sorry I am for all the trouble you've been through. I had no idea." The man shook his head.

"Thank you, Mr. ..."

"Wallace. Mark Wallace."

The name cut Katherine like a knife, and she took a step back and stammered. "Y-you're his..."

He nodded. "I was Jonathan's partner, yes. I feel so foolish that I never realized what he was doing." He shrugged, then ran a hand through his hair before tugging at his collar. From the redness of his face and the roll of skin almost folded over the collar, he was long overdue an up-size in shirts. "Look, do you have time? Can we talk? I've found out some stuff that I think you should know."

Despite having other things on her mind at the moment, Mark's words piqued Katherine's curiosity. There were so many unanswered questions about Jonathan. Perhaps Mark had some answers. "Yes, alright. But not at your office."

"I quite understand. Would you like to have coffee perhaps?" Mark's breathing had slowed a little, but his face still resembled a tomato.

"Yes, okay. Coffee sounds good."

They walked in silence to the coffee bar and placed their orders, then chose a table across from the bathrooms at the back of the cafe, away from the millennials in their knee-less designer jeans drinking their designer macchiato lattes with a twist of soy.

Once seated, Mark placed his briefcase on the table and opened it. He rummaged around inside it for a moment, then extracted a folder and placed it on the table, before shutting the briefcase and putting it on the floor beside him. He rested his hands on top of the unopened folder.

"Miss Walters."

"Call me Katherine, please. You said you'd found something."

"Yes. I had to clear out Jonathan's desk when he..." Mark unclasped his hands and flicked the edge of the folder with a fingernail that looked as if it spent a lot of time being nibbled. "Well, first of all, I found this." He opened the folder and took out a photograph, which he slid across the table to Katherine.

She stared at it. A woman in lacy underwear stood beneath an arch of red roses. Her stance was overtly sexual, her ample breasts barely covered by her skimpy bra, her red lips forming a pout as if she was blowing kisses to the person behind the camera. If it wasn't for an age difference of maybe ten years older, the woman might almost be Katherine's twin. The resemblance was uncanny, although Katherine doubted she would ever pose for a photograph in such skimpy underwear.

Katherine glanced at Mark, then back to the photograph. "Who is she?"

"Look on the back."

Katherine turned the photograph over. Written on the back in a faded scrawl were the words:

'My darling Jonathan, I know you always find me sexy in this, so now you can look at me whenever you want. All my love on your 13th birthday, Mummy.'

A shudder of revulsion ran through Katherine, and she thrust the photo back across the table to Mark. She gagged and rushed for the toilet, just making it before throwing up. Her knees buckled, and she sank to the floor, clutching the sides of the toilet bowl.

Had Jonathan and his mother...been having sex? Katherine shuddered and vomited again. Is that why he was so infatuated with her? Because she reminded him of his mother? And that archway of roses looked very much like the roses at her orchard gate. Surely not. She'd have to have another look at the photograph to know for sure, and she certainly didn't want to do that.

She returned to the table, still shaking, and sat, thankful that Mark had put the photograph away.

"Tell me that's not really his mother," Katherine said.

"Unfortunately, I think it is. I found letters, too."

"No, I don't want to see."

"I quite understand. But there are things you probably do want to know."

"I'm listening. For now, anyway."

"From what I've found, it seems that Jonathan had a 'relationship' with his mother, but then ten years ago, she died. She fell down a set of stairs and broke her neck."

Seventy-Seven

Katherine gasped. The cup slipped from her hand and clattered back onto its saucer, spilling coffee over the table and Mark's folder. Mark snatched up a bunch of napkins and began mopping up as a server bustled over.

"I'm so sorry," Katherine said, close to tears again.

"It's alright." The server, Debbi—according to her name tag—wiped the table. "Can I get you another cup?"

"Yes, please." Katherine tried to smile at the young woman.

"I'll have another too, if I may," Mark said.

"Certainly, sir." Debbi made a funny little half bow, half curtsy and walked away.

When she was out of earshot, Katherine leaned toward Mark. "Jonathan killed my mother by breaking her neck."

Mark slumped back in his seat. "I didn't know. I'm sorry."

"At the time, I didn't know he'd killed her, of course. He told me just before... he died." Katherine averted her eyes. Despite being ultimately responsible for Jonathan's death, she still couldn't come right out and say she killed him.

"The house you bought, on Dartmoor, it was Jonathan's. Did you know?"

Katherine shook her head. “Jonathan’s? No, that’s not right. It belonged to someone called Christian Bennett. I signed the contracts, remember?”

Mark leaned forward in his seat again. “That was Jonathan's middle name and his mother’s maiden name. Well, Christina Bennett anyway. I’m presuming that Jonathan’s father was an ‘Irving’, but I don’t know for sure.”

“Dear God, this just gets weirder by the minute.” Katherine shook her head. So the arch of roses was indeed the one by the orchard gate. She placed her elbows on the table and rested her head in her hands, thumbs pressing into her temples as if to ward off a headache.

Debbi arrived with their coffee. “Are you alright, Miss?”

Katherine looked up and smiled. “Yes. It’s just been a trying day.”

Debbi’s brow lost its crease, and she smiled back. “I know what you mean, Miss. I’ve got five-year-old twin boys, so I have days like that all the time!”

Katherine smiled. “You poor girl. Twins!” The image of her unborn baby popped into her mind, and her smile faded.

After Debbi left again, Katherine picked up her coffee and sipped before replacing the cup in the saucer. “You’d better tell me what else you know before I pick up my cup again.”

Mark nodded. “Okay. Some of this is conjecture on my part, you understand, but Jonathan had been acting so weird since he met you. I must admit I’ve done some snooping since he died.”

Mark opened the folder again, and Katherine steeled herself for another photograph, but Mark only extracted two sheets of paper. He didn’t give them to Katherine, but placed them in front of himself.

“I’ve written down the salient points so I don’t forget anything.” He gestured toward Katherine’s cup. “Want another mouthful before I start?”

Katherine took another sip and set her cup down.

“You’re not the first,” Mark said.

“Sorry?”

“There have been at least two others before you. Both are very similar in looks to his mother, but you are definitely the closest.”

“That just makes me feel sick. How do you know this?”

"Jonathan had no family, you see, and although I didn't know it, he'd named me as executor of his will, so I ended up with the unenviable chore of clearing out his house. I found scrapbooks labeled with names. One was 'Mummy', then there was 'Sarah', 'Chloe' and..."

"Katherine, I suppose."

"Yes, yours."

"What happened to Sarah and Chloe?"

"Well ... Sarah, I don't know about her . She must have been before Jonathan and I became partners, but I remember Chloe. She went back home to Australia."

"Australia? That's a coincidence. Jonathan lost a mate there; taken by a shark when they were surfing. He wore the Southern Cross tattooed on his arm as a tribute."

"Is that what he told you?" Mark chuckled wryly as Katherine nodded. "Load of bollocks, if you'll pardon my expression. He had that done when she was here to prove how much he loved her. It didn't make any difference though; she still shot through."

"Lucky Chloe," Katherine said. "I wish I'd..." Her bottom lip quivered, and she trailed off. Her eyes brimmed with tears, and she hung her head, hoping Mark hadn't seen.

"Katherine?" Mark touched her hand. That was all it took for the dam to burst. She sobbed quietly, tears falling on the table and her shuddering shoulders the only visible signs of her distress.

Mark's hand enfolded hers and held it, squeezing it gently. His hand was warm and comforting.

Katherine sensed someone beside her.

"She's okay, Debbi, just give her a minute," Mark said softly. Then they were alone again.

When she had herself under some semblance of control, she withdrew her hand from Mark's grasp and tucked both hands beneath her legs. She met Mark's eyes, a deep brown, nothing like Jonathan's. She didn't think she'd ever find blue eyes attractive again.

"I wish I'd never met him, Mark." If she hadn't, her mother would still be alive.

"I know. But it's over now. He's gone and can't harm you anymore."

Katherine sniffed and shook her head, a wry smile on her face. "Oh, you don't know Jonathan! He's still making my life hell."

A puzzled frown creased Mark's forehead. "I don't understand."

"Mark, I'm pregnant."

Mark's mouth dropped open, and his eyes widened. "What?"

"The night he killed my mother, he drugged me and raped me after I passed out. I only figured it out today."

"Bloody hell. What are you going to do?"

Seventy-Eight

Katherine lay on her side in a private room of Derriford Hospital. Her labor had not gone well, resulting in an emergency C-section and hysterectomy. She should have expected it. Nothing to do with Jonathan had ever been easy, and once again, he'd made her suffer. Through the open door of her room came the excited chatter of new mothers, the crying of newborn babies, and the bustling of the nursing staff. Then there were the fathers, their booming look-at-me-aren't-I-the-top-dog voices announcing their fertility proudly to the world. She hated them all. Her own baby was gone, taken away without her having seen the little boy. She didn't want to see him, didn't want to build a picture of the child in her mind.

She had received assurances that her baby would be well cared for. People who could not have children of their own would be overjoyed to give her little boy a loving home.

It was the right thing for her and for the child, so why did she feel so empty? So emotionally numb. So bereft. She'd always hoped that someday she'd have children with someone she loved and who loved her; to be a family. But now that option had been taken away from her completely.

An ache jagged its way through her heart, and, turning her face into her pillow, she cried. Tears of loss, grief, and despair. Did she make the right decision? Should she have kept her baby? But how could she? Every time she looked at the little boy's face, she would remember the horror that was Jonathan. No, she'd made the right decision.

Jonathan's face floated ethereally behind her closed eyes. His cold, blue eyes stared unblinking at her. She thumped her fist on her pillow. "Go away!" she muttered. But his eyes, full of dead light, continued to stare.

"GO AWAY!" Katherine's voice was louder now as she threw her pillow across the room, oblivious to the crash of her water jug as it fell to the floor.

In her mind, Jonathan laughed at her. "You're mine, Katherine. You'll always be mine!"

"GO AWAY! YOU'RE DEAD!" Katherine screamed, her screams mingling with his laughter as his words repeated their loop again and again.

"Always be mine, Katherine, always be mine."

Seventy-Nine

After Katherine's meltdown, nurses had kept her door closed, and had medicated her to calm her. She'd dozed on and off, waking each time someone entered the room. A *whoosh* sound signaled the door opening again, but Katherine feigned sleep so as not to have to converse with whoever it was.

Female voices spoke in hushed tones as two nurses checked and cross-checked her chart, her blood pressure, and then straightened up her blanket.

"You know who she is, don't you?" one voice said. Katherine recognized the accent of Ellen, the New Zealander. A gorgeous Māori woman with long black hair, flawless dark skin, and sparkling brown eyes.

"I recognize the name from somewhere, but I don't know why."

The second voice was unfamiliar, but she sounded very young, almost at the pitch of a schoolgirl.

"It was in all the papers. She killed her boyfriend after he'd kept her in a dungeon for months," Ellen said, a note of triumph in her voice.

"Gosh, now I remember," the second voice said. "Poor girl. Now I understand why she didn't want to keep her baby. Of course, that must be who she was screaming about. The bastard killed her mother, too, didn't he? All because he supposedly loved her. What a sicko."

"Yeah," Ellen said. "Bloody sicko, alright. They say he was having it off with his mother. His own mother! Can you believe it?"

The voices fell silent a moment, then Ellen said, "God, I'm glad she killed him."

Gentle fingers stroked the back of Katherine's hand, and Ellen whispered. "Don't you worry, Katherine, I'll look after you. You've been to hell and back, but you're safe now."

~

Katherine sat on the edge of the hospital bed. Showered, dressed, and packed. She glanced at the patient care board on the wall. Five days she'd been here, and today she would be discharged. The door opened, and Ellen strode in, a broad smile on her face.

"So, you're going home?" Ellen flipped open a patient folder and began checking off the discharge paperwork, ticking boxes, flicking pages, scribbling notes. "Bet you're glad to be getting out of here, huh?"

"Yes, I'll be glad to get back to my novel."

"You should have brought it with you, plenty of reading time when you are in hospital."

Katherine chuckled. "No, I mean to writing my novel. I'm a writer."

Ellen looked up, her eyes wide, awestruck. "Really? A writer? Wow, that's so cool. What do you write? Will I have read any of your books?"

"No. I haven't been published yet. But I'm working on it. I've finished my first novel, and I need to find an agent who'll represent me. Meantime, I'm busy writing my second and have an outline for a third."

"That's fantastic. I couldn't write if my life depended on it, but I read heaps. I get lost in books. Absolutely love reading. Never go anywhere without my trusty Kindle." Ellen let the folder slide onto the bed, paperwork forgotten. "I like books about women and the struggles they go through. Don't suppose you write that kind of thing, by any chance?"

Katherine laughed. "As a matter of fact, that's exactly what I write."

"Well, when you get published, you make sure you let me know so I can be one of your first fans. I want a signed, first edition, so I can have bragging rights that I knew you before you were famous." Ellen's enthusiasm was infectious. She seemed almost as excited at the prospect of Katherine being published as Katherine herself.

"Let me have your address, and I'll make sure you get one." Katherine fished in her handbag for a notepad and handed it to Ellen, who scribbled down an address and phone number.

Katherine glanced at the address. Roborough. Just outside Plymouth on the road to Tavistock. She'd driven through it many times.

"It's only a couple of miles up the road, so it's really handy to the hospital," Ellen said.

The door opened with its all too familiar *whoosh* sound. Ellen snatched up the discharge folder and opened it at random. "Now don't forget, if something doesn't feel right, please see your doctor, or go to the emergency department." She turned to the orderly waiting just inside the door. "And we're done." She closed the folder with a resounding clap and held it out to the orderly. "Pop that in the 'discharged' pigeon hole for me on your way, please, Bill, while I strip the bed."

"Sure, will do." Bill took the folder and tucked it under his arm.

"So, I guess this is goodbye, then," Ellen said, addressing Katherine. "I hope your time here has been, if not pleasurable, at least comfortable."

"Thank you, Ellen." Katherine patted her handbag where the notepad containing Ellen's address now resided. "For all you've done. Your kindness and compassion have meant so much to me." A tear welled in Katherine's eye as a matching one spilled over in Ellen's.

Ellen sniffled, then reached for Katherine. "Come here, silly." She wrapped her arms around Katherine and hugged her, both women dissolving into tears.

Behind Ellen, Bill coughed. "Um, I'll wait outside." His words were followed by the *whoosh* of the door.

Katherine giggled. "Look at us, what a pair, eh?"

Ellen released Katherine and reached for the box of tissues, pulling out a few and wiping her eyes before blowing her nose with all the grace of the Titanic's foghorn. This set Katherine off giggling again, Ellen now joining in the mirth before finally pulling herself together.

"Now, you. Out. Before you make me lose my job."

"Thanks again." She pecked Ellen on the cheek and started for the door.

"And call me!" Ellen yelled as Katherine reached the door. Katherine gave her a wave of acknowledgment, not daring to turn around for fear of another attack of the giggles.

Part Three

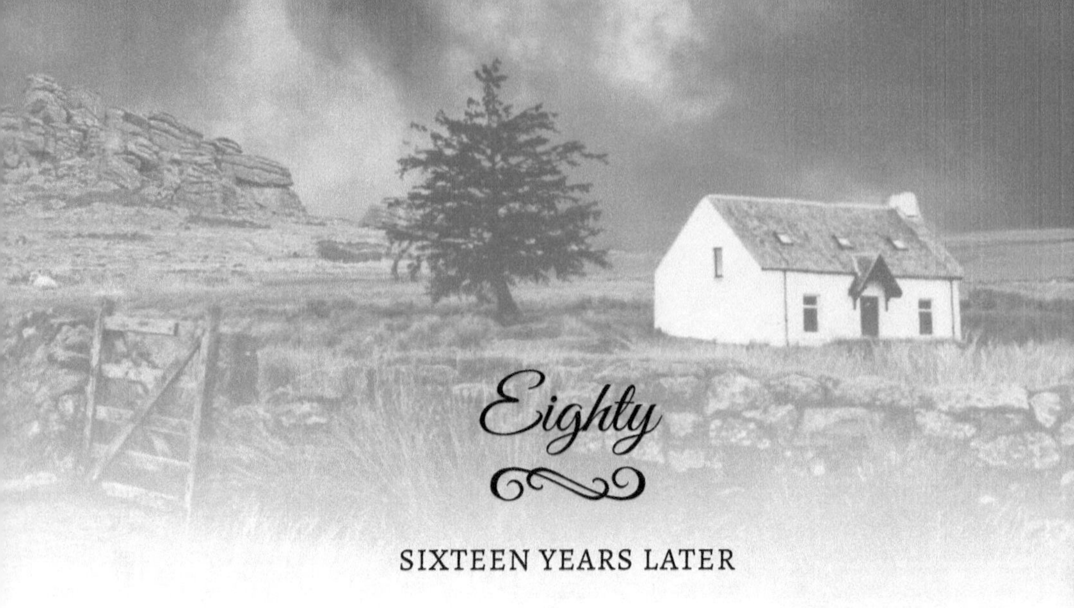

Eighty

SIXTEEN YEARS LATER

Katherine half-watched the evening news, her mind focused on her upcoming book tour. A tour that would take her to cities all around the country, along with Ireland and the Isle of Man. She'd done several now, so she knew what to expect, but always at the back of her mind was the dread. What if nobody came? What if she sat at a table laden with piles of her latest book and nobody came? What if she stood at a lectern reading an excerpt from her book to an almost empty room? Or worse, that people started leaving as she read? She had to stop thinking like this. Perhaps a glass of wine would calm her nerves. In the kitchen, she opened a bottle of Australian Shiraz, poured a glass, took a large gulp, and headed back to the living room.

Her book was being launched at WH Smith in Plymouth, where she would read an excerpt and also sign copies. At least in Plymouth, she knew she'd have at least one customer. Ellen always came and bought a copy of the latest book, even though she'd read the story at least twice before it even reached Katherine's editor. She had, in fact, taken over from Monica as Katherine's main critique reader.

Monica had passed away perhaps ten years ago. Her health had steadily failed with the progression of her MS, and the end was possibly a release. Not only for her, but also for Jim. Katherine still visited Jim on his farm, but not as often as she should. Katherine had moved away not long after she'd had the baby. Just too many memories. Too much guilt, too much pain, and way too much sadness. And every time she'd seen that arch of roses, the horror flooded back. She'd cut the roses down and removed the arch, but still the memories persisted. She'd needed to start again, so she moved to a small village a few miles outside of Plymouth, where she'd found a real chocolate box cottage, complete with thatched roof, lead-light windows, exposed beams, pretty yellow roses—she didn't think she'd ever like red roses again—climbing over the entry porch and a huge beech tree in the corner of the garden.

Ellen loved the cottage, too. It was so vastly different from her own modern home. She said it was like stepping into a time warp every time she visited. When she stayed over, they loved to curl up in the window seat with their coffee, catching the morning sun and watching the squirrels playing among the branches of the beech.

Now, Ellen was about to head off to the wilds of Sierra Leone, so they'd made plans to have a final catch-up following Katherine's book launch. One last hurrah. It had been a couple of months since they'd last spent time together, despite living only a few miles apart. That last time, they'd spent a long weekend hiking in Snowdonia. Katherine wanted to walk to the top of Mount Snowdon, but Ellen said, *Blow that, I'm catching the train.* So they'd compromised and caught the train up and hiked back down. That evening, after each had soothed their aching muscles by soaking in the bath, they'd dressed up and hit the bar, spending the night drinking and laughing with the locals. It had been quite a night.

She'd miss Ellen, but she hoped to make a surprise visit to Sierra Leone if she could squeeze it into her schedule.

As she raised her glass to take another drink, Katherine glanced at the television and paused, the glass halfway to her mouth. Something about the image on the screen looked familiar. A reporter, wearing a solemn expression, stood outside what appeared to be Ellen's house. Maybe they're doing a story about her upcoming missionary work. She grabbed the remote and turned up the volume.

"*... mutilated body found in this house behind me has been formally identified as Ellen Anne Mehrtens. Miss Mehrtens, a nurse at Derriford*

Hospital for 20 years, was stabbed numerous times. Police have not yet arrested anyone in connection with this brutal and sadistic murder. A murder that has shocked and frightened residents of this normally peaceful neighborhood."

What? Ellen murdered? No, it couldn't be.

The camera panned back, revealing a woman standing with the reporter. Katherine recognized the woman as Ellen's neighbor, Rebecca, who had popped in once or twice when Katherine was visiting.

"Mrs. Forest, you lived next door to Miss Mehrtens and found her body. What can you tell us?"

"We're all in shock. Ellen was such a kind, caring, and decent woman. She delivered my babies. Who would want to do such a thing? To tie her up, slit her wrists, and cut her throat? And then to stab her so many times after she was dead." Rebecca was on a roll now, seemingly enjoying her moment of fame, gory as it may be. *"Do you know he stabbed her in the face? Left the knife buried up to the hilt."*

Acid burned in Katherine's throat as her stomach rolled, and she clapped a hand over her mouth and dashed to the kitchen, bending over the sink a split second before her stomach heaved, emptying itself of wine and the remains of a recently eaten Caesar salad. Again and again her stomach clenched, and Katherine sank to the floor as her knees turned to jelly. When her stomach eventually quieted, she got shakily to her feet and rinsed the sink.

After washing her hands and splashing cold water on her face, she returned to the living room. The local news had finished, replaced by the national news and its lead on President Trump and his on-again, off-again trade tariffs, and the missing Epstein list.

Katherine turned off the television, her mind reeling with thoughts of Ellen and the manner of her death. She couldn't take it in. Who would want to harm Ellen? And why?

Her glass of wine still sat on the table, but the thought of it made her feel sick again. She snatched it up and went back to the kitchen, and poured it down the sink.

She spent the rest of the evening trawling through news reports online, but found no further information. Finally, she went to bed, but sleep was a long time in coming, and when it did, Jonathan returned, his sightless eyes staring fixedly at her as he shambled toward her, his arms outstretched, his leather bracelet still circling his wrist, his index finger pointing at her. "You killed me, Katherine. All I wanted was for you to love me, but you killed me." Katherine backed away, but Jonathan's arms grew longer, longer, reaching, reaching, until they closed around her neck.

Eighty-One

Katherine woke, her scream still echoing in her mind. Had she screamed out loud? She lay, staring into the darkness, willing herself to relax, slowing her breathing. Eventually, she slept again.

Dark clouds lay heavy over Plymouth the day of Ellen's funeral, reflecting the mood of the gathering. No celebration of life or pop songs, no funny stories or jokes to farewell Ellen. The manner of her death demanded and deserved a serious, somber, and solemn occasion.

Katherine sat at the back of the church and looked around at the congregation. So many women and so many children, ranging from toddlers to late teens. How many of these children had Ellen delivered over the past twenty years?

Funny how things turn out sometimes. When Ellen had given Katherine her phone number and secured a promise that she would receive a signed copy of Katherine's first book, there was no way either of them could have foreseen the deep, rewarding friendship that would develop between them. Katherine's life had changed so much in the sixteen years since they'd met.

Sixteen years. It seemed like a lifetime. Her baby would be a young man now. Katherine still sometimes wondered what had happened to him, whether he had inherited her own gentle softness or Jonathan's narcissistic, psychopathic tendencies. She hoped, for the sake of the child and the adopting family, that the boy did not take after his father.

In order to register the baby's birth, she had to name the little boy, as well as record the father's name. She hadn't wanted to acknowledge Jonathan in any way. Not after what he'd done to her. But it wouldn't be right to withhold that information from the child, so she'd reluctantly noted Jonathan as the father and named the little boy 'Christian' after Jonathan's middle name.

Of course, the guilt of giving up the baby still haunted her. That and the manner of Jonathan's death. His broken, bleeding body still stalked her nightmares, his steel-blue eyes fixed and staring. Staring at her. Questioning her. Accusing her.

The service over, six pallbearers hoisted Ellen's coffin on their shoulders and carried it from the church, the congregation shuffling in a line behind.

At the grave, the mourners gathered around, and Katherine hung back, not wanting to see her friend lowered into the cold, damp earth. Another prayer for Ellen, and then it was over. Tears rolled down Katherine's face, and she made no effort to stem them, just stood and cried as the mourners gradually drifted away from the grave.

A small woman approached. "You're Katherine Walters, aren't you?"

Katherine groaned inwardly. Normally, if someone recognized her, she'd be thrilled, but right now, she didn't want to talk about her books. But what could she do? She couldn't very well deny who she was. She reluctantly nodded.

The woman moved closer and extended her hand. "Ellen spoke so highly of you." Her eyes, already red from crying, filled with fresh tears. "I'm Grace Mehrtens, Ellen's mother." Her voice cracked on the last words and the tears trickled down her cheeks.

Katherine's heart broke for his poor woman who had traveled halfway around the world to bury her daughter. She took Grace's hand

and then embraced her, holding her as they both sobbed and cried, sharing their pain and sorrow and grief.

A tall, dark-skinned man came up to them and put his hand on Grace's shoulder. "You okay, Mum?" He smiled at Katherine, but it was a sad, thin smile, as though all the joy had flitted away, leaving just the outline behind.

Grace released Katherine and turned to the young man. "Yes, dear. I'm okay, just sad. This is Katherine Walters."

The young man extended his hand. "Pleased to meet you, although I wish it were under better circumstances. I'm Alex."

Katherine shook his hand. "Yes. Me too, Alex."

"We'd better go, Mum, they're waiting for us." Alex took his mother's arm. "Katherine, you'll join us for some refreshment, won't you?"

"Yes, thank you. I'll see you there." She waited for them to get some way ahead and then walked to the edge of Ellen's grave. From her handbag, she took her latest book, *Tracy's Troubles*. The cover depicted an anguished-looking woman holding two babies. One with curly black hair and dark skin, the other fair-skinned with wisps of blond hair. She'd signed the book, of course. *To my dearest Ellen. Words cannot express how much you've meant to me, nor how much I will miss you. Farewell, my friend.* She looked around to ensure she was alone and then dropped the book into the grave. It landed with a muffled, hollow thud, and Katherine winced at the sound. She stood a moment, head bowed, and said one last prayer for her friend. Then she turned and walked away.

Two long trestle tables, each one loaded with plates of food, stood in the center of the church hall. People milled around drinking cups of tea, nibbling on sandwiches, cakes, biscuits, cheeses, dips; chatting, sharing stories. Katherine spied Ellen's mother and was about to walk over to her, have a quick chat, and make her excuses, but a voice behind her spoke her name. A voice with the smooth richness of Lindor chocolate. She turned around, and her heart didn't just skip; it frolicked. The voice belonged to a cliché. The kind of cliché that adorned the cover of every steamy romance novel. He was tall, dark, and oh, so handsome, and he was looking at her with eyes that might well be responsible for global warming. Katherine didn't just want to drown in this man's eyes; she wanted to go scuba diving.

Eighty-Two

He held out his hand. "I'm Ben Mehrtens, Ellen's brother."

Katherine could think of nothing to say. Her body was clamoring out for this man. To kiss him, strip him naked, and make love to him. But she had to do something, say something. She reached for his outstretched hand. His touch was electric. Sparks exploded through her body, and the babble of conversation that had been so loud around her faded to white noise. Nothing else existed but this man and her. Her knees turned to mush, and she wobbled on her high heels.

"Hey, come and sit down." Ben held her up, one arm around her waist, the other supporting her elbow as he guided her toward a chair by the wall.

"Thank you," Katherine stammered as she sat.

"Let me get you a cup of tea. I'll be back in a moment."

Katherine watched him, her eyes fixed on him as he walked away. She'd known Ellen had two brothers, but her friend had neglected to mention how utterly gorgeous Ben was. He'd ignited feelings in her she had never known. If she had to describe her feelings, it would be unadulterated, unashamed lust. Of course, the timing could not be worse. To have this happen at her best friend's funeral was a million shades of wrong.

She must get a hold of herself. She breathed, slowly and deeply, calming herself, focusing herself, the way she did before a public appearance. By the time Ben returned with a cup of tea, she was once again in control. "Thank you." She smiled at him and took the cup.

He sat down beside her. "Are you okay?"

Katherine nodded and sipped her tea. "I'm fine. Just somewhat overwhelmed." Hopefully, he'd think it was the funeral that affected her, not his presence.

"Yeah, I know. It's so hard to take in. We've all been knocked for six."

This was safer ground. If the conversation stuck to Ellen, Katherine might get through without making a fool of herself. Hopefully.

"I still can't quite get my head around it," she said.

He seemed about to reply, but a young couple approached, and he rose to greet them. While they talked, Katherine finished her tea. Now would be a good time to excuse herself. She stood up and walked away, not daring to look back.

Mrs. Mehrtens stood chatting with two women Katherine recognized as work colleagues of Ellen's. She'd met them a few times at various parties that Ellen had invited her to. Katherine greeted them and then addressed Ellen's mother.

"I'm going to head off, Grace. I'm glad to have met you, just sorry it had to be under these circumstances."

"You take care, my dear. Thank you for coming, and thank you for being such a good friend to Ellen."

They embraced, and when they parted, both had tears in their eyes. Katherine turned away before hers spilled over. She made a beeline for the door, wanting to escape, but Ben blocked her path.

"Katherine, don't leave. I need to talk to you," he said, his tone insistent and somewhat urgent.

"Oh?"

"I just— "

"Excuse me." A woman cradling a tiny baby in her arms interrupted Ben. "This is Georgina." She looked lovingly down at the sleeping baby. "She was born the day Ellen, um, died. Ellen delivered her."

"She's lovely." Ben's face softened, and he gently touched the little one on the cheek. "I'm sure Mum would like to meet you and Georgina."

Katherine edged away, but Ben's hand on her arm stopped her. He took out his phone.

"I really need to talk to you. Can I have your number?"

Without hesitation, and with her heart doing flip-flops in her chest, she took the phone from him and keyed in her mobile number, then handed it back. He tapped the screen a few times, then put the phone back in his pocket.

"Thanks. I'll call you." He took the young woman's arm and guided her to where his mother stood, with Alex still beside her. Katherine watched Ben walk away, her heart settling back to a more normal beat.

Finally, Katherine escaped the hall and made her way back to her car, where she kicked off her heels and slipped on a pair of flats that she kept in the car for driving. She hated driving in heels. On the odd occasion when she'd done it, she never felt fully in control and ever since Jonathan, she was always very careful to be in control, whether it be with cars or men. After all, as Ellen liked to say, *if it's got tires or testicles, it's gonna be trouble.*

Back home after the funeral, Katherine opened a bottle of Oyster Bay Sauvignon Blanc from Marlborough in New Zealand. It had been one of Ellen's favorites. There was a particular flavor in Sauvignon Blanc from that region that she'd never found in similar wines from other parts of the world. Interesting that the same grape variety could taste so different depending on the region, the climate, and the winemaker. She hadn't eaten all day, hadn't felt like it, but if she didn't have something sensible now, she'd end up snacking on potato chips or cookies at midnight. There was no point looking in the fridge; it was pretty bare. She'd meant to do some grocery shopping while in Plymouth, but couldn't bring herself to undertake such a mundane task after burying her best friend. So, she'd have to make do with whatever was in the pantry. Which, she found on opening the door, was almost as bare as her fridge. Dinner looked like being a tin of soup. Potato and leek or cream of mushroom.

She heated the mushroom soup and made toast with the remains of the three-day-old bread. She took it into the living room and curled up on the sofa, legs beneath her to eat her meager meal, promising herself that she would shop tomorrow. And eat something nourishing and sensible.

Her phone vibrated on the coffee table, then started jingling its tinny tone. She picked it up. An unknown number; she swiped to answer.

"Hello."

"Katherine, it's Ben Mehrtens."

Katherine's insides turned to jelly at the sound of his voice. Heavens, he'd have women swooning all over him if the response exhibited by her hormones was anything to go by.

She swallowed her heart back down. "Hi Ben... " She managed to stop herself from gushing and saying something stupid like 'how lovely to hear your voice'. Why was she like this?

"Look, I'd really like to talk to you. Can we meet?"

"Um, I guess so." What on earth would he want to talk to her about? Well, obviously, Ellen, but what did he hope to learn from her?

"Great. How about tomorrow? Maybe I could drop by in the afternoon if that suits."

"Yes, that would be lovely." Christ. Why on earth did she agree to that? She knew nothing about Ben other than that he was Ellen's brother. And the most deliciously desirable man she'd ever set eyes on of course. But even Jonathan had seemed charming initially, and what a nightmare he'd turned out to be. She'd been cautious of men ever since. Never invited a man to her house, even if she'd known him for months. Nor would she go to a man's home. On the odd occasion that she slept with someone, she insisted on staying in a hotel. Yes, it was paranoid, and no doubt cost her any chance of a proper relationship, but she couldn't, and wouldn't, risk another Jonathan in her life. And now she'd agreed to Ben calling around. No, it wouldn't do. She'd have to get out of it somehow.

"Look, on second thoughts," she said quickly before the thought of

Ben in her bed had a chance to change her mind. "I've got to go to Plymouth tomorrow. Maybe we can meet for coffee, somewhere."

"Okay, but how about lunch instead?"

"Fine. Where shall we meet?"

"Perhaps you can meet me at Ellen's. Mum and Alex are flying back to Christchurch tomorrow, but I'm staying on to finalize things."

Ben's voice broke on the last word, and Katherine's heart ached in sympathy. What a terrible thing to have to do. Not only bury your little sister, but then have to clear out her belongings. She'd had to do that when her mother died, laying bare all of her mother's most intimate secrets. Secrets a mother would never want her daughter to find. Things such as the pair of men's slippers beneath the bed. Slippers that definitely weren't her father's. Things such as the small bundle of letters addressed to 'my darling Jacqui' from a man named Gerard. Things such as the vibrator nestled in her mother's bedside drawer.

"I can be there about eleven, if that's okay," Katherine said, not relishing the idea of seeing where her friend died, but not having the heart to put Ben off again.

Eighty-Three

Katherine pulled up outside Ellen's house and sat a moment, steeling herself before getting out of her car and walking up the short path. The door stood open, and Katherine froze on the step. She couldn't go in, just couldn't. Her friend had died just inside, at the bottom of the stairs. Ellen's beautiful cream carpet was gone, fortunately, but some spatter stains on the wallpaper remained. Ellen's blood.

"Hell, Katherine, I'm sorry." Ben bounded down the stairs, bundled his arms around her, and turned her away from the doorway. "I shouldn't have left the door open."

She looked up at Ben, her heart aching so much she'd swear it would break. "I never ... you've ... oh God. Her blood. She's really gone." Sobs racked her body, and she buried her face in Ben's chest as she cried. It was true. Even though she'd been to the church service, seen the coffin in its grave and offered condolences to Ellen's family, it hadn't seemed real. It was as if she'd viewed the events through a filter of some kind. Well, the blinkers were well and truly off now thanks to the bloodstains, and the truth had come crashing in on her in a way nothing else could.

Ben held her while she cried. He stroked her hair and murmured soothing sounds. When she quieted a little, he put a hand under her chin, tilted her head up, and gently wiped her tears away with his thumb.

"You okay?" he asked.

Katherine shook her head and shrugged. "I don't know. It's just hit me suddenly. Ellen really is gone." She pulled back a step from him. "But how are you? How are you coping with ..." She fluttered a hand toward the house.

Ben chuckled, but there was no mirth in it. "We're a tough breed, us Māori. I'll get by." He gave her a sad half-smile. "I'm really sorry you saw her ..." He trailed off as if unable to say the words.

She reached up and touched his cheek. "Don't apologize. It wasn't your fault."

He half-closed his eyes and leaned toward her touch with a soft sigh. After a moment, he said, "Do you still want to have lunch, or would you rather not?"

"No, I'm okay, really."

Ben frowned. "So, was that a yes or a no to lunch?"

"Sorry. It's a yes." She paused, then added, "I think."

He chuckled. "I'm taking that as a yes, then. I just need to grab something." He strode back into the house, then returned a few moments later, slipping a brown leather bomber jacket over his pale blue shirt. Coupled with slim-fitting jeans and boots, he once again looked as if he'd stepped from the cover of a romance novel. *My God, he's gorgeous.*

"Ready?" he asked.

She nodded, not daring to speak in case the words spinning in her head accidentally found their way out of her mouth. Now was certainly not the time to say, 'forget lunch, just take me to bed.'

"Did you have a place in mind?" Ben asked.

"Um, I hadn't thought." There was that restaurant she'd been to with Ellen a few times, but that would bring back too many memories. There was a new place near Crownhill Fort. It wasn't too far away, and there'd been a write-up in the paper about it recently; it got a good rap.

"I know just the place. Want me to drive or would you prefer to take your car too?"

"More than happy for you to drive. Drivers are all mad over here. They scare the crap out of me every time I get behind the wheel."

Katherine laughed. Ellen once told her that New Zealand drivers were the worst in the world. She climbed behind the wheel of the Range Rover and started the motor.

"All set?" she asked once Ben buckled his seatbelt.

"I guess." Ben shrugged and then gripped the grab handle with both hands.

Katherine drove as sedately as possible, stealing glances across at Ben every so often, smiling to herself when he appeared to relax and then let go of the grab handle. His deer-in-the-headlights look finally replaced with a softer, more at ease expression as he looked around instead of staring straight ahead.

Over a lunch of breaded scampi and freshly grilled haddock, they chatted about mundane matters as though neither of them wanted to bring their mood down by talking about Ellen. But of course, they'd have to at some point.

That point came when they lingered over coffee. Katherine folded her napkin and placed it on the table. "Now, Ben, you said you wanted to talk to me, yet all we've done is chatter about everything and nothing. What did you want to talk about?"

"Ah," Ben said, putting his cup down and reaching into an inside pocket of his jacket. "This." He placed a notebook on the table between them. "It's Ellen's address book."

Katherine looked at the book and then up at Ben. "I don't understand. What does this have to do with me?"

"Your name's not in it." Ben tapped the cover of the book with one finger. "And it should be."

"What do you mean? I'm not following you."

"This address book has pretty much every person Ellen ever met in it. She's had it for years. Mum sent it to her for Christmas about ten years back. See?" He flipped the cover open. Written on the inside of the cover was *To Ellen, with love at Christmas. Mum.*

"There used to be matching note-paper and envelopes, too. They're long gone, of course. But she kept the book."

"I'm sorry, Ben, I'm still not following."

"Where is the 'W' page?" Ben pointed to the alphabetized index pages and followed down with his finger. The 'W' was missing.

Katherine frowned. Then Ben opened the book to where the page should have been to reveal a torn edge, as though someone had hurriedly ripped the page out. The page beneath had been lightly gone over with a pencil, revealing an imprint of what had been written on the torn-out page. Katherine's name, her phone number and her email address.

She grabbed the book and peered at it closely. "Who did this?"

"Who did what? Tear out the page, or use a pencil to make out what was on the ripped-out page?"

"Well, both, I guess."

"I'm responsible for the pencil. As to who tore out the page, I have no idea. Did you and Ellen have a falling out by any chance?"

Katherine glared at Ben. "No, we certainly did not. What made you leap to that conclusion?"

"Look, don't fly off the handle. I'm not accusing you of anything. I'm just trying to make sense of things."

"A page is missing from her address book and you think Ellen ripped it out because we'd fallen out?"

"No, it's not just that. Katherine, please bear with me. Perhaps I'd better just lay out the whole shebang instead of piecemeal."

Katherine sat back in her chair and folded her arms across her chest. "Yes, perhaps you should."

Eighty-Four

Ben leaned his forearms on the table. "Okay, here goes. Ellen wrote home every month and in those letters, she always mentioned you. What you'd done together, places you'd been. She talked about your books, how she bought every single one in hardback, how you'd signed them and how pleased you'd been to see them on her bookshelf. So, the thing is, there are no books of yours on the shelf."

Katherine's brow creased and she unfolded her arms. "What? That can't be."

"But it's true. Ellen was a neat freak, as you know. I mean, who else would have a white carpet for God's sake? She filed all her books in alphabetical order by author. There's a large gap where your books should have been, but they aren't there. And the thing is, they aren't anywhere."

"So where are they?"

Ben shrugged. "Who knows? But it's a mystery, particularly considering your name being torn from her address book."

"What do the police think?"

"I haven't spoken to them about it yet. Guess I'll do that tomorrow."

"Want me to come with you?" Shoot, now why did she volunteer to do that? The way this man affected her hormones, she shouldn't be putting herself in a position to be near him.

"No, that's okay," Ben said with a sigh. "I hate talking to coppers. They have a knack for making me feel guilty when I know I haven't done anything."

Katherine nodded. "I think they go to a special school to learn that technique."

After a few moments, Ben signaled the waiter for the bill, handing over his credit card. Then he pushed his chair back, but didn't stand. "I'd better get back to it, I suppose." Tears welled in his anguished eyes. "It's horrible, Katherine, just horrible. Everywhere I look, everything I touch reminds me that my little sister is never coming home. I hate that her life has been reduced to a pile of boxes for Oxfam. It's just so unfair." He dropped his head, his tears dripping one by one onto his jeans, his shoulders shuddering as he sobbed.

Katherine got up, crouched beside him and held him, trying to comfort him the way he'd done for her. Her heart ached so much to see this man in tears. How he must be hurting. Should she offer to help him pack up Ellen's things? God, no. She couldn't bear that. It would be just too hard.

"Come on, let's get out of here." She took her car keys from her pocket and put them in Ben's hand. "You wait in the car. I'll only be a moment."

Ben nodded. She patted his shoulder and hurried to retrieve Ben's card from the waiter. After a moment, the bell on the restaurant door tinkled and she glanced over to the table they'd shared. Ben was gone. She thanked the waiter and left the restaurant.

Ben sat in the passenger seat, his head bowed, his fingers fiddling with the zip of his jacket. He glanced quickly at her when she got in, but lowered his gaze again immediately.

"Are you okay?" Katherine asked, watching him.

He nodded. "Look, I'm sorry about that. I feel stupid."

She grabbed his wrist, somewhat harder than she'd intended, but it had the desired effect. He looked at her as she glared at him. "You have nothing to apologize for and don't you ever feel stupid for loving your sister." Her tone was harsh, almost angry. She let go of his wrist and softened her voice. "And don't ever be ashamed to show it, either."

"I can see why Ellen liked you so much. You're very kind." Then he laughed, a dry, humorless laugh. "But if you ever tell the lads I coach in Rugby that I blubbered like a baby, I'll revise that opinion."

Katherine made a motion as if zipping her lips. "It's a deal." She stuck out her hand.

Ben clasped her hand and shook it vigorously. Then held it, perhaps a little longer than necessary, before letting go. Katherine turned her attention to starting the Range Rover, as though it was the most complicated piece of machinery in the world.

They drove in silence the few miles back to Ellen's home and Katherine pulled up outside. She kept the motor running, but turned to Ben. "Will you be okay?"

"Yeah, I guess so. Have to be." Then he squared his shoulders and winked at her. "Told you. We're a tough breed."

He unbuckled his seatbelt and opened the door, then turned back. "Almost forgot. Mum asked if she could have your address. She wants to send out notes. For...you know."

"Yes, of course." Katherine leaned over and opened the glove compartment, taking out a pack of business cards. She slipped one from the pack and took a pen from behind the sun visor and began to write her post office box address. She was very secretive about her real home address. Of course, the people living nearby knew who she was, but with some of the weirdos around these days, it didn't pay to be too public. A weirdo couldn't easily stalk a post office box.

But this was Ben. Her best friend's brother. Despite their recent meeting, she felt like she'd known Ben for years. Ellen talked of her big brothers constantly, sharing with her all the news from 'home' each time she received a letter or email. Katherine knew Ben had been married, but that it had ended in an acrimonious divorce after only a few years. He'd not had a serious relationship since. Alex, on the other hand, was happily married with two teenage daughters who thought the world of their uncle Ben. She scrunched the card up and dropped it onto the floor. Grabbing another card, she quickly scribbled her home address on it and handed it to him before she changed her mind.

He looked at it, then tucked it in his jacket pocket. "Thanks." He got out, shut the door and then came around to the driver's side. Katherine lowered the window.

"I'll let you know what the cops make of the address book. Okay?"

"Yes, of course. It's certainly got me stumped."

Ben turned and walked away, giving a wave when he got to Ellen's door. Katherine drove a little way to where she had room to turn her car around and headed back out of the street. Ben still stood by Ellen's door. He waved again.

Eighty-Five

"Dammit!" Katherine highlighted a passage on her computer and hit the delete button. Things weren't going right for her this morning. She'd been writing for an hour and a half, and all she'd managed was two pages, and no doubt when it came to editing, those two pages would be ninety-five percent crap.

Her mind kept wandering from the novel she was in the middle of writing, a story of revenge set in the world of corporate high fliers. Surprisingly, though, her mind wasn't drifting to thoughts of the book tour, but to a certain incredibly good-looking man who'd visited her in a dream last night. And what a dream. She still felt the tingling glow where her dream self had been touched, caressed, and kissed by him. No wonder she couldn't concentrate on killing off her characters one by one. If there had been a love scene in this book, now would have been the perfect time to write it, but unfortunately, it was all greed and revenge and murder.

Despite the messages her body was sending her, Ben was not for her. He lived halfway around the world for a start, so any thought of a relationship was out of the question. All they would ever have would be a fling, a one-night-stand, a wham-bam-thank-you-sir. While she had no objections to a fling, the timing was all wrong. Ben was grieving the death of his sister and also had the unenviable task of closing off Ellen's affairs, shutting down the last vestiges of her life. The last thing he'd be thinking of was hopping into bed with his sister's best friend.

No. It wasn't going to happen, and that was all there was to it. So she'd better knuckle down and get on with her work.

Half an hour later, after several more false starts and deleted paragraphs, she got up from her laptop. She must do something to get rid of the sexual tension in her body and get her mind focused. A good workout might help. Not that it would satisfy the sexual urges, but it might leave her exhausted enough not to notice. She changed into a lycra crop top and shorts, tied her hair up in a messy ponytail, and loaded her favorite exercise routine video on her phone. Tapping the key to cast the screen to her television, she adjusted the volume and followed the aerobics instructor.

She stretched, jumped, sprinted, punched, kicked, and spun, and when the routine finished, she restarted it and followed through again. Sweat soaked her hair and her clothes by the time she'd completed the second routine, and she flopped down on the floor, wanting to cool down a bit before heading for the shower.

Someone was knocking on her door. She didn't get many visitors, which was just the way she wanted it, so hopefully this would be a neighbor and not another religious zealot wanting to save her soul. With a sigh, she got up off the floor and went to the door, but as she swung the door open, she froze in horror.

Ben stood on the doorstep.

Eighty-Six

Fuck. The man of her dreams was standing on her doorstep, and here she was, looking like something out of a nightmare.

"Ben! Hello. I wasn't expecting you."

"Sorry, I should have called. I wanted to give you this. It was Ellen's favorite, and I thought you might like it." He held up a long, slender greenstone pendant on a silver chain. Katherine had seen Ellen wear it on occasions; she'd even remarked on how beautiful it was. Her eyes misted with tears as she took it from Ben.

"Thank you; that's so thoughtful of you. I shall treasure it always. Come in." She stood aside for Ben to enter, noting he had to duck to avoid cracking his head on the lintel. Once inside, Katherine closed the door and led Ben through to the living room.

"Have a seat. Better watch your head on the beams, too."

Ben made for the closest chair, ducking under each beam. "I'm glad Ellen had normal-height ceilings. Are all old houses in England like this?"

"A fair number. Look, I've just finished a workout. Do you mind if I take a quick shower and get dressed?"

"Of course not. Take your time."

"Thanks, make yourself at home. The kitchen's at the end of the hall if you want a cup of tea, and there's whiskey in the decanter on the sideboard. Help yourself." She trotted up the stairs and turned the shower on, shedding her gym gear while the water warmed up. Phew, she stank of sweat. It's a wonder Ben didn't run a mile at the sight and smell of her. She scrubbed her skin until it tingled, shampooed her hair twice, rinsed and worked conditioner through it, combing it with her fingers before rinsing again. Satisfied that she no longer stunk like a skunk, she turned off the shower and wrapped a towel around her body. She used another towel to dry her hair as she walked back along the landing toward her bedroom.

She stopped and gasped, heart clamoring, pulse racing to keep up with the desire flooding her system. Ben stood at the top of the stairs, casually leaning against the newel post.

"Katherine." His rich velvety-chocolate voice set her secret places tingling.

He took a step toward her, his gaze locked on hers. "If you don't want me, just tell me to go."

Eighty-Seven

Again, she felt the tingling glow from the previous night's dream. All those places he'd kissed her, touched her. Her lips, her throat, her breasts, her stomach. They all yearned for the real thing. She longed to have him inside her, the weight of his body on hers. What should she say? What words could ever articulate the way she felt? That she'd wanted him from the first moment he'd spoken her name.

She said nothing, merely kept her eyes focused on his and let the towel fall to the floor.

His eyes widened, his mouth gaped, and then he was kissing her, wrapping her in his arms, lifting her, carrying her to her bedroom. She lay on the bed and watched while he removed his shirt, revealing a smooth, athletic body, strong, well-muscled arms. He took off his jeans and then hooked his thumbs in the top of his underwear, pushing them down, letting his erection spring free.

Katherine held her arms out to him, and he came to her, lying half beside her, half on top of her. He kissed her mouth, and she put her arms around him, one hand caressing the smoothness of his back while the other held his head, keeping his mouth locked on hers. She kissed him hungrily, sucking his tongue into her mouth. He cupped one breast, flicking his thumb over the hardened nipple. His knee pushed between hers, and she parted her legs, allowing him to move between them, his erection hard against her thigh.

He groaned. "I don't suppose you have a condom."

"Top drawer." She pointed to her bedside table.

Once he'd donned a condom, he placed his hands beside her head and supported his weight on them, looking into her eyes, one eyebrow raised in question.

"Are you sure?" His voice trembled with emotion.

Was he asking her permission? She'd never had anyone stop and ask if it was what she wanted too. She reached up and caressed his cheek. "Yes, Ben. It's what I want."

Without another word, he lowered his body onto hers and guided his erection inside her. Slow movements initially, but gradually increasing the speed and depth of his thrusts. Katherine wrapped her legs around him, holding him to her, moving with him. A wave started deep inside her, spinning and spiraling outward, gathering speed, multiplying, gaining momentum, engulfing her whole body. The waves rose to a peak, paused at their zenith, and then tipped over in a tumble of orgasmic pleasure, Katherine crying out and clinging to Ben as she rode each wave down.

Ben kissed her gently, first on her forehead, then her eyelids, and then her lips. He still moved inside her, and Katherine wanted him to experience the pleasure he'd given her. She grasped his firm buttocks and pulled him to her, locking her ankles behind him, keeping him deep within her. He moved faster, his breathing rate increasing, his eyes closed, his upper teeth biting down on his lower lip. Katherine rocked beneath him, keeping in rhythm with his movements as they became harder, harder, faster, faster until his body stiffened and his back arched with one final thrust as his orgasm swept through him.

Katherine held him and caressed him as he'd done for her as she'd come down from her own climax. After a few moments, he withdrew and lay beside her, gathering her in his arms. They snuggled together, enjoying the afterglow of their lovemaking. Katherine, more satisfied than with any other man, closed her eyes and drifted off to sleep.

A hammering on the front door pierced Katherine's peaceful doze, and she opened her eyes. Ben still lay beside her, his eyes open and gazing at her. He kissed her lightly on the lips.

"I think there's someone at the door," he said, smiling.

Katherine stretched. "I'm not answering it." All she wanted to do was luxuriate in Ben's arms. And make love to him a second, third, maybe even a fourth time.

"I think it might be the police," Ben said, in a voice no more urgent than if he'd told her it might rain next Thursday.

"What?" Katherine sat up. "The police!"

"Uh huh. Forgot to tell you. A detective— Pearce, I think his name was. Said he was going to drop around."

Eighty-Eight

Katherine sprang out of bed, pulling on her jeans and quickly buttoning her shirt. Ben chuckled and lay back on the pillow, his arms behind his head, feet crossed at the ankles, body stretched out like a Greek god, or in Ben's case, a Māori god. His now flaccid penis, glistening from their encounter, languished amid a tuft of black pubic hair. Under her gaze, it began to stir.

"Not a sound," Katherine said, and quickly left before she changed her mind. She ran down the stairs in bare feet.

~

"Ah, Miss Walters. I'd almost given up on you answering the door," the detective said when she opened the door.

"I'm sorry, I was just tidying up upstairs." She laughed, a high-pitched, nervous laugh.

"I'm Detective Sergeant Pearce. We need to have a word. It's about Ellen Mehrtens' murder. May I come in?"

Katherine stood aside and let him through the door. As she closed it, she caught sight of herself in the hall mirror. Bloody hell, she looked a sight. The term 'bed hair' didn't come close to describing the mess that her black curls had become. And she'd buttoned her shirt wrong. No time to fix it now. She just had to hope the detective wouldn't notice. Of course he'd notice. That's his job, to notice things that weren't quite right.

"Miss Walters, Ben Mehrtens came to see me earlier this morning. He believes you are connected with his sister's death."

"No! That's ridiculous. I had nothing to do with Ellen's death. How dare you? How dare *he* accuse me?" Of all the nerve. He comes over, uninvited, takes her to bed, and now she finds out he's accused her of murder. At this moment, she hated the man in her bed.

"Miss Walters, calm down." The detective made a patting motion with his hands, the way a mother would soothe a child. "He simply said you were connected, not that you were responsible. Please let me explain."

Katherine sat on the edge of a chair. "Yes, I think you'd better."

"He showed me his sister's address book and explained about the missing page. He also mentioned that his sister owned all of your books, and yet they are missing from her bookshelf."

Katherine nodded. "Yes, I'm aware of that."

"Now, I've got to say, I'm really struggling to make some kind of connection between those two pieces of—let's call them evidence for want of a better description—and Ellen Mehrtens' murder." The detective shook his head. "I just can't figure out if it's important or a red herring. Can you think of any connection?"

"No. None."

"Any strange phone calls or emails?"

"No. None," she said again.

The sound of the upstairs toilet being flushed had the detective glancing upward, one eyebrow raised. Heat crept up Katherine's neck, flaming her cheeks.

The detective looked back at her and smiled. "Well, if you do get any strange calls or emails, please let me know. And now I'll let you get back to your, um, tidying up, was it?"

If a chasm appeared in her living room right now, Katherine would gladly jump right in. If the detective hadn't previously had any inkling of what she'd really been doing upstairs, well, he sure as hell did now.

But why should she be ashamed? The detective didn't know it was Ben. It could be her boyfriend for all he knew. Rather than cover her face with her hands, which is what she wanted to do, she held her head high and walked with the detective to the front door.

She opened it, and the detective stepped outside. Then he turned back with a smile on his lips and a twinkle in his eye. "Tell Mr. Mehrtens I'll be in touch, would you? That is his rental parked just across the street, isn't it?"

If her cheeks were on fire before, they now burned like lava. But she gathered her decorum and smiled back. "I'll be sure to pass on your message."

"Enjoy your afternoon, Miss Walters." The detective walked away and Katherine shut the door and leaned on it, eyes closed, trying to calm her frazzled nerves and douse the fire in her cheeks.

Eighty-Nine

When she opened her eyes, Ben stood at the top of the stairs. Naked. He smiled. "Come back to bed."

Katherine ran up the stairs to his waiting arms.

They made love again, but when Katherine reached for him a third time, Ben stopped her.

"Phew, give me a bit of time to recover. I'm not as young as I used to be, you know, but if you want more, I'll give you more." He pushed her back onto the bed and kissed her, moving his lips and his tongue over her entire body, kissing, licking, sucking. She giggled when he kissed her toes, but when he licked his tongue up her leg and found her clitoris, her giggles turned to moans of ecstasy. He brought her to the brink of orgasm and then entered her.

When they were both spent, Katherine lay beside him and snuggled close. "You know, for a forty-something, you recover pretty quickly."

Ben kissed the tip of her nose. "You know, for a forty-something, you're pretty hot!"

~

Ten days after Ellen's funeral, Katherine sat at a table in WH Smith, surrounded by copies of her latest novel, *Tracy's Troubles*. A dozen or more people stood in an orderly queue, each clutching their own newly purchased copy, awaiting their turn with Katherine.

She'd already signed over twenty books, and her writing hand was aching. Thank God for computers. She'd hate to write a manuscript longhand. Some people did it, apparently, but she couldn't see herself doing it. Not in a month of blue moons.

But no matter how tired she was, she still greeted each purchaser with a smile, thanked them for their purchase, and asked how they would like the book signed. Just before she handed the book back, she would slip in a bookmark advertising her other books. Shameless maybe, but it was all part of marketing.

Little by little, the queue diminished, and finally, she was done. Katherine put down her pen and flexed her fingers. She'd never imagined having to sign a little over fifty books. A couple of older women still browsed the bookshop, but each already clutched a copy of *Tracy's Troubles* as if it were an ingot of gold.

It had been a good day; the reading went well, and sales had been steady. The one sad note was, of course, Ellen's absence. Every time Katherine heard the swish of the automatic door, she'd glance up, expecting to see Ellen walk in, a beaming smile on her face, to pick up at least two copies of her book. One for her and one for her mother.

But on a brighter note, Ben dropped in and purchased a copy to take home to his mother. Katherine hated the thought of him going back to New Zealand. Since the 'day of the detective', they'd spent most evenings together. Evenings that turned into Ben staying over and them making love time and time again. Never had Katherine felt so satiated, so comfortable with a man, so fulfilled. Ben was everything she'd ever wanted in a lover, a partner, a—dare she say it—husband. Everything was perfect except for the fact that he lived halfway around the world. Right at the start, she'd known their time was limited, but her heart still ached at the thought of him leaving, and the endless stretch of lonely nights in her lonely bed with only a memory to keep her warm.

The automatic door swished, and she glanced up. A young man with a hoodie pulled low over his forehead, hands thrust into his pockets, stood aside and let the two women exit before he entered the shop. He didn't look like the kind of buyer for her book, so she quickly dismissed him from her thoughts.

"Here, you look like you could use a coffee." Lesley, the store manager, put a cup beside her.

"Thanks. You're a life-saver." She picked up the cup and sipped. Strong, dark, smooth. Just like Ben. Her mind drifted to the way he'd made love to her that morning, slow, luxurious, building her up slowly, teasing her with his lips, his fingers, his tongue.

"I'm dying to go to the loo," Lesley said. "Can you look after the shop for me? I'll only be a minute."

"Sure, go ahead." Katherine returned to her daydreams.

After a few moments, the young man in the hoodie thrust a book in front of Katherine. "Can you sign this for me?"

"Sure," Katherine said, putting her coffee down and picking up her pen. She looked up at the young man, but with his head bowed, she couldn't see his face. Still, she smiled at him the way she did for anyone who purchased her books. "How would you like me to sign it?"

"To Christian with love, Mother," he said.

Katherine looked up, brow creased in puzzlement. "Sorry?"

The young man threw back his hoodie, and Katherine looked into a face that had haunted her dreams for over sixteen years. His ice-blue eyes still chilled her soul.

"Jonathan," she whispered.

"Hello, Mother," Christian said, raising a gun.

Ninety

"I had to kill people to find you. Now it's your turn, Mother." His chilling tone left no doubt in Katherine's mind that she was about to die.

Mustering every ounce of strength, she pushed the table at him, spilling posters, books, her coffee, and a jug of water as the edge of the table rammed into his upper thighs. She threw herself to one side as he fired the gun, the bullet missing her by what could only have been inches.

"You fucking bitch! You killed my father! I'm your son, and you dumped me like I was garbage. I hate you!" Spittle flew from the young man's mouth as he shouted at her. Then he raised the gun again.

She had only seconds. If this were to be the end for her, she wasn't going down without a fight and, if at all possible, she'd take him with her. She launched herself at him, head down in a shoulder charge, catching him unawares. Her shoulder connected, sending pain zinging down her arm and up to her skull. He stepped backward onto the slickness of the wet posters, and his feet slid from under him. He went down with a thud; the gun discharging again.

Katherine leaped on him, a knee on his chest, her hands gripping his, trying to wrestle the gun from his grip, but he held on to it, pointing it at her, laughing as his finger found the trigger.

Again, she was fighting for her life, just as she had all those years ago with Jonathan. That time she'd won. Would she be so lucky this time around?

"No, you fucking don't." She screamed at the man beneath her and pushed all her weight down on her arms, forcing his hands back.

The sound of the gunshot rang in Katherine's ears, deafening her, but there was no pain, no fear, no anything. She looked down at the young man. He no longer laughed. Blood gushed from the side of his head, and as Katherine stared at the horror beneath her, he shuddered, and one final bubble of blood gurgled from what remained of his mouth, and he lay still. His remaining blue eye, so much like Jonathan's, took on a faraway stare.

She slumped, sensing, as if from a distance, hands circling her waist, lifting her as dizziness replaced the adrenaline. She went willingly, letting the blackness close in and obliterate the bloodied mess that had been her son.

"Miss Walters, can you hear me?" A disembodied voice reached into Katherine's subconscious, and she forced her eyes open. She was seated on a chair, half hidden behind a bookcase at the back of the shop, but with no memory of how she got there. A woman dressed in a paramedic uniform crouched before her, patting the back of her hand. Katherine shook her head, trying to clear the cobwebs cocooning her brain. Memory flooded back, and she tried to jump up, but hands held her down.

"Just relax, Miss Walters. I'm Sarah. I'm a paramedic, and I need you to remain seated while I check you over." She wrapped a cuff around Katherine's arm, fixed an oxygen monitor on her middle finger, then got a small torch and shone it in each of Katherine's eyes. Sarah suggested taking Katherine to the hospital for observation, but Katherine shook her head. "I'm okay, really. A bit shook up, but I don't need to go to the hospital."

As the paramedic packed up her gear, she stressed that if Katherine became dizzy or faint or nauseous, she should seek medical help immediately.

"Where's Jonathan?" Katherine shook her head. No, that wasn't right. It wasn't Jonathan. She gripped Sarah's arm. "The young man. Will he be alright?"

Detective Pearce appeared at Katherine's side. "I'm afraid not, Miss Walters."

Katherine slumped. So her son was dead at her hands, just like his father. Her emotions see-sawed from grief to relief.

Detective Pearce cleared his throat. "I need to ask you some questions, if you're up to it."

He opened his notebook, and without waiting for Katherine's reply, he launched into his questions.

"Now, witnesses say Christian Bayley was claiming to be your son. Was he?"

"I believe so," Katherine replied.

The detective frowned, and his eyes narrowed. "You *believe* so?"

The emphasis he'd put on his question made it clear he had no idea what was really going on. If the circumstances were reversed, Katherine would have thought it an odd answer, too.

She sighed. "Let me explain."

The detective pulled a chair across the floor and positioned it in front of Katherine. He sat and motioned for her to continue.

She took a deep breath. "Many years ago, I was involved in a relationship with a man who kept me locked in a cellar for four weeks." She paused as the detective held up his hand in a stop sign.

"It's okay, Miss Walters. After my last conversation with you, I looked you up on the police computer. The statement you made following the death of Jonathan Irving made very disturbing reading."

"So you'll understand why I didn't want to keep his baby."

"There was no mention of the child in your statement."

"It was only later I found out that Jonathan drugged me the night my mother died and raped me."

"I see. So, what did you do?"

"I gave the baby up for adoption when it was born."

"And Christian Bayley claimed to be that child?"

"Yes. I've no doubt that he is. He looks like Jonathan, especially his eyes. Those eyes have haunted me for over sixteen years. He's definitely Jonathan's son."

"Right." The detective stood. "We'll leave it there for now. I'd like you to come down to the station this afternoon if possible and make a formal statement." He handed her a card. "Shall we say three p.m.?"

Katherine sighed. "Yes, of course."

When the detective left, Lesley brought her another cup of coffee. "Here, drink this. It's a double shot, and you look like you need it."

Katherine accepted it gratefully. "Thanks." She took a sip, tears stinging her eyes. "I'm so sorry about today, Lesley. Everything was going so well, too."

Lesley perched on the edge of the chair recently vacated by the detective. She patted Katherine's arm. "Don't you worry about that. We had good sales, and several people have already signed up to be notified of your next release. As for that ... " she hesitated, as if searching for the right words. "That unfortunate business, I can guarantee you that there'll be triple the number of people through that door in the next few days. They're a macabre lot; they'll all be wanting to see where it happened."

Katherine shuddered. "That's awful."

Lesley smiled a mischievous grin. "It's true, though. Won't do your sales any harm, either. If anyone in Devon hadn't heard of you before, tonight's television news will change that, judging by the reporters and camera crews outside. The only thing stopping them from barging in here is a couple of burly coppers at the door."

Katherine peeked around the corner of the bookcase. The shop itself was empty, save for the police. A mobile screen hid her son's body from view. Through the door, she could see the shoulders of two police officers almost blocking the entrance. Beyond them, heads bobbed and strained, trying to get a glimpse inside. Lesley was right. A macabre lot.

"Is there someone you want me to call for you?" Lesley asked softly. "You probably shouldn't be alone."

Ben. She wanted Ben, but she didn't want to have to tell him her life story here. He didn't know that she'd borne a child. No, she'd call him when she got home.

"I'll be fine. My car's parked behind the shop. Can I sneak out the back way?"

"Sure. I'll check that the coast is clear and let you out."

Katherine drove home and called Ben.

That evening, curled up on the sofa, Ben's arm around her shoulders, she told him the whole story, from her very first meeting with Jonathan, her mother's death, her incarceration in the cellar, Jonathan's death, the birth of her child, culminating in the events at the bookshop.

Ben held her close, his body trembling. "My God, Katherine, you might have been killed." He drew back a little, then tilted her head back, kissing her tears away, then holding her in his arms again.

That night, their lovemaking was soft, tender, and sensual, and they fell asleep with their arms wrapped around each other.

Two days later, Katherine returned home from the police station in a daze. Detective Pearce had called early in the morning, asking her to come in. She'd obliged with some annoyance. They'd already taken her statement, and she wanted to put the whole thing behind her. Surely they couldn't have more questions.

As it turned out, Detective Pearce had new information. Information that had left her reeling. Christian's adoptive parents had died in an explosion and resultant house fire, and there was some suspicion that it had not been accidental. Detective Pearce didn't come out and actually say as much, but Katherine got the impression that Christian might be a suspect.

Christian had left Barnstaple after the fire and turned up in Plymouth a couple of days later, according to his former girlfriend, Jacinta Lane. He'd applied to find his birth parents, and when it was unsuccessful, he'd found a job at Derriford Hospital. According to Ms. Lane, he'd hoped that by working at the hospital, he'd be able to track down his birth parents.

Alarm bells clanged in Katherine's mind. Christian worked at the same hospital as Ellen. Had he quizzed her about his birth mother? Had Ellen refused to answer and so he'd tortured her until she told? Was that why Katherine's books were missing and why that page had been torn from Ellen's address book? Had Christian killed Ellen? Was that what he'd implied when he'd said he'd had to kill people to find her? Could he have committed such a brutal act? She brought to mind his face when he'd confronted her, the pure hatred in his eyes. Eyes so much like his father's. Jonathan's eyes had shown the same anger and hatred that last day. Yes, Christian could have, and probably did, kill Ellen.

Katherine shared her thoughts with Detective Pearce, who'd scribbled furiously in his notebook. He seemed eager, even excited at the prospect of a connection between Ellen's murder and Christian. He promised to keep Katherine informed of developments.

A week passed before Katherine again heard from Detective Pearce. When he did telephone, he requested Ben be present too, if he wasn't already there.

"Well, at least he won't catch me with my pants down this time." Ben winked at her as he sprang out of bed and pulled on his jeans. Katherine made a show of bending over from the waist to pick up her underwear.

"On second thoughts," Ben said, gripping her hips and rubbing his body against her bare bottom.

Katherine laughed and skipped away from him.

Ben pointed to the bulge in his jeans. "Now look what you've done."

She sauntered seductively toward him, put a hand on his crotch, and stretched up to kiss him, then at the last minute she ducked away. "Later, big boy."

Seated in the living room with cups of tea and a plate of chocolate digestives on the coffee table, Detective Pearce told them that, according to Ellen's colleagues, Christian had questioned her directly about his birth parents. Questions she refused to answer. Further, there was compelling evidence that Christian was responsible for Ellen's death. A search of Christian's flat had turned up a carrier bag containing several hardback novels, all signed 'To Ellen' by Katherine, along with a blood-spattered paperback and blood-soaked fibers from a rope. DNA testing matched the blood on the book and the rope to Ellen, and fibers similar to that found in Christian's flat were also embedded in Ellen's wrists and neck.

Ninety-One

When Katherine shut the door after the detective left, she returned to Ben, who sat stone-faced on the sofa, his forearms resting on his knees, hands clasped together.

"Ben?"

He raised his head to look at Katherine. The stone in his face cracked and crumbled. Tears formed and fell. Without a word, he rose and hurried out of the room. His footsteps pounded up the stairs, and then the bathroom door closed with an audible thud.

Should she go to him? Let him alone? His sobs reached her, every one stabbing like a dagger in her heart. This was all her fault. Jonathan was dead because of her. Ellen was dead because of her. Her son was dead because of her. And now Ben's heart was breaking because of her.

She couldn't bear it. She climbed the stairs and knocked softly on the bathroom door.

"It's open." Ben's voice was thick with emotion.

She opened the door. Ben sat on the edge of the bathtub, staring at the opposite wall, his body shaking with each sob. Katherine put a hand on his shoulder. Ben looked up, his haunted eyes swollen and red, his face wet with tears. He pulled her to him and buried his face in the softness of her midriff. She held him while he cried, her own tears falling onto his dark hair. Eventually, his sobs subsided to snuffles and he drew back.

"Sorry about that melt-down," he said, reaching for the box of tissues on the shelf. He pulled out a handful and wiped his face, blew his nose. "I've always been a bit of a softy where Ellen's concerned. When we were little, she fell and grazed her knees badly. I cried more than she did." He blew his nose again, lifted the lid of the toilet and threw the used tissues in the bowl. "Did that bloody copper really have to go into so much graphic detail? Couldn't he just have said that the boy did it and spare us all the forensic stuff?"

He stood and reached for Katherine's hand. "Come on, I don't know about you, but I need a bloody stiff drink."

Seated on the sofa with a large whiskey each and the decanter on the table in front of them, Katherine told Ben of her fears—that it was her fault Ellen died, and that he'd blame her for the heartache his family were going through. Ben's answer was to take Katherine's glass from her and put it, along with his own, on the coffee table. Then he rose, picked her up and carried her up to her bedroom where all thoughts of Jonathan, Christian and Ellen disappeared from Katherine's mind as she kept her promised appointment with Ben.

Katherine stood at the entrance to passport control at London's Heathrow Airport, clinging to Ben, her tears soaking into his shirt. She'd known this day would come, that he would go home, and had been dreading it. Now it was finally here, and they were saying goodbye. Ben hadn't wanted her to come to the airport, but she'd insisted, if only to delay the inevitable by a few hours. She'd driven up with him and planned to catch the train back to Plymouth the next day. By the time she returned home, hopefully, she would have picked up the shattered pieces of her heart and put them back in their designated slots.

Ben pulled back, breaking their embrace, holding her hands by her sides. "Katherine, I have to go."

She nodded, not daring to speak.

He kissed her forehead. "Should I call you when I get home?"

She nodded again, still not trusting her voice.

He kissed her softly on the lips, and then he walked away. Just before the airport swallowed him up, he turned and waved to her, a sad smile on his face. She waved back, her throat burning, heart aching, tears cascading down her face.

The automatic doors closed behind Ben, and it was over. The man she was fairly sure she was in love with was gone. Katherine stumbled away, making her way to the ladies' room, where she locked herself in a cubicle and sobbed. Three weeks she'd had with Ben. Just three weeks. She'd known it wouldn't, and couldn't, last, but that didn't make the parting any easier. Three weeks just weren't enough. She wanted more. She wanted a lifetime with him, and even that wouldn't be enough.

Some time later, she emerged, splashed cold water on her face, and regarded herself in the mirror. She could repair her tear-stained face with fresh makeup, but nothing would disguise her swollen, red eyes. She wadded up some paper towels, soaked them in warm water, and washed away her makeup. Delving into her handbag, she set about making herself look halfway respectable again.

Job done, she held her head up, set her shoulders, and strode out of the ladies' room, determined that she wouldn't shed another tear over Ben Mehrtens.

Ninety-Two

TWO MONTHS LATER

For the first time in Katherine's writing career, she'd written a romance. A short, steamy romance. She still ached for Ben, still missed talking with him, still missed laughing with him, still missed making love with him.

As he'd promised, Ben had telephoned when he'd arrived in Christchurch, but their conversation had been stilted. She'd tried to keep her emotions in check. Only at the end of the call, when they said goodbye for the last time, did emotion crack in her voice.

"I miss you, Ben."

He sighed. "I'm sorry, Katherine."

"Ben, I… " But she was talking to a dead line. He'd hung up.

He hadn't called again.

She'd taken solace in her writing, pouring all her feelings, all her emotions, all her yearning into a new story. But unlike her own torment, her story had a happy ending. Her character had married her man, and together they'd walked off into the sunset. How terribly clichéd, and no doubt the editing process would fix that. If only her own life could mirror her story. But it was not to be.

She would put her novel aside for a few weeks and then start editing. Right now, though, she'd visit Jim. She hadn't seen him for over three months, and it would be good to catch up with him. Would she find him at home or striding the moor? Perhaps hiking boots would be a good idea. Just in case.

When she pulled up in Jim's yard, he emerged from the barn, wiping his rather dirty hands on an even dirtier rag. Even though it had been some years since Jim had buried Felan, she half expected to see him by Jim's side. The weathered wooden cross at the end of the barn bearing Felan's name always gave her a pang of sadness.

But what was this? A border collie puppy scampered out of the barn and trotted alongside Jim as he walked to greet her.

"Well, you be a welcome sight, young lady."

Katherine ran the few steps to him. "It's so good to see you." She wrapped her arms around him and hugged him close, despite his dirty clothes. Then she reached down and let the puppy sniff her hand. "Who's your new friend?"

"This," he said, bending down to pick up the squirming puppy, "is Jasper."

Katherine scratched Jasper behind one ear, remembering how much Felan had enjoyed the same attention. "He's lovely. He must be good company."

Jim looked toward Felan's grave, pressed his lips together as if the pain of losing his best friend was still raw.

"Aye, that he be," he said after a moment, then smiled. "Felan will always hold a special place in my heart and my memories. But it was time to put the past behind me and move on. I can never replace Monica or Felan, but I can still find room in my heart to love again."

He put Jasper on the ground, and the pup sat obediently, looking up, eyes alert, so much a scaled-down version of Felan.

"Come on in and I'll make us a cup of tea," Jim said. "I can do with a break. That damned tractor will be the death of me, I swear."

"What's wrong with it?"

Jim looked sideways at her. "Without putting too fine a point on it, I'd say she's knackered."

Over tea, Katherine told Jim about Ellen's death, about Christian, and then, with tears in her eyes, she told him about Ben.

Jim patted her hand across the table. "You love him, don't you?"

Katherine sobbed, her heart breaking. She nodded.

"Is there any chance?"

"None. He lives in New Zealand. Our last conversation was awful. Stilted and uncomfortable, as if we didn't know what to say to each other. He broke my heart." She looked up. "Oh, Jim, what do I do? I've never felt like this before."

Jim scooted his chair around to sit beside Katherine, his arm around her shoulders. "Aye, it hurts, lass. When you lose the one you love, you feel you can't go on, that there's nothing left worth living for." He snuffled and scrubbed at his face. "When I lost Monica, I was like that. But you go on. Somehow you muddle through."

Katherine nodded. Somehow, she'd have to muddle through.

Ninety-Three

Katherine returned home just after dark. She'd spent longer than she'd intended with Jim, but it had been worth it. She felt much more settled now. That was one thing she loved about Jim. He had a way of grounding her, helping her see what was actually important, and mooning over a man with whom she had no future was a complete waste of time and energy.

So. No more. She'd had a great time with Ben, but it was over, in the past, and she would move on.

Humming softly, she opened a bottle of wine, poured a glass, and sipped it while she threw together a salad. She sat at the table, but before she'd even managed a mouthful, someone knocked on the front door. Bother. She half toyed with not answering, but the knocking came again, so reluctantly she got up and went to answer it, hoping to get rid of the caller as quickly as she could.

On opening the door, she gasped and put a hand out to steady herself from falling. Standing in front of her was the last person she'd expected to see.

"Ben!"

Without a word, he wrapped her in his arms and kissed her, long and deep. Her plans of moving on from him disappeared like a snowflake in a furnace. He finally released her and she could breathe again.

"I love you, Katherine, and want to be with you. Come home with me."

"What? You mean New Zealand?"

"Yes. Or wherever you want home to be."

"I don't understand." This entire conversation was surreal. It had to be a dream. In a few minutes, she'd wake up and none of this would be happening.

"You're a writer. I'm a software developer. We can work anywhere in the world we want. All I need is an internet connection."

"Ben, this is too much. You can't be serious. Think about what you're saying, what you're asking."

Ninety-Four

He clasped her hands in his. "I have thought about it. I've thought of nothing else since I left England. I've thought about you night and day. Everywhere I go, everything I do, you're there—in my mind and in my heart. I want to live the rest of my life with you."

Katherine realized she hadn't invited him in. They were still standing on the doorstep. "I'm sorry. Would you like to come in?"

Ben shook his head. "No. I mean, I'd love to, but I won't. If I come in, we'll end up in bed and, as delicious as that thought is, I want you to take your time and think carefully about what I've said. Will you do that?"

Katherine nodded. "Okay. I will."

"Great. I'm staying at the Hyatt in Plymouth. Room 188. I'll be there till Wednesday." He kissed the back of her hand and held it against his cheek. "I hope you'll come."

Katherine watched him cross the street to his car and drive away. She closed the door and leaned against it. Was any of that real? Did it actually happen, or was she dreaming? She touched her lips where his kiss still lingered. That must have been real; her lips still tingled. As did the rest of her body.

Back in the kitchen, Katherine re-capped the wine and put it in the fridge, along with her untouched salad. Right now, she didn't want to eat or drink. All she wanted was Ben.

At forty-nine, she'd pretty much given up on finding love. Real love; the kind of love that lasts a lifetime. Ben was offering her that. She thought back to Jim's words. He was right. It was time to move on. Time to take a chance on love.

Running up the stairs, whooping with joy, she pulled her suitcase out from beneath her bed and stuffed it with clothes, toiletries, and her laptop. Then she locked up her house and drove to the Hyatt. She hurried through the deserted hotel lobby to the lift, wheeling her suitcase behind her. Her heart pummeled her chest and excitement trembled through her body. She held her breath as she knocked on the door of room 188.

The door opened and Ben stood before her, dressed only in a pair of gray sweat pants. He raised an eyebrow, then glanced down at the suitcase on the floor beside Katherine. When his gaze met hers again, his eyes sparkled. He quickly pulled the suitcase inside the room, then lifted Katherine up in his arms and twirled her around, laughing, before putting her back on her feet.

"You came," he whispered a moment before his lips found hers.

About the Author

Barb Evans spent her childhood in Devon, and has always had a love of the wilds of Dartmoor, where this novel is set. It's a place she has returned to many times since moving to Australia in her early teens.

When not writing or planning their next holiday, Barb can be found doing chores out on the small farm she shares with her partner.

www.ingramcontent.com/pod-product-compliance
Lightning Source LLC
Chambersburg PA
CBHW032054050726
47590CB00001B/265